No Backup

A Crime Novel

Jake Jacobs

ISBN 978-1-62806-389-9   (print | paperback)
ISBN 978-1-62806-390-5 (ebook)

Library of Congress Control Number 2023918067

Published by Salt Water Media
29 Broad Street, Suite 104
Berlin, MD 21811
www.saltwatermedia.com

Cover art by Tobie Jacobs

No Backup

CONTENTS

AUTHOR'S NOTE

This is the second book in the Detective William Brogan series; fictional crime novels based on authentic experiences and events occurring today. Working twenty-five years with the Maryland State Police, a detective for twenty of those, opened my eyes to many of the horrors men and women visit upon the weak or unsuspecting.

Very few people wake up in the morning thinking they're going to become a victim. Those are the prey upon which the predators target their evil. Despite being outnumbered and outgunned, people like Detective Brogan stand ready to run toward danger when things go sideways.

Policing has taught me one thing I remember to do each morning before I leave my home; I never let my guard down, and I never trust a stranger. Even though I live in a peaceful beach town, bad things can and will happen.

Welcome back to Sandpiper.

1

SHOTS FIRED

The gusts of wind were causing little tornados of dead leaves and pine needles to tear across yards and streets. November means dead leaves and abundant pine needles are part of the ambiance of this near-ocean community. Trees swayed back and forth, making swooshing sounds like a giant moving through the forest, adding to the foreboding atmosphere. The lofty pines made it easy to understand why this community was known as Tall Pines. The ocean was a scant two miles away.

This had been a thick forest before developers cut in roads and housing lots, creating an investment paradise for those who loved to visit the ocean resort town of Sandpiper. Houses sprang from the ground in different shapes and sizes. If there were building codes and restrictions being enforced, they would be difficult to point out. The one consistent landmark was the pine trees that populated nearly all the lots. Developers and home buyers removed only enough trees to squeeze in their homes and a short driveway. Many driveways remained unpaved, but a rustic and forest-like feeling was prevalent because of the needles that fell and blanketed the ground.

The ground cover and trees made this a muted place. The vegetation swallowed the sounds. The original developers decided against installing streetlights, with only the glow of house lights creating a dark and quiet setting that made every fall evening a tribute to the spirit of Halloween. Street signs were difficult to see and only a few lights showed in the windows of scattered homes. Ghosts and spirits surely lurked in the dark waiting to rush out and devour an unsuspecting soul. Tonight, the temperatures were dipping into the low forties heading for the thirties before the sun would rise. Luckily, a partial moon prevented a total blackout.

It was approaching 1:00 a.m. Kelly sat quietly in her rented, nondescript, black Honda sedan. She had backed into the driveway of an unoccupied residence. More than half the population of Tall Pines lived here only in the summer. Vacant homes were plentiful at that time of the year. Kelly never considered getting permission to park in a stranger's driveway. Her needs this particular night superseded those of the homeowner. With the car turned off, she sat low in the front seat to reduce the chance of being seen. A dark blanket was draped across her torso to provide a layer of warmth against the invading chill. A thermos containing now-lukewarm coffee sat in the center console cupholder, but was consumed sparingly. Having been in place for nearly five hours, she had left the protection of the car only once to relieve herself next to the darkened house. She never took her eyes off her target. She knew leaving a surveillance in progress was a cardinal sin; as soon as you got out of sight, you'd miss the event you were waiting to see. She disabled the overhead light so her exiting and re-entering the vehicle would go unnoticed by anyone in the area. An uneaten peanut butter and jelly sandwich remained bagged on the front passenger seat.

This driveway was selected because it provided the best view of the home she was watching. From her position, she saw both the front, the rear, and one side of the dwelling of interest. The driveway was short, and a lone Chevy pickup truck was facing out - either black or dark blue. Lights were on in the front of the house, the curtains drawn. At 1:30 a.m., Kelly saw a person walking along the darkened street toward the target residence. Using a small set of Vortex binoculars, she determined it was a female. The subject was wearing dark clothing, including a hoodie-style sweatshirt with the hood pulled up, concealing most of her facial features. Using binoculars aided in seeing blonde or light-colored hair peeking out from the hoodie. She had a slim build and looked to be around five foot four. She cut across the lawn, going directly to the front door of the house.

Kelly saw her knocking on the door. The front door swung inward; the home's interior light flooded the unlit front porch for a moment. Positive identification of the female was made. The subject of the surveillance was now entering the target residence. The woman disappeared quickly inside the house. As she passed through the door, a White male with thick, dark hair leaned out. Appearing to be taller than the woman, he looked about the area before he ducked back in and closed the door. The porch went dark.

Using her blanket for concealment and a penlight, Kelly jotted an entry in her notebook, logging her observations and time. Surveillance was long, boring, and frequently non-productive—but tonight appeared to be that rare occasion when patience, planning, and a little bit of luck had all come together. She shed the blanket that warmed her and sat straighter in the seat. Now the real work began.

It was extremely important to track and log everything that happened. If the opportunity presented itself, a photographic record of what was taking place would also be made. Kelly hated domestic cases, but they paid the rent and kept the lights burning, so she did what she had to do. With her binoculars focused on the house, she saw shadows moving across the window of the lighted room. The curtains were closed, preventing a clear view of the interior. Patience was back in play. It was a waiting game and you never knew how it would turn out.

An hour after the female entered the house, the lights in the front went out. A light then came on in a room in the rear of the house. Luckily, it was also on the side in view of the surveillance vehicle. Kelly decided to wait about thirty minutes before approaching with her cell phone set to video. She hoped to at least capture recordings of conversations, and maybe even some video. Warrants and trespassing were not considered, as any evidence gathered would not be used in a criminal case, and more likely would never be shown more than once to help move a divorce settlement along. She's wasn't a cop. Her threshold of legality was set lower.

Kelly was startled by movement in the pine trees, behind the target house, twenty minutes into her wait time. Almost an apparition, a dark figure moved from the edge of the pines across the short backyard to the rear of the house. Internal alarms started going off and she quickly checked her hip for her holstered gun. Her cell phone was in her jacket pocket. She called 911, gave the address, and said, "Possible home invasion." She killed the call and knew there was no time. She exited her car and began moving cautiously toward the house.

She had barely cleared the front of her vehicle when she heard the sounds of shattering glass and splintering wood. The dark figure had breached the back door. Kelly now had her Glock in hand and moved as fast as caution permitted toward the back door. An instant later, she saw three bright flashes in the backroom of the house, accompanied by the sounds of gunfire. She was now in a full sprint that brought her to the broken rear entrance to the house. She peeked through the open door and saw a dark kitchen. Down a short hall, light flooded from an open door. Kelly heard a scraping noise emanating from somewhere down the hallway. Knowing there was a great likelihood that someone may have been shot, and seconds could make the difference between life and death, she quickly passed through the kitchen after clearing the room with her gun raised at shoulder height. Gun still raised, she moved to the open doorway and glimpsed, at an angle, into a bedroom. The view was not what she expected. Two naked bodies lay sprawled on top of each other across the bed. Neither was moving, and there was the presence of blood on the back of the top body. This was a sphincter-tightening moment when Kelly knew she must act, but by doing so she had to put her own life on the line. Training told her never to center an open doorway, as it became a fatal funnel where many good men and women had met their maker. She heard a noise coming from the right side of the room, but she was unable to see that portion of the room from her position.

Kelly thought about her movements. *Did I make any noise while approaching the open bedroom? Is the shooter waiting on the other side of the wall to shoot me when I enter the room?* She needed a distraction and quickly searched her surroundings and found nothing. Kelly then realized she stood on a possible distraction. She reached down with her free left hand and slid her left shoe from her foot.

It's not much of a plan, but it's all I've got. Using her left hand, she hurled her shoe into the room, over the prone bodies on the bed. It struck the wall above the headboard and fell to the floor. Before the noise of the shoe had even registered, a gunshot rang out. The doorframe shattered and splinters of wood flew about head high. Kelly spun around the corner of the doorway, keeping a low profile, with her gun pointed out before her. She locked eyes with the shooter. There was a moment of recognition as the shooter began to redirect his weapon, pointing it directly at Kelly. Her Glock barked twice, and the assailant was pushed back against a bedroom wall by the impact of two rounds striking him center mass. His gun dropped from his hand and he slid down the wall, leaving streaks of blood behind. When he came to rest, his legs were out straight in front of him and his chin was resting on his chest.

"Oh shit! Oh, fuck! I just killed my client," Kelly said aloud, although no one else in the room could hear her. She moved forward, kicking his gun away, and spoke to him, calling him by name, but there was no response. She checked for a pulse but found none. Kelly pulled his head up, only to look into dead eyes.

She moved quickly to the bed and found the top body was that of the client's wife. She had been shot in the middle of her back and again in the back of her head. She had no pulse. Leaning over the dead woman, she saw the White male with thick dark hair. He had been shot in the face and was unresponsive.

As she again dialed 911, Kelly thought, *What a shit show this is!* She proceeded to the back door, first placing her gun on the kitchen table. She sat on the back stoop with only one shoe on. She told the 911 operator "I will be waiting for the arrival of the police at the back door." A few minutes later, she heard the first drone of a police siren. She thought, *You never know how things will turn out.*

She speed-dialed her lawyer. Marie answered on the third ring. A quick explanation and Marie said, "I'll meet you at the PD. Tell them your lawyer has told you not to say anything until she gets there. I'm on my way." Dead air. Marie had hung up without waiting for a response.

Flashing red and blue lights illuminated the yard. Kelly considered her situation. Butterflies began to swarm in her belly. *Listen to your attorney. Keep your mouth shut.* A feeling of loneliness and despair swept over her. *I just killed another human being. I did the only thing I could do. How is this going to work, now that I'm a PI?*

2

WHO IS KELLY?

K elly's brother, James, an Army veteran twelve years her senior, introduced her to martial arts when she was eleven years old. After years of study, she had a fifth-degree black belt in two styles of martial arts. Martial arts introduced her to cops and the ways of law enforcement. While fighting her way into a predominantly man's world, a lot of glass ceilings had been broken before she became a police officer.

She was blonde, blue-eyed, and easily misread by those who crossed her path. Her disarming smile allowed her to gain access to the unsuspecting. Because of her confidence and training, she stood eye-to-eye and toe-to-toe with her opponents. Also, her physical abilities were bolstered by her five-foot-eight frame and toned body. These qualities were assets in the world she traveled.

She carried a gun and a badge and dedicated her life to defending and protecting herself and others. For all these reasons, she was chosen to be a member of the Baltimore County Dignitary Protection Unit after only two years on the job. Kelly Hart was a badass.

3
NOT ALL GLAMOUR

Kelly Hart's working days and nights for the next eight years with Baltimore County PD were spent protecting the county's politicians, movers, and shakers. In the field of dignitary protection, those being protected were known as "The Principal." When working a Principal, Kelly was expected to run interference from any perceived threat and diffuse any negative situations that might arise. Diplomacy and de-escalation skills were paramount. Knowing and planning escape routes was equally important.

Thought to be glamorous work by the uninformed, it was a grueling task to keep the Principals safe. They had little to no idea of danger and thought that living in their protective bubble of wealth and fame was enough to keep them safe. The dignitary protection agent was often mistakenly used as waitstaff. Most Principals never grasp the concept that the protection agent needed both hands free at all times.

During the spring of her ninth year in the Dignitary Protection Unit, Kelly was assigned to accompany the county executive's wife, Melisa Collins, to a fundraiser being held on his behalf at a local hotel. It was by invitation only, commanding a five hundred dollar-a-plate dinner. It was sold out. Kelly had worked with Mrs. Collins before and had found her polite and cooperative.

Recently, the County Executive, Barry Collins, had taken a very controversial stand on the issue of arming teachers in public schools. A strong proponent of law enforcement and the second amendment, he was in favor of this tactic. He was convinced that properly vetted and trained teachers would act as the first line of armed defense against an active shooter. Anti-gun advocates were voicing their displeasure, and many threats were being flung about. A demonstration was planned outside the hotel, with members of both sides expected to attend. Police were on high alert and extra officers were assigned to monitor the demonstrators.

Inside, the party was just getting started with an abundance of hors d'oeuvres and champagne being served to guests; while the county executive and his wife worked the room greeting and glad-handing the attendees. Kelly stood near, but not too near, Mrs. Collins. Another protection agent was assigned to the County Executive and stood within arm's reach of him. An outer ring of protection agents encircled the County Executive. All the agents were connected by radios with coiled wires going into their earbuds. A single sharply spoken word came to Kelly's ear, "GUN!"

No other words were necessary. Kelly reached for the arm of Mrs. Collins, pulling her back and down, while she searched for the threat. The County Executive was surrounded by his protection team from the outer ring. Soon enough, the threat was visible. An older White man dressed in a dark suit and tie, but clearly not at the level of the other guests, emerged from the crowd, forcing his way toward the County Executive. His right hand was raised, and he started firing rounds from a semi-automatic handgun. The shots were not well aimed, but people in the inner circle began to fall.

By now, Kelly had placed herself between Mrs. Collins and the approaching danger. She had drawn her service weapon and looked for a clear shot. It worked both ways. The clear shot came simultaneously with that of the perpetrator. He fired. She fired. A sharp pain in her right forearm registered—she had been hit. A second impact slammed into the middle of her chest and told her she had been shot again. Her ballistic vest saved her, but the impact was like being kicked in the chest. If her first shot hit the attacker, he was unfazed and continued forward. An adrenaline rush coursed through Kelly's body. She looked through her gun's sights and lined up her next shot. She fired, and it held true, striking the oncoming attacker in the center of his forehead. He dropped like a marionette whose strings had been cut.

4

AFTER THE CHAOS

After the chaos that always follows such an incident, it became clear that two people had died: one a paying guest, and the assailant. Two other protection agents had received minor non-life-threatening wounds. They were treated and released that evening. Kelly was rushed into surgery to try and save the lower portion of her right arm. The bullet had passed through her arm, but left a path of damage and destruction. Luckily, Baltimore had one of the best hand-trauma hospitals in the nation and Kelly was there within thirty minutes of being wounded. The shot to her chest was checked and had caused bruising, but no other damage.

After six hours of microscopic surgery, Kelly's arm was judged to be stable. It would take time to see if it would be a usable appendage. When Kelly awoke from surgery, she found herself in a private room with a nurse attending to her IV line. Her arm was numb and the fingers protruding from the bandages failed to move when she ordered her brain to wiggle them. She found that taking a normal breath was hampered by a pounding pain in her chest. The nurse immediately recognized Kelly's stress and her heart rate and blood pressure began to increase. The nurse's nameplate identified her as Sharon. She laid a hand on Kelly's left shoulder, gently pushing her back onto her pillow. "Take it easy and go slow," Sharon said. "You've had extensive surgery on your arm, and what you're experiencing right now is normal. The doctor is being summoned to come in and talk to you about your surgery and your prognosis."

Kelly's parents had been notified and, after arriving at the trauma center, were ushered in by the nurse. Both looked extremely worried and relieved at the same time. Sedated and pale, Kelly did not present well. But she was alive and it appeared her arm had been saved. Kelly dozed as they awaited the arrival of the doctor.

True to the nurse's promise, the doctor came in about ten minutes later. Kelly, being heavily medicated for the pain, was impressed. He was tall, with dark features and unusually bright teeth that gleamed when he revealed a breathtaking smile. A starched white doctor's coat and a stethoscope wrapped around his neck completed the television-like character. The mandatory iPad was tucked under his left arm. "Hello Kelly." He offered his hand to her mother and father. "Mr. and Mrs. Hart, I'm Dr. Gary Treadwell." His voice was warm and encouraging as he began to address them.

Dr. Treadwell said, "Officer, you've had quite a time this evening. I'm told you were able to take action that prevented death and injury to a lot of innocent souls. Unfortunately, while doing so, you were injured. The bullet that struck your right arm has created a lot of damage. You were in surgery for about six hours while a team of micro-surgeons put your arm back together."

Kelly asked him, "Will my hand and arm be okay?"

"Recovery and rehabilitation are going to take time. There is also the possibility that additional surgery may be needed. Right now, there is swelling in your arm, so don't panic because you can't move your fingers. Your arm is currently in a surgical harness that will keep it immobile and against your body. That will come off in about twenty-four hours and we'll check your wound to see how it's doing."

"How long will it be before I can use my hand?"

"You are fortunate that your injury was treated so soon after it occurred. You are in an excellent hospital for treating such injuries. I will be honest with you. The return of full use of your hand is in question. Only time and extensive rehabilitation will determine at what level you will be able to use your right hand. I know you have more questions, but right now, it's too soon to have all the answers. I will try to address them tomorrow."

"What about my injuries from the shot I took to my chest?"

"I can tell you that the bullet that struck your vest did no damage. You are bruised, but there is no damage to your bones or organs. You're going to have some pain while taking deep breaths for a couple of days. Try to get some rest tonight and the job of getting better starts tomorrow. You have a whole team who will be working with you to get your life back in order. And officer, thank you for your service. You did a good thing today. Do you have any questions?"

Kelly had stayed focused on the doctor as he spoke. "No, thank you." Her mind stayed awake long enough for her to begin to fear the ramifications of having limited use of her right hand. *What about my career? My martial arts and defensive tactics? I've overcome hurtles in the past. I'll overcome this and be back at the job sooner rather than later. I can do this. I know I can.* A drug-induced sleep consumed her.

"Joe, go home and get some rest," Mrs. Hart directed her husband.

"What about you, Debbie?"

"I'm staying," she continued as she took a position in the chair next to the bed. She wasn't going anywhere. "My only child is hurt and I'm staying to watch over my baby."

Visitors, colleagues, friends, and even police brass were turned away at Mrs. Hart's insistence. They were advised not to return before the next afternoon, after the hospital staff reexamined and evaluated Kelly. None of the hospital staff considered asking her mother to leave. On the contrary, they brought her a blanket and pillow to help make her comfortable throughout the coming hours.

The media was on the story and was being held at the main entrance to the hospital. A Baltimore County police officer had stood her ground and saved members of the county executive's family in a blazing gun battle. She had killed the attacker. A hero had been born. Reporters clamored to get more information, which remained sketchy. The police spin doctors would be at work throughout the night, putting together a story that would shine a bright and positive light on the police department and its leadership, even though the leaders were nowhere in sight when the bullets had been flying. Ceremonies and photo ops were already being planned. Everyone in the Baltimore area would soon know who Kelly Hart was.

5
MOMENTS OF FAME

The news cycle was slow at the time of the attack and the story stayed front and center on TV, cable, print, and social media for nearly four days. They hailed Kelly a hero and lamented the fact that she had been seriously injured and her future was uncertain. Several reporters tried to interview her, but that never happened. "No comment," was her response to all questions. Undeterred, the media found sources, both inside and outside the police department, more than willing to share what they had seen and what they thought happened that night. Each individual was getting their fifteen minutes of fame and was constantly checking social and print media. Most were sadly disappointed when they found nearly all they had to say had ended up on the cutting room floor. The talking heads ran with the ball and spoke as if they had been there themselves. When the next heinous crime occurred in Baltimore, the typical media circus died quickly.

Released from the hospital three short days after the surgery, Kelly faced a myriad of problems with a cast on her right arm and unable to use her right hand. *How will I drive, cook, do my hair, apply makeup, and get dressed?* She'd never felt so helpless.

Joe and Debbie Hart had always been good parents and tried to come to the rescue. Her Mom suggested that Kelly move back home where they could help her for as long as it took. Kelly resisted, countering with the agreement she would accept their help, if they would move in and stay at her apartment. "I want to be near my stuff and get back to as close to normal as possible," she explained. In reality, she couldn't wrap her head around going home to Mommy and Daddy at her age.

Her mother acquiesced with some reluctance. "Alright, we'll try it your way. Although your apartment may be a little tight for the three of us."

After two days at Kelly's apartment, they all realized the situation was not comfortable for anyone. Kelly's place was not large enough to handle even two people living there, let alone three. It was a one-bedroom apartment with a sleep sofa in the living room. In addition to the difficulty of unfolding the sleeper and then refolding it in the morning, Debbie Hart was a little too old for a sleep sofa for any length of time. On the third morning, Debbie broached the subject in her normal forthright manner. "Kelly, I'm not helping your recovery staying here. To sum it up, one bathroom, two women, and your father frequently visiting is way too cozy. You know I want to help you with dressing and showering. But, to be honest, I believe we are both feeling claustrophobic at best, and at worst, frustrated. We've tried. Neither of us have complained. But it's just not working, is it?"

She knew her mom loved her and genuinely meant well. But she was right. Kelly actually felt relieved. "Thank you,

Mom. I appreciate everything. I really do. But I'll be fine on my own."

However, Debbie wasn't finished. Mom had made an executive decision and told Kelly her alternate plan. "I think it would be best for you to stay at our place in Sandpiper. Being on the beachfront will be the perfect atmosphere and location to help you heal. The kitchen is fully stocked and the living room is large enough when you're feeling ready for visitors."

Kelly took a minute to think. Their family apartment at the Driftwood resort was a third-floor beachfront. with two large ocean-facing bedrooms complete with ensuite bathrooms and a powder room off the living room hallway. Even more important to Kelly right now; it was serviced by an elevator. And because her family visited several times a year, it was well maintained.

Debbie completed the sale of the idea, "Also, rehabilitation sites are available in Berlin, just a few short miles from the condo. And the outside deck will be a wonderful area for you to relax. You can walk on the beach every day and breath in the warm, fresh air."

Kelly jumped on the idea. She had been going to the beach since she was a kid and still went down a few times during the summer. She had her own key and spent time there in the winter just reading and kicking back by herself. It was a great idea.

Kelly hugged her mom, "Thank you. You're the best."

Smiling, her mother added, "Your father said he would come down when he could." Kelly knew her dad's part-time job as an investment advisor would limit his visits, but this felt like a neutral place rather than staying in her mom and dad's home in Baltimore.

Within six weeks, Kelly had both hard and then soft casts removed. The surgery had been declared a success by her surgeons, supported by physical examinations and X-rays. They believed her immediate treatment had prevented infection from taking hold, eliminating one of the most dangerous situations created by gunshot wounds. They all agreed she was extremely lucky, considering the circumstances.

But Kelly didn't feel so lucky. A thin, red, ugly line ran from her forearm to her elbow, showing the track of the bullet and subsequent surgery. A bone was shattered and replaced with a short titanium rod. The damaged muscles, ligaments, veins, and arteries were all reconnected and functioning. She could wiggle her fingers and partially close her hand, but not grip anything. Now the full extent of the damage would present as she took on the challenges of physical and occupational rehab.

The police-involved shooting investigation cleared her of any wrongdoing. She had followed agency procedures throughout the incident and fired her weapon only to protect herself and others from a clear and present threat. An autopsy of the attacker revealed her first shot struck the assailant in his side, but passed through without striking any vital organs. This allowed him to continue to move forward and continue shooting.

A background investigation revealed the perpetrator to be Ralph Sheldon, a politically far-left individual who often boasted of what he would like to do to the government officials who were driving the country to the right. In his mind, guns should not be allowed for anyone. Even the police should be disarmed. A search of his house revealed he had several hidden guns. Two of the guns were previously reported stolen from a neighbor and a relative. Rules for thee, but not for me.

The months that followed were dedicated to rehabilitation. Kelly worked tirelessly doing the strengthening and flexibility exercises provided by the rehab center. Improvement was slow and sometimes measured in millimeters of movement. She frequently traveled with her mother back to the Baltimore area to meet with doctors who evaluated her progress and encouraged her to keep going. Checking in with Dr. Fry, the physician with the police department, and human resources director, Mrs. Day, was mandatory. Kelly was collecting workers' compensation, but the day would eventually come when she would receive a medical release saying she had reached maximum recovery. She would receive a permanency rating on her loss of the use of her right hand. This would determine her future as a police officer.

In addition to rehabbing her right hand, Kelly took the initiative to make herself ambidextrous. She focused on using her left hand for everything she did, despite the fact she had some limited use of her right. She even practiced simple martial arts strikes and kicks, making her left side her lead. It was like starting all over again, but she didn't give up.

Soon she was able to drive herself and perform the daily tasks as they presented themselves. Mom and Dad agreed to leave her alone at the beach. They sensed she needed her own space and time to deal with the emotional side of her injury. It threatened her career and her future remained unclear.

Kelly sought out and made friends with a Maryland-licensed firearms dealer and instructor, Jackie Gitcher, who had a pistol range and could qualify applicants for handgun permits. He heard her story and was eager to help. She wanted to learn to shoot with her left hand while still trying to reach a point where she could again shoot with her right. As to be expected, shooting left-handed did not go well for a while, but many boxes of bullets later, she began to improve consistently. She shot every day. While her left-handed shooting was improving, she tried shooting with her right hand but found she could hardly lift her gun to shoulder level and when she did it was impossible for her to hold it steady. Despite all her effort, she would begin to shake wildly making it impossible to align the sites on the target. She even tried pointing the gun just a few feet in front of her and shooting it into the ground. She almost cried when she realized she didn't have the strength to pull the trigger. *More exercise has to be the answer.* She decided she would just double her efforts at the rehab center, maybe adding more trips to the gym where additional equipment would be available to help her strengthen her shoulder, arm, and hand.

One morning, after a three-mile jog on the beach, she visited a local market shortly after it opened to grab a bottle of water. She pushed the front door open with her left hand. She was wearing sweatpants, a T-shirt, sneakers, and a baseball cap with her hair pulled into a ponytail sticking out the back. A windbreaker was tied around her waist and a fanny pack rested on her hip carrying her cell phone, a Kubaton issued by Baltimore County PD, a set of keys attached to the Kubaton, and her badge.

The first thing Kelly heard was a loud voice barking in a berating tone. She quickly assessed the situation and observed a young female clerk in tears, suffering the wrath of a middle-aged man standing across the counter from her. Moving in behind the man, Kelly determined from the one-sided conversation that he was upset about an item he was trying to return. She glanced around the irate man and saw a pair of sunglasses laying on the counter.

The young clerk said, "The store policy is that you must have a sales receipt to show the item was purchased from the store before I can refund your money." She continued, "We don't sell that brand of sunglasses, sir."

"The hell you don't. I got them right here and they aren't the quality I paid for. I want my forty dollars back right now," the man exclaimed. "If I have to, I'll come around this counter and get my forty dollars, so just give it to me now!"

Kelly moved next to the man at the counter and said, "I think you need to tone it down a notch. This young lady doesn't need you trying to intimidate her with your voice and your demeanor. May I see the sunglasses?" she asked while picking them up from the counter.

A quick examination told her they were old and battered. Both lenses were heavily scratched and on their very best day, they were probably worth between five and ten dollars. She laid them back on the counter and turned to the man without saying a word.

He knew his scam was meeting unexpected scrutiny, and he puffed his chest up and said, "Who the hell are you, and what business is it of yours?"

"I'm Detective Kelly Hart and I'm making it my business. Now show me some identification or we can conclude our business at the station house."

His entire persona deflated as he floundered for words to cover for his ill-conceived plan to rip off the young store clerk. "I'm sorry officer, this is just a mix-up. I guess I got these glasses at another market that looks like this one. I'm just trying to get my money back. You know how all these places look alike."

Kelly calmly said, "No, I don't know how all these places look alike, and I'm still waiting for you to produce some identification." Reluctantly, the man produced a very worn wallet with a driver's license. His name was Bernard Sampson and his address was Montgomery County, Maryland.

"Mr. Sampson," Kelly said, "Do you still live at this address?"

"Yeah, most of the time, that's my mom's address."

"What will I find if I run a criminal check on you, Mr. Sampson?" Kelly inquired.

Making no eye contact and bowing his head, Bernard said, "I've been arrested for possession of weed and theft, but nothing major, and I've stayed out of trouble for the last two years."

"Why are you in Sandpiper, Mr. Sampson?" Kelly pushed.

"Just came down with my girlfriend for a couple of days. We're supposed to go back later today."

Kelly produced her badge from her fanny pack and covered the portion that said Baltimore County with her finger. Once Sampson had a glimpse of the badge, she returned it to her pack.

"Here's what's going to happen, Mr. Sampson. You're going back and find your girlfriend and you are both going home right now. Do you understand me?"

Sampson nodded his head rapidly. "Yes ma'am, I do understand."

"Okay, we have an understanding. If I see you later today, you're going to jail for attempted theft by means of fraud. Are we clear?" Kelly asked. Before handing back his ID, Kelly took a picture of it with her phone. "Now apologize to the clerk and get on your way."

"I'm sorry Miss for the mix-up and my loud voice. I won't be causing you no more problems," Sampson said while moving towards the door. Without another word, he slipped out onto the street and disappeared.

"You okay?" Kelly asked, addressing the young girl behind the counter.

"I am now," she responded. "I was really afraid before you came in. My name is Olivia. Thanks for helping me."

"No problem," Kelly said, extending her hand across the counter. Kelly got an enthusiastic handshake from the young woman.

Kelly instructed Olivia to tell her boss what happened and that the guy was just trying to run a scam. They both looked down at the sunglasses still sitting on the counter. "Don't worry, he won't be back for them," Kelly said.

Kelly got a bottle of water and left the store with mixed emotions. She stood up to a bully and helped the young girl out. *What would have happened if that asshole had broken bad? Would I have been able to deal with him with one hand and two feet? Yes, I think I could have. All you need is to have bigger balls than your opponent.*

6
OPPORTUNITY

Time ran out for Kelly. The day of reckoning came and went. All the rehabbing and extra effort put into returning her right hand to its previous state failed. There had been a vast improvement, but she still fell short of the physical requirements of a sworn police officer. An independent medical review confirmed the police department's findings. Her workers' compensation benefits ran out and she was forced into medical retirement. She was awarded sixty-six and two-thirds of her current salary tax-free and would be eligible for cost-of-living increases in future years.

Colonel Bakey, who oversaw the Dignitary Protection Unit, met privately with Kelly. Bakey said, "Kelly, I'll find you a civilian position somewhere within the department, but I admit it will be a desk job with a salary far less than you had been earning as a sworn officer."

Kelly responded, "Thanks colonel, I appreciate your kindness and I'll consider the offer." Before she reached her car, she had considered it and discarded it. *I was a cop and I belong on the street.*

A feeling of depression began to seep into her world. She gave up her apartment in Baltimore and decided to live full-time at her parent's condo in Sandpiper, a situation she could not fathom herself in at this stage of her life.

Days after receiving her medical discharge from the police department, Kelly's cell phone rang. She didn't recognize the number but answered it anyway. "Hart."

"Kelly?" the caller asked. "Is that you?"

Not recognizing the voice, she answered cautiously. "Yes, who's this?"

"This is Marie Barnett, from the police academy—we went through together. Do you remember me?"

Kelly said, "Yeah, I do remember you, dark hair cut short. Always laughing and seeming to have a good time. I heard you left the job to go to law school. What happened?"

"I did it," Marie answered. "I became a lawyer and have had my practice for about five years now. I specialize in insurance claims, but I do take some criminal defense and civil cases when I get the opportunity. I read about what happened to you and heard you were in Sandpiper. I was wondering how you're doing. I heard they forced you out on a medical."

"Afraid so," Kelly responded, almost tearing up when she finally heard it said by someone else. Marie picked up on the despair in Kelly's voice and immediately went on. "That's the reason I'm calling. I know you and I know what a hell of a cop you've been. Awards and plaques for being a hero don't give you a future. I have a proposition that may help us both. I have to confess a self-serving interest in making this call."

Kelly's curiosity peaked. "What's on your mind, Marie?"

"Well, the thing I didn't tell you is my practice is in Berlin, so we're about five miles apart right now if you're in Sandpiper. If you have some time, I'd like to meet face to face and lay out my thoughts and get your feedback. You may find it interesting."

"As it happens, I am in Sandpiper and all I have is time. Text me where to meet you." Kelly responded.

They met at 3:00 p.m. at Wild Horses on Main. It was a small restaurant on Main Street in Berlin serving great food. There was also a small bar. A lot of locals used it as a hangout after work. The two had the place pretty much to themselves. They chose a booth along a side wall where they would have the privacy to talk, and in true police tradition, they would be able to observe anyone entering the establishment. Once a cop, always a cop.

Kelly and Marie hugged and immediately sat down. A server came over and introduced herself. "Hi, I'm Kim. Let me tell you about the specials."

Marie interrupted her rehearsed menu list and expressed, "We're old friends and are going to be catching up for a while, so could you bring over two iced teas for now?"

Kim said, "Sure thing. I'll leave the menus on the table. Take your time and just give me a wave when you're ready."

Marie was dressed like a lawyer on her way to court: a black shirt dress, black heels, a pair of Prada sunglasses, and carrying an expensive leather briefcase. Her hair was touching her shoulders and wore the sheen and shape of a good hairstylist. She still had the easy smile that seemed to have her lips perpetually turned up at the corners.

Kelly came in a normal Sandpiper beach outfit. Casual as casual can be open-toed sandals, jeans, and a tee shirt with a penguin on the front. Her blonde hair was pulled up in a knot on top of her head. Kelly actually looked more appropriate for the venue.

Marie got right to the point. "Kelly, have you made plans on what you're going to do with your life now that you're not a cop?"

"No, I was hoping against hope that I'd get back on the job, but now that's been taken away. I guess I'm sort of floundering right now, but nothing seems to fit my needs."

"Have you ever considered being a private investigator?" Marie asked. Kelly's mouth opened and her eyes widened.

"Before you answer, let me tell you why I wanted to meet with you. After five years in practice, I'm beginning to get more and more clients and, of course, more and more cases to work. Success brings with it certain requests."

"What kind of requests Marie?"

"I want to grow my practice and I think you may be able to help me. I'm still not big enough to hire a full-time investigator, but I do need someone to serve my process, interview witnesses and potential clients, and conduct investigations for me as the need arises."

"Marie, are you asking me to work for you?"

"No! You would be your own boss and be able to take on any investigation or assignment that comes your way, as long as it was not in direct conflict with one of my cases. You would be a natural with your background."

"So, this is what you meant by a PI?"

"Kelly, you can set your competitive hourly rate and I'll have my clients pay you directly for your services. I will determine what is necessary for my cases. I suggest you have them give you a retainer before you do anything for them and have them replenish the retainer as needed. That way, you never have to wait for your money."

"This is interesting, handle your clients, but also have the ability to bring clients in on my own. I'm intrigued, Marie, I have to say."

"Sandpiper could use someone like you. I know other attorneys who are always looking for a PI. Just so we're clear. Never, ever trust a lawyer to pay you for your work. Always get your money upfront. Lawyers can be a nasty bunch. I know because I'm now one of them."

Marie looked across the table at Kelly and continued. "I've already checked and there would be no prohibition with you being a private investigator. Your physical disability is not a disqualifier, and your ten years of police experience make you eligible to run your own agency."

I can't believe Marie has checked into all of this for me.

"If you can qualify with a handgun, you are also eligible to obtain a concealed-carry permit. I spoke with Maryland State Police investigator, Jenny Carter, in the licensing section. She told me that with your background and notoriety, she felt your vetting would move smoothly and quickly through the system. I have her name and phone number if you want to speak with her after our meeting. She's a friend of mine and has empathy for you and your circumstances."

Kelly sat back in her seat, overwhelmed by the presentation and potential opportunity. She gazed off and her thoughts started to churn. *Never thought about being a PI. It would allow me to do most of the things I've already been trained to do. Even personal protection details.*

Marie spoke again, "Let me sweeten the pot just a bit more while you think about it. My office is right down the street. It's an old and narrow building that runs from Main Street to an alley. Are you familiar with the area?"

Kelly said, "Not exactly."

"I'm renting it with an option to buy, so I have use of the entire space. It is set up for two suites. I've been using the front four offices for my law practice, but there are two more offices, a separate bathroom, and an entrance in the rear of the building. I would allow you to use them rent-free for the first year while you get your feet on the ground. Having you close at hand would be worth it to me. Right now, they just sit empty."

"Well, how would this work?" Kelly asks.

"We can whack up the rest of the monthly bills based on the square footage. There is already a separate phone line going into those offices. I have a receptionist we could share while you're out of the office. She works normal business hours. There's some old office furniture back there that you can use or toss if you want to bring in your stuff. One of my four offices is a small conference room that I'm willing to share with you when you need one. There is a door in the hallway that separates the two suites, which would give us both complete privacy and autonomy. You can even hang a sign in the alley showing people where you are. Parking is tight, but people always find a way."

Now Kelly was flabbergasted. As Marie ticked off the positives about the proposal, she removed all the questions that had been forming in Kelly's mind. She was hard-pressed at the moment to think of any reason why she shouldn't try to make this work. Kelly looked down at herself and her face reddened. She looked Marie in the eyes and said, "I apologize for the way I look. I had no idea I was coming to a career opportunity. Please forgive me for not being more professional."

Marie laughed, "Believe me, girlfriend, if this wasn't a workday, I'd be dressed just like you. What do you think about my offer?"

Kelly stuck out her hand. "I'm in!"

7

I'M A PI

The following eight weeks were nothing short of mayhem. Kelly traveled to the State Police Licensing Division and met with investigator Jenny Carter. Carter welcomed Kelly and said, "Let me help you complete all the necessary paperwork for getting your PI license so we can make sure every I is dotted and every T is crossed."

Carter knew of Kelly's background and felt a little special treatment was in order. Carter followed up to make sure Kelly's file did not linger on anyone's desk for days or weeks. Even the background checks—including criminal history—were performed and verified. Personal and professional references were checked. Kelly knew this because a couple of her references had reached out to her saying they had been interviewed. All investigative reports were submitted in a timely manner. Nothing improper or illegal was done, but the grease was definitely on the skids.

The concealed-carry permit was much the same. Gitcher qualified Kelly using her left hand. Kelly scored ninety-two out of a possible one hundred.

Kelly spent her waiting time making her new offices shine. "Hey Marie, do you mind if I give these old walls a facelift?"

Marie laughed, "Be my guest."

Kelly added, "I might as well have the carpet professionally cleaned while I'm at it."

Kelly's mom and dad were enthused just to see her excited for the first time in over a year. They pitched in during the cleaning and bought her a nearly new desk and office chair. Kelly was able to purchase the rest of the office furnishings at HomeGoods.

Kelly got a call on her cell while working at the office "Hi Kelly, how you doin'? It's Mike Haynes. I'm in your area and wanted to see if you have time for a coffee."

Kelly was happy to hear from Mike who was her old partner in her unit back in Baltimore. Kelly responded, "It's good to hear from you. Sure, I would love to grab a coffee. I'm at my office. Why don't you come by and I can give you a tour, and then we can go for that coffee. I'll text you the address."

Fifteen minutes later, Mike arrived at the law office of Marie Barnett, Kelly heard Mike's voice when he came through the door. She went up the hallway to greet him. Both smiling and happy to see one another, they shared an awkward hug because Mike was carrying a package under his left arm. Kelly guided Mike back to her office and gave him the Nickel-tour. Mike laid the package on her desk. Kelly looked at Mike, "What's this?"

"It's a little something from the unit back in Baltimore, so you don't forget us. We all pitched in on this." As Kelly opened the package, she saw a sign for her new business. It was a custom-made sign of dark brown wood with raised white lettering saying, Kelly Hart ~ Private Investigator. Mike told her,

"We thought this would be suitable for hanging outside your alley entrance." Kelly said, "It's empowering to have so many people rooting for my success. Thank you and thank them for this gesture."

Off they went for that coffee and catching up. At the end, they vowed to stay in touch and get together whenever Mike was in town. *Tomorrow I'll send a thank you note to the office in Baltimore.*

Unrelenting, Kelly found the time and energy to spend her evenings serving; subpoenas, summons, and other court documents for Marie. In Maryland, the only requirement for serving process is to be eighteen years of age. The fee for the service of process varies from county to county, ranging from forty to one hundred and twenty dollars. In the world of process serving, you only get paid for papers that you serve. Attempts to serve net you nothing.

Kelly quickly learned some of the tricks of the trade. Lying, trickery, using costumes, or hiding in the shadows were all acceptable behaviors. She found it fun and somewhat stimulating. Her success now weighed heavily on the use of her imagination to overcome obstacles. While not making big money, she was making Marie a very happy camper. A couple of other attorneys asked Marie if her server was willing to serve their court process. Marie directed them to Kelly, so she could discuss their needs for her service and review her terms about pick-up and payment. Marie's advice about retainers had saved Kelly from a very expensive lesson most PIs learn the hard way.

Kelly was already accumulating a treasure trove of stories about serving papers. At one address, an older man answered the door in a tattered robe. "Hey, You Joe Sturns?" asked Kelly. When he saw a woman at the door, he casually let his robe fall open fully exposing himself and said, "Yeah, I'm Joe." Kelly had seen far worse behavior and was unimpressed by what he was showing her. She stuck out her hand as if to shake Joe's hand, but when he reached for her hand, she used her left hand to put a rolled piece of paper in it. "Mr. Sturns, you've been served." She turned on her heel and walked away. Making money one serve at a time

At another residence, she'd been there twice. No one would answer the door. She heard voices and the television playing, so she knew people were there. She went to a nearby pizza place and ate a dinner consisting of a personal-size pizza, ordered to go. For an additional five bucks, she had Wally, the teenage employee, loan her his baseball cap with their logo.

She returned to the residence wearing the hat and carrying the almost empty pizza box. This time she accompanied the knock with a shout-out, "Pizza delivery!"

The door sprang open, and a young girl said, "You have pizza for us?"

"I have an order for Larry Bane. Is he here?"

The little girl yelled out, "Hey Larry, there's a pizza here for you."

A tall, thin man came to the door saying, "I didn't order any pizza."

Kelly said, "It's already paid for. Are you sure you're Larry Bane?"

The guy said, "I'm Lawrence Bane and I'll take the pizza." He reached out and took the box. Suspicion crossed his features when he noticed how light and small the box was. He opened it and saw a rolled piece of paper. More confusion as he unrolled the document. While he was unrolling it, Kelly turned and walked away from the door, turning and looking over her shoulder: "You've been served, Mr. Bane."

Kelly heard the words, "You fucking bitch," as she closed her car door and drove away.

She knew these hard serves would probably be a no-show at court time, but she got paid for the service, not the appearance. Failure to appear or comply with a court document usually ended up with the judge issuing an arrest warrant for failure to appear. A sheriff's deputy would soon be calling on these assholes.

These difficult situations were not the norm. Usually, the service of a summons or a subpoena was as simple as knocking on a door and asking for the person to be served and handing them the paper. Sometimes the blank look on the recipient's face would cause Kelly to take the extra time to explain what they needed to do, when, and where they needed to go. Kelly always felt good for taking the extra time with those folks.

One day all Kelly's work paid off when the mail carrier delivered both the private investigator's license and the concealed-carry permit on the same day. Miracles never cease! Coupled with an official-looking PI badge she ordered on the internet, Kelly was now the real deal.

She sat at her new desk and looked around her office at all the paraphernalia gathered to make her legit. She thought to herself, *I did it. I'm a PI. What a hoot! Now, what do I do?*

8
A NEW SUIT

The Sandpiper Police Department has a small detective unit consisting of three investigators. The lead detective was William Brogan. He came to Sandpiper from Baltimore City Police Department where he was a seasoned homicide detective. A politician who failed to be able to influence Brogan's honest policing policies hastened him to seek a new jurisdiction to continue his police career. The politician's son went to jail for murder and Brogan went to Sandpiper PD. The town of Sandpiper became the benefactor and their lead detective had earned the admiration and respect of everyone involved in law enforcement in the county including the State's Attorney and the Courts.

Detective Brogan's ability to set his hours allowed him to cover the day shift and a small part of the evening shift. He liked to have as much personal contact with as many officers as he could. Sometimes he came in at 5 p.m. and worked until 1 a.m. for the same reason. Everyone, including the chief, understood he was a man of all shifts and it helped everyone stay on their toes, not knowing when or where Brogan would show up. His cell phone was never turned off; he was available twenty-four-seven.

Brogan's workday in Sandpiper began at 10 a.m. that particular morning. It was raining lightly making the streets shine. The slick blacktop caused the normal amount of low-speed traffic accidents keeping the uniform guys busy. People never seem to learn to slow down and keep their space or to put their cell phones down. Fortunately, low speeds normally result in damage without injuries.

Brogan was dressed in his navy single-breasted suit with a fresh white shirt and light blue tie. His gun rode comfortably under his left arm in a brown leather shoulder holster. He was ready to protect the town he loved. The weather did not lessen his good mood.

The police radio came to life drowning out Brogan's Luke Bryan country tune on the radio. "Carjacking is in progress at 47th Street at the laundromat." There was a moment of silence and the police communication officer (PCO) continued, "The car is a red Toyota and a woman is reporting her 18-month-old baby is in a car seat, in the rear. The car was last seen heading south on Ocean Highway."

Brogan picked up his mike and said, "This is Car 3 to headquarters, call the bridge and have them raise it and leave it up until further notice. Send two cars to Ocean Highway and Route 90 and two cars to the Delaware line. Have them remain in place until relieved, and notify the Delaware authorities of the situation and ask if they have a car available at Lucy's on The Bay. Recall all cars on lesser calls and have them begin patrolling the streets south of 47th Street. I'm currently at 33rd Street and will remain at this location. All cars are directed to go to radio silence unless they have new information concerning this carjacking and kidnapping."

PCO responded, "Car 6 and 9 report to Route 90 intersection. Car 16 and 19 report to Delaware line. All other patrol cars begin to filter south and patrol streets south of 47th Street. All cars, FYI south bridge is in the up position. Delaware authorities MSP and Sheriff's office have been notified."

Brogan responded, "10-4 Headquarters."

Brogan barely pulled to the shoulder before he observed a red vehicle headed south, moving in and out of traffic at a high rate of speed. He checked his side-view mirror and pulled across three lanes of northbound Ocean Highway and into the left turn lane at 33rd Street. The red car blew by him in the southbound lanes. The driver recognized the unmarked roller and sped up even more. Brogan threw his blue bubble light on the dash, and with the light flashing, he negotiated a U-turn while other southbound cars moved out of his way. When he straightened the wheel to head south, he saw the red car make a dangerously sharp right-hand turn on 28th Street.

Brogan called in his sighting on the radio, "Car 3 to Headquarters, suspect vehicle sighted turning on 28th Street. I'm in pursuit."

"10-4 Car 3," PCO responded. "Headquarters to all cars, Car 3 is in pursuit on 28th Street toward the bay."

Brogan made the turn onto 28th Street just seconds later. The red car was nowhere in sight. Brogan accelerated for a short distance and then let off the gas as he approached a sharp left-hand curve in the road. The driver of the red Toyota was apparently unfamiliar with the road. The fence that protects the road from a water feature on the right was shredded. He had driven through it, plunging the car into the water.

The car was already up to its windows and sinking fast. The suspect was exiting through the driver's window, leaving the child to fend for itself. Brogan called over his mike, "Car 3 to Headquarters, vehicle in the water at 28th Street curve. The suspect is a blonde-haired kid wearing a green sweatshirt. I'm going into the water after the baby."

Not waiting for a response, Brogan threw his gun and cell phone under his front seat and left the vehicle with his keyless remote—locking the vehicle as he ran to the edge of the water. He lifted a large rock and placed the remote under the rock for safety. The sinking car was still visible, and Brogan could hear the shrieking voice of a baby in distress. Not knowing the depth of the water, he walked in and was quickly in waist-deep water. The cold water smelled of rotting vegetation and was a murky greenish-brown color. The muck pulled at his shoes, slowing his progress. The car appeared to be settling on the bottom with the roof still above the water. The water level was easily covering the child, who was sitting low in a car seat in the back. Brogan took five long and strong swimming strokes and arrived at the side of the car. No sounds were coming from the car, and Brogan could see the child was completely submerged.

Without hesitation, Brogan jerked the backdoor handle but found it locked. He moved to the driver's door and pulled it open. He leaned in between the two front seats. He reached further in and felt the baby struggling against the seatbelt that held the child in place. Brogan has carried a three-inch clip knife in his front pants pocket since his first day as a police of-ficer. He kept it razor-sharp. He withdrew his hand from the struggling child and grabbed his knife, flicking it open with practiced skill. He wedged himself sideways between the two front seats and went to work on the seatbelt, cutting through it like butter. The baby began to float out of the seat. Brogan pulled the child to him and twisted out of the grasp of the car seats. Feeling his own need for oxygen he quickly surfaced and stood up, bringing the child over his left shoulder, well out of the water. The child bounced off of Brogan's shoulder as he struggled back to the shore. The bouncing action with the child facing down had a CPR effect and suddenly there was violent coughing, followed by an ear-splitting scream. Brogan smiled at the greatest sound he had heard in a long time. He brought what turned out to be a little girl down off his shoulder and looked into her eyes. Her blue eyes matched his. His bright eyes and wide smile somewhat startled her. She quieted for a moment and then began a soft sob capable of breaking anyone's heart.

Brogan finally looked up at the shoreline and saw a group of cops staring back. A soggy, wet, blonde teenager was wrapped in a blanket, hooked-up, and closely guarded. A young woman, tears streaming down her face, was held in check by a police officer. She was the mother, brought to the scene by this equally young officer. As Brogan reached the shore, he turned the little girl around so she could see her mom and then held her out at arm's length so her mother could reach and pull her in. Officers immediately wrapped both mom and baby in a blanket. A few looky-loos joined the many officers and they began to applaud the rescue. For a few moments in time, everyone was happy, except the soggy teenager.

Brogan retrieved his car remote and made his way up to the road. Sergeant Burton was smiling as he handed him a blanket. The mother clung fiercely to her daughter as a paramedic tried to examine the baby. "Good job detective," Burton said. "Hope that wasn't your favorite suit!"

Brogan smiled and said, "No, my favorite suit is the one the town is about to buy me."

Burton slapped Brogan on the back and said, "I'll tell the chief you'll be a little late getting into the office."

Chief Richards ordered all to return to normal duties. Brogan arranged the blanket on his front seat and was about to enter when a hand landed on his shoulder, pulling him around to look into the tear-streaked faces of the mother and child. The baby had calmed, but the mother not so much. She leaned in, crushing the child between them, and gave him a peck on the cheek. Breathlessly, she said, "I'm Bonnie. I can never thank you enough. My daughter, Katie, is my everything. Thank you."

"Glad I was there to help," Brogan responded stoically. He smiled at the little girl as she reached her little hand out to him. He took her hand in his and squeezed gently. "Have a wonderful life, little one."

He nodded to her mom and entered his car. She moved back, allowing him to re-enter the road and drive away. Other Sandpiper officers closed around to help her through this traumatic experience. The perp was placed in the backseat of a patrol for transport to the PD. A tow truck was pulling up to remove the car from the water. Town employees arrived to make temporary repairs on the fence. A sense of normalcy returned to Sandpiper. Another Sandpiper detective was arriving at the PD to assist with the arrest and charging of the suspect. Brogan headed home to restart his day.

9

BRING HER HOME

K elly sat alone in her office. She'd been there since 7:30 a.m. No one had called or knocked on her door. Marie and the receptionist weren't due in until 9. She could hear cars moving in the area, but she had no window facing the street or the alley. Her only window was nailed shut and faced the brick wall of the next building, with a narrow space separating her from the wall. She had curtained the window to give the appearance of a view, but the only thing to see was the depressing brick.

Her mind wandered. *Is this what PIs do? Just sit and wait for someone to call or come in? Hell, nobody knows I'm a PI or where I'm located.* Her box of fresh business cards sat in her desk drawer. She had placed some in her briefcase and a few in her car's glove box. Marie took ten and the receptionist placed a few in a card holder on the credenza behind her chair. As far as Kelly knew, not a single card had fallen into the hands of a potential client. Marie had nothing pending that needed an investigator. *Is this a mistake? A fantasy of a new career? Is Kelly Hart, PI, doomed to fail before I even get started? Maybe I should advertise on the radio or in the paper? Or go on Facebook to get the word out? Would that make me look desperate? I need to calm down! This is my first full day as a licensed PI. What am I expecting? A line around the building with people eager to pour their problems and money at the new investigator in town? Get a grip, Kelly!*

At 9 a.m., Stacy, the receptionist, arrived and put on a pot of coffee. Stacy was in her early thirties—maybe five foot, four inches tall, with beautiful green eyes. Stacy was always pushing her mousey brown hair out of her eyes, which was distracting when talking with her. She was a warm and welcoming person, and Kelly had already begun to like her and saw the strong bond of trust and loyalty between her and Marie.

Five minutes later, Marie came through the front door, dropped her briefcase on her desk, and headed for the coffee pot. Kelly came to the front of the building, drawn by the sounds of office activity.

Marie said, "Hey Kelly, how long have you been here?"

Kelly responded, "Since around 7:30. Nothing going on so far."

Marie laughed. "This town is hardly awake at 7:30, so don't be disheartened that nothing is going on yet. I have something in my briefcase that may change that for you. Grab your notebook and a coffee and we can talk in my office."

Kelly said, "Good morning Stacy," as she passed by walking into Marie's office.

"Good morning."

Marie told Kelly, "You can leave the door open. I've found it better to let Stacy know what's going on with my cases so she can better handle incoming calls. Stacy files all of my paperwork so she has insight into everything happening in the office. She has never leaked a word about any of the cases passing through here. She can be trusted, Kelly." *Trust is hard-earned in the police world. I have to work on that.*

Marie pulled a thin folder from her briefcase and centered it on her desk while sipping her coffee. "Last night, I had dinner with some friends at their home here in town. Ken and Renae Brightfield. They're good people and have been my friends for years. They told me they were afraid for their daughter's safety and sought my counsel."

Marie looked at Kelly, "Their daughter's name is Debbie Brightfield. She's eighteen years old and has recently taken up with a boy from Baltimore. Two weeks ago, they left Sandpiper together in his car to go to his place in Dundalk. Debbie told her parents she was just going for a visit and would probably be back the following weekend. The same day she left, she called her mother and gave her the address in Dundalk and said everything was fine and she was having a good time. Debbie called her mom twice more during the week, telling her everything was good and she'd be home soon.

"The Brightfields explained the weekend came and went with no contact from their daughter. Renae called Debbie's cell phone on Monday. After several rings it went to voice mail, but about an hour later, she received a text from Debbie's phone saying everything was good and she was sorry she hadn't made it home yet, but decided to stay in Baltimore for another week or so and signed off, 'LOVE, DEB.' This sent up a red flag to Renae because Debbie never referred to herself as Deb. Debbie would correct people who would call her Deb stating she preferred Debbie. Renae being concerned, texted back, asking her to call her as soon as she got a chance. Renae received no response to her text.

"It was clear to me that Renae and Ken had good reason

to worry about their daughter. Ken seemed frustrated and angry. Renae called and texted Debbie's phone every day for the next four days. Renae received a couple of short text responses saying she was busy and would reach out soon. On the fourth day when Renae called, the phone went right to voice mail, and Renae knew the phone was turned off. At that point, she was really scared.

"During the time Renae and Ken were telling me the circumstances, Ken erupted, 'I've had enough! I'm going to Baltimore and bringing Debbie home. And if that boyfriend of hers gets in the way, I will deal with his little ass!' I talked Ken down and expressed he should not take matters into his own hands."

"Marie, do you really think Ken would go to Baltimore?" Kelly inquired.

"Not sure but there is a good possibility.

"I asked Renae if they had called the police. She explained Ken had called Baltimore County PD and told them the story. He spoke with Corporal Schmidt. Schmidt informed him, since Debbie was eighteen, she could come and go as she pleased, and there was really nothing they, as parents, could do to stop her. And since there had been no report that indicated Debbie was in trouble or distress, there was nothing the police could do. Schmidt told him to give it a little more time and see if it doesn't work itself out. Ken was told he could call back next week if they were still concerned, and the PD would send an officer around to check on her.

"I felt bad for Ken because he hung up feeling he had been blown off. Ken said, 'Fuck the police. We're not going to wait another week. Something needs to be done NOW!' I could see Renae was visibly upset. Renae said, 'I'm afraid for both

Debbie and Ken. Ken's a great guy, a great husband, and an exceptional father, but he's also a big-game hunter and will carry a gun if he goes to Baltimore. No telling what he could do if provoked. I need to find my daughter, but I need to protect my husband from doing something stupid.'"

Kelly asked, "Marie, are these folks helicopter parents? Do you think they are overreacting?"

"No, it's funny you ask that. Renae thought they may be overreacting, but her gut was telling her they needed to do something. I know through my past conversations with Renae, my longtime friend, that Debbie had always suffered from low self-esteem because of her red hair, freckles, and the fact she developed early. She was not ready for what puberty had in store for her. Renae would tell her often she was attractive, but Debbie never believed her.

"I looked at Renae as she looked down at her hands, folded in her lap, and asked, 'What's wrong, Renae, what are you thinking? 'That boy spent more time looking at my daughter's chest than her face when they were together. Debbie had gone to some counseling hoping to overcome her self-doubts, but I know she jumped at the first attention given to her by this boy, whom she had just met at a nightclub in Sandpiper. She apparently had some phony identification that allowed her to get into the clubs.'"

"So, Kelly what do you think? I told the Brightfields about you and suggested you might be able to help them. I told them just a little bit of your history as a police officer and how much I respected your work. I said I would talk with you this morning, and ask you to call and maybe even meet with them. They know you're a PI and need to be compensated for your time, so they are prepared for that. They have money and never asked how much you charge. I told them you would ask for a retainer and lay out a plan of what action you would take for them."

Marie pushed the file across the desk to Kelly and said, "Inside the file is all the information the Brightfields have on the boy from Baltimore. They have his name, address, and a physical description, and a description of his vehicle. Their daughter's cell phone number is in there too, along with a photograph of her. Their phone number and address are also in the file. Can you reach out to them this morning?"

Kelly studied the information for a few moments and then said, "I'll get right on it. My gut also tells me something is not right. I'll get them the answers they need. This is my first case and I'll do the best I can to make sure Debbie is all right. Thanks for trusting me with this. These are your friends and I won't disappoint you either."

Marie responded, "That's why I called you in the first place. I know your work ethic. Go to it, investigator."

Kelly called the Brightfields and spoke with Renae. Kelly introduced herself and said, "Renae, I assure you I will do whatever it takes to help you and your family."

Ken jumped on the call and said, "Can you come to our home immediately?"

Forty-five minutes later, Kelly walked through the front door of the Brightfield residence and found herself in a well-appointed colonial home. She could tell that either they were gifted with an artistic flair or a professional designer had played a role here. She felt like she was in a model home. The word beautiful came to mind, but that was even inadequate for what she saw.

Ken and Renae shook Kelly's hand and thanked her for

coming so quickly. Ken was a strong-fit man built like a Ken doll with a full head of hair. His hands were soft to the touch, but firm and strong. His grip left little doubt he was someone to be reckoned with, but his face showed his stress and anxiety. He needed answers sooner than later. He said, "I would like to address the financial part of your investigation and get that behind us so we can focus just on Debbie."

Renae was a woman with light red hair and a beautiful smile. If Debbie took after her mother, she was gorgeous. Renae had the physical presence of an athlete, perhaps a tennis player. Her grip was strong, and she looked Kelly in the eye when she shook her hand. She looked as if she had been crying recently, but had pulled herself together and was ready to find out what was going on with her daughter. She appeared relieved to see Kelly.

Kelly told the Brightfields, "Let's get some housekeeping out of the way. I charge eighty-five dollars an hour, plus any expenses incurred during the investigation. This includes mileage and possibly lodging if I have to stay overnight somewhere. I require a two-thousand-dollar retainer. The retainer may need to be replenished or returned in part to you based on how my investigation goes."

Ken said, "Let's sit at the dining room table and talk about what you intend to do." He had already placed his checkbook on the table before Kelly had arrived. He asked if a check was okay and when she nodded, he filled out a check for two-thousand dollars and handed it to Kelly saying, "Whatever it takes."

Kelly began the conversation, "You know, I was briefed by Marie as to what you told her. Now I need more facts. All information is pertinent; no detail is too small."

Kelly said, "Let's start with the boy, his appearance, his

car, and any conversations you have had with him."

Renae began, "He told us his name was Zack Ward and he was twenty years old. He was about six-foot tall, but reed-thin. His almost blackish-brown hair was shaggy and often fell across his eyes. When we saw him, he was wearing jeans that appeared to be clean and a teeshirt with a cartoonish guy on a skateboard."

Ken said, "I remember he had a tattoo on his right fore-arm, but it was faded and I could not identify what it was."

Renae touched her fingers and said, "His fingernails were dark. He mentioned he worked in an auto shop and it was difficult to eliminate all the grit despite repeated washing—claimed it was the sign of a working man. He also said he was taking some community college classes at night at Essex."

Ken said, "I noticed the car was cleaned and appeared to be well cared for.

Kelly asked, "Give me details about the car, what color and make of the car was it, two-door or four-door? Were there any stickers, accident damage, or anything that would set it apart from other vehicles?"

Renae was able to get the color down to the blue of a US flag, with a dent in the trunk on the passenger side. Both were sure it was a Honda.

"There was also something hanging from the rear-view mirror," Ken added.

Both Ken and Renae conveyed that while he was very po-lite, he gave them the uneasy feeling, that he was making up his story as he went along.

Ken said, "I noticed Debbie was hanging on every word and desperately trying to make us accept this guy who had just come into her life. In the end, we tried to support her effort to leave the nest for the first time and try to find herself outside Sandpiper."

Renae said as she looked up at Kelly, "Although he was far from what we hoped our daughter would be attracted to, the boy did not seem threatening while in our presence. We now wish we had found out more about him."

Kelly told them her plan was straightforward. "Tomorrow morning, I will go to Dundalk and make face-to-face contact with Debbie. I will check out the living conditions and determine if she is safe and well. I'll share with Debbie the worry that you are going through because of her silent treatment. I will also get eyes on Zach and determine if his employment and participation in college are real or made up. Finally, I'll encourage Debbie to call home to reassure you of her well-being and urge her to keep an open line of communication with you. I'm going to offer Debbie an exit ramp to this relationship by offering to drive her back to Sandpiper. If I find anything criminal in nature, I will call Baltimore County PD and be sure they address the situation before I leave Baltimore."

Kelly asked Renae for a word or something that no one else would know, maybe something from Debbie's childhood. Kelly said, "Debbie will not know me and if I share this with her, she will know she is safe and can trust me." Renae thought for a couple of seconds and said, "Dino. When she was little, she had a stuffed dinosaur with a long neck she used to carry around all the time. It was always her favorite, even after it became worn and dirty. I would clean it after she was asleep, otherwise, she would not be parted from it. She could never say dinosaur—but settled on Dino. I still have it in the attic."

Kelly promised the Brightfields that she would call them as soon as she knew the circumstances surrounding their daughter and keep them fully informed. She expressed she would also listen to any input they had before returning to Sandpiper. Kelly gave them one of her new business cards and told them to call her anytime and especially if they thought of anything important or if they spoke or received a message from Debbie. Nothing would stop the face-to-face meeting she intended to have with Debbie. She also planned to talk with Debbie away from Zach. The Brightfields were on board with the plan and again thanked Kelly for helping them. As they showed her out the front door, Ken said, "Please bring our girl home." The worry in their eyes for their little girl's safety was evident.

"I will if I can," Kelly responded, giving them a look of determination before letting the door close behind her.

10
A CHANCE MEETING

Kelly went back to her office and got everything she felt she would need for her mission. She left a note for Stacy saying she would be out of the office tomorrow. She placed a note on Marie's desk saying she would be in Dundalk and have her cell phone on if needed.

Kelly had gone from zero to full speed in just a few hours. Elated that she had her first case to work on and two thousand dollars in the bank to prove it, she decided to go out to dinner and have a good meal. A glass of wine would be nice, and the alone time would give her a chance to sharpen her focus on her plan for tomorrow.

At 16th Street and the Sandpiper boardwalk, she found an upscale restaurant that provided a view of the ocean to enhance the occasion. It was a busy place and Kelly elected to sit at the bar. The bartender took her drink order and gave her a menu.

A tall, dark-haired man took the empty stool next to her. She had noticed the stools were bigger and softer than most bar stools she had sat on. They were spaced so you didn't feel cramped. The man appeared to pay her no attention. He ordered a Coors Light beer and a shot of Yellowstone bourbon and also took a menu. He was easy on the eyes as Kelly stole a glance or two. When he spoke with the bartender, he had a low soulful voice. Kelly could not help noticing the fine, tan dress pants, expensive, brown Italian shoes, a light blue dress shirt buttoned almost to the neck, and a dark blue jacket. His freshly shaven face and a hint of cologne caught her nose. *Man, a guy with no stubble, nice!* The jacket hid his masculine build. *Modest to boot!*

When the bartender brought his drinks, he and the man exchanged light banter like they knew each other. *Maybe this guy was a regular. File that away for future use: a paid investigation, a good meal, a good wine, and eye candy. Things are definitely looking up.*

She quietly ate her meal and drank her wine. Her unknown companion did the same. Kelly was a little disappointed and a little surprised he had not tried to start some dialogue with her. She thought she was looking pretty hot. *Maybe he's gay.* He did look a little polished for Sandpiper.

Liquor bottles lined the shelves behind the bartender, and behind the bottles was a mirror. Kelly hadn't paid attention to it when she sat down, but now she looked into the mirror and found a set of dazzling blue eyes looking right back at her. A smile raced to her lips before she could stop it. She was the first to break contact. He didn't seem to care she had caught him eyeballing her. *Wow, a quiet man who made her melt with just his eyes.* It had been a long time since Kelly had shared herself with a man. This guy held promise.

She caught herself, *Jesus Christ, this is the same shit that happened to Debbie. What the hell am I thinking?* In her mind, she was already in bed with this stranger, and he was fulfilling her every need. *Good grief, I'm writing my own PI romance novel. I need to get out more. I need to get laid.*

He finished before she did and the bartender brought him his bill. He paid with a credit card, signed his name on the receipt, and pushed it to the rail. As he stood and turned to go, he leaned into Kelly's space and said, "You look really nice this evening. Maybe we'll see each other again sometime." And then he was gone.

What was that? What had just transpired? She caught herself giggling, like a dizzy teenager. That was definitely a first. The bartender was busy at the other end of the bar, so she quickly reached over to the receipt that lay at the rail, pulled it to her, and read just a single name. Brogan. *Who is this Brogan guy?* She quickly put the receipt back in place. A few minutes later she paid her bill and walked out onto the boardwalk. On the way to her car, all her senses were heightened. *Will he be somewhere waiting for me? He probably will make his move with some kind of bullshit pickup line that would ruin the entire fairy tale meeting.* But he wasn't. He was gone and all she had was a name.

No time to contemplate. Big day tomorrow. She needed to be on top of her game. Debbie may need to be rescued, or maybe just didn't give a shit about her parents. *We'll see.*

11

I WILL COME FOR YOU

The Chesapeake Bay Bridge was coming up, and so was the sun. Kelly left Sandpiper at o-dark-thirty and it was a magnificent sight. With the sun at her back, the metalwork of the bridge glistened. The calm waters of the Chesapeake Bay were visible as her vehicle began to climb the structure, leaving the Eastern Shore behind.

As she began her descent onto the Western Shore, her mind churned with thoughts of what she may face this morning. *Always plan for the worst and enjoy the times when it never happens.* She was about forty-five minutes from Dundalk. She had patrolled the Dundalk area in her first years on the job with the PD. It was a blue-collar town with the normal mix of good folks and assholes. Sometimes, it seemed the number of assholes was gaining a distinction.

The address she had was for a residence on Dundalk Avenue. Some homes on the avenue had kept their original dignity, with fresh paint and manicured postage-stamp lawns. Some houses and even entire blocks had fallen into disrepair as poverty seemed to encompass the community. She came to the address in her file and was not surprised to see it was well into its downward spiral. It was one of six adjoining row homes. She slowed down and cruised by to check it out. It was 7 a.m. and either no one was moving about or they were already gone. Zach's vehicle sat directly in front of the residence. It matched the description in every way. She jotted down the tag number on the inside of her file. It felt funny not to call it in on her radio, have the PCO run it in the MVA files, and give Kelly instant information. *I'm not a cop anymore.* A PI had to obtain information in different ways. She had already run Zach Ward's name through the publicly accessible Maryland Judicial System database. It had revealed that Zach was in the system more than once. Records of various misdemeanor charges, malicious destruction of property, disorderly conduct, theft, and multiple traffic citations did not paint a very favorable picture for a guy who was only twenty years of age.

Kelly had found his first obvious lie. Records showed that Zach was actually twenty-six years old pretending to be much younger. *Was it to win the heart and attention of a younger, naïve woman? Strike one against Zach.*

Rather than rush into a confrontation that early in the morning, Kelly elected to park nearby and watch the house for a while. Perhaps she would gain additional intelligence, which she could use to bring a peaceful resolution.

At 7:50, the front door to the residence swung open and the storm door pushed outward as Zach exited, pulling the interior door closed behind him. He let the storm door bang shut. He had a lit cigarette dangling from his mouth. *My god this guy is wearing the same outfit the Brightfields described in our meeting.* The jeans and the T-shirt were the same, down to the ratty cartoon character on the front of the shirt. *Did this guy like this shirt or never change his clothes?* He moved at a hurried pace directly to his vehicle, climbed in behind the steering wheel, started the engine, and pulled abruptly from the curb. No signal, no caution. Just get in and go. No wonder he had citations adding up.

The opportunity was knocking. Not sure where Zach was going or how long he would be gone, Kelly saw her chance to talk to Debbie. Kelly was wearing a light baseball-style jacket, concealing her shoulder-holstered handgun. She had a Benchmade flick knife tucked in her front jean pocket. Her newly acquired PI badge was clipped to her belt but placed well to her side so it would not show unless she intentionally lifted that side of her jacket. Kelly left her car where it was parked and made the short walk to the front door. She decided she would not reveal her status as a private investigator unless necessary. It would hold very little sway with a really bad guy who would know it carried little authority.

The storm door pulled open on well-oiled hinges. Kelly rapped lightly on the door in a non-threatening manner. She moved to the side of the door, using the protection of the house. In the police academy, she was taught never to stand in front of a door unless you know what was on the other side.

A few seconds passed before a female voice said, "Who's there?"

Kelly answered, "Hi it's Kelly, I'm a friend of your mom."

The door opened about two inches and a single eye peeped out. "Who are you and how do you know my mom? I don't know you."

Kelly quickly remembered the secret password. "Your mom said to tell you that Dino is at your house waiting for you."

The door opened wider, allowing Kelly to put her foot inside enough to prevent it from being closed. Kelly recognized Debbie from the Brightfields' description and photograph, but she also saw the anxious look on her face. Debbie tried to see beyond Kelly, looking for something or someone. It was only then Kelly observed how Debbie was dressed. The short shorts and a gauzy fabric top revealed she was wearing no bra and did little to contain her breasts. Debbie was barefoot and her hair looked unwashed and unkempt. Kelly thought this was a far cry from the picture she was carrying in her file.

"Debbie, we need to talk. May I come in?"

Debbie seemed to mull over the question and finally said, "I don't think so. I'm not supposed to let anyone come in while Zach isn't here."

Kelly said, "This is important and I'm sure Zach wouldn't mind you talking to a friend of your mother."

"Who's at the door, Debbie?" a male voice called out.

"It's okay, Sammy. It's a friend of my mom," Debbie said, stumbling over the words.

"What does she want?" the male voice asked. "Zach doesn't want strangers in his house, so find out what she wants and tell her to hit the road."

Kelly had heard enough. She pushed through the door into a semi-dark living room. A fat, ugly guy lay on the couch behind a small wooden coffee table. The table top was scarred with burn marks, probably from the overflowing ashtray that currently had a burning cigarette wedged in it. This Sammy was a visual nightmare, wearing dirty jeans and a stained T-shirt that was so short it had not met his jeans in years that exposed his ugly belly and pubic hairs in a disgusting swirl. He was shoeless and looked as dirty as his surroundings.

Kelly ignored Debbie and addressed Sammy. "Who are you and what are you doing here?"

Kelly's voice carried the authority of someone who needed to be answered.

Sammy sat up a little straighter and said, "I'm Sammy. I'm a friend of Zach's."

Kelly repeated, "What are you doing here?"

"Zach told me to stay here and keep an eye on Debbie until he gets back."

"Why would Debbie need you to watch her?" Kelly demanded.

"I guess so she doesn't leave," Sammy answered meekly.

Kelly assessed this guy as having the IQ of a rock. "Where do you live?" Kelly asked.

"About three blocks from here," Sammy answered. "I came up here on my bike when Zach called me and said he had something for me to do."

Kelly pushed her position. "I'm here now so you need to go home. I'll tell Zach I told you to go."

Sammy looked confused and asked, "Are you a cop?"

Kelly raised her voice and stepped closer to Sammy. "What the fuck do you think? Are you stupid or something?"

Sammy was grabbing for his shoes. "Okay, lady, I'm out of here. Tell Zach you made me leave."

Kelly lowered her voice. "I will. You be safe going home."

And like that, Sammy was out the door. Kelly stood at the door and watched him pedal away.

Then she turned her attention to Debbie, who had remained silent during the entire exchange with Sammy. "Debbie, tell me what's going on," Kelly asked with a concerned voice.

That's all it took. Debbie seemed to dissolve and collapse into a small chair near the door. Her head fell into her hands, and she began to sob. She began a mantra, "I'm so sorry, I'm so sorry, I'm so stupid, please help me. I fucked up. He said I was special. He's a pervert and I couldn't see it. Now it's too late." Kelly knelt in front of her and gently lifted her face so that they were eye to eye.

"I'm here to help you. You are safe now. Just please tell me what has happened."

The whole sorted story tumbled out of Debbie between tears, sobbing, and gasping for breath. It was hard to watch, but not hard to believe. Unfortunately, Kelly had seen it all before during her patrol days. Debbie began telling her story. "Zach was the perfect guy on the trip to Baltimore, laughing and seeming so happy to have me in his life. He said he couldn't wait for us to get to his place and have quality time together. It started just fine, although I was a little startled by the deplorable conditions he was living in. He told me being single allowed him to be a little sloppy in the housekeeping area, but promised to clean the place up now that I was there."

Kelly continued to listen while Debbie went on. "It didn't take long for the two of us to start making out and eventually end up in Zach's bed. We made love for hours at a time, and Zach still seemed normal. I was no stranger to sex, so I was into it in the beginning. When Zach went to get a beer, I called my mom to tell her I was safe and to give her the address where I was staying. I purposely didn't tell her the condition of the house."

"Why wasn't Zach at work?" Kelly asked.

"Zach told me he had just lost his job because he was supposed to be working when he was down at the beach with me. I felt like I may have created a problem for him, but he assured me he could get a job anywhere and not to worry."

Debbie paused a moment before continuing. "We screwed all day long and ordered pizza when we got hungry. Sammy came over that night and hung out for a while. I didn't like him much. He was always undressing me with his eyes. When

I talked about calling home, Zach told me I was a woman now and needed to stop calling mommy every day and grow up. I snuck in a couple of calls and texts the first week when Zach wasn't around."

As tears formed in the corners of her eyes, Debbie said, "Zack took me to a local mall and had me try on some shorts and tops. He made me model them in the store and he selected shorts that were way too short and extremely tight. The top he picked out was so sheer I could see my bra. When we got home, he insisted I wear them, minus the bra of course. He was always horny and made me do some things that embarrassed me, but pleased him.

"One day, he demanded I remain naked all day long. I relented when he stripped naked himself and told me I was being a prude. Nobody was around, he said, so why get dressed?

"He took me multiple times throughout the day. When I asked him about going to his night classes at Essex, he told me he quit because he already knew more than they were teaching him.

"When the weekend approached, I told him I was ready to go home, but he said he was hearing a knocking sound in his car engine and he wanted to have a buddy look at it over the weekend.

"When I said I would call my mom to come to get me, he got angry and took my cell phone away from me. Later, he said he had texted my mom and told her I would be staying for another week and everything was good. He refused to show me the text and said, 'You spend too much time worrying about your mom and your damn phone.' I eventually found my phone in his sock drawer, but by then the battery was dead and I didn't have a charger. His phone never left his pocket and there was no house phone. And his car never left the house during the whole weekend.

"I begged him to let me call home or to please take me home. He said he would, but never lived up to the promise. Last night, Sammy had come over for a couple of hours and I was extremely upset that Zach had made me wear the tight shorts and the see-thru blouse. Sammy got an erection and didn't try to hide it. Zach had to notice but said nothing. After Sammy left, Zach told me that Sammy had been his friend since elementary school and had always had a problem with his weight and his looks, so he felt sorry for him."

Kelly reached out and touched Debbie's arm, trying to re-assure her. Debbie continued, "Zach asked me if I would con-sider giving Sammy a blow job the next time he came over. Nothing serious, he said, just friends helping each other out. I almost threw up just thinking about it, but realized Zach was serious and would probably push and maybe insist I do it." Now the tears came. Kelly saw a box of tissues on the floor and reached for one to give to Debbie.

After wiping her tears and blowing her nose, Debbie took a deep breath and continued. "Early this morning, Zach said he had to run to the store to pick up some stuff, and I saw my first opportunity to pack my stuff and get out of here. He had me put on the shorts and the top before he would leave. About an hour before Zach left, Sammy showed up riding his bike. Zach had told Sammy that he had to leave and told him to stay and watch me. It felt like there was a secret going on between them.

"As soon as Zach left, Sammy started flirting with me say-ing how good-looking I was and how he liked the clothes I wore. His eyes bored holes into my breasts and I could tell he was getting aroused. I stayed away from him but caught him stroking himself through his jeans as I came back into the living room. I had the sinking feeling that this was going to be the day I would be forced to pleasure this fat fuck that

Zach called his friend. I was scared of both of them, but mostly Zach, because he was quick-tempered. He had never struck me or physically harmed me, but the verbal intimidations and lewd insinuations had reached a point I knew he was ready to act on them."

Debbie told Kelly that when she heard the knock on the door, she thought it was Zach, coming home and signaling Sammy the time had come to share their prize. "I was so surprised when I saw you. That's why I looked over your shoulder to see if this was part of Zach's plan and if he was just waiting to jump out and make me do terrible things."

Kelly stood up and then pulled Debbie to her feet. "Get that outfit off and pack your stuff. You and I are out of here now. I'm taking you home. If you forget anything, it stays here because you're never coming back. Do you understand?"

Debbie nodded her head but remained in place.

"Now!" Kelly barked. "Fucking move your ass!" Debbie ran to what Kelly assumed was a bedroom.

While Debbie was packing, Kelly toured the living room and kitchen area. The carpet in the living room was filthy and smelled like cat piss, the kitchen was piled high with discarded food containers and empty beer and soda cans. *This whole place should be condemned*, Kelly thought. The girl had made a serious mistake in judgment, and had probably come within a hair of being gang raped, and passed along to Zach's friends. It would take time to heal from this, but a lifelong lesson had definitely been learned. Kelly was unsure how Debbie's parents would handle the information. It was Debbie's story to tell. Kelly would strongly suggest to Debbie that the healing would begin when she bared her soul to her mother. If Kelly could get this girl home safely, her financial compensation will have been well earned.

Kelly heard the water running and guessed it was from a bathroom. Pacing the living room, Kelly yelled, "Let's go, let's go!" The water stopped and Debbie appeared at the bedroom door. She had splashed water on her face, and it was still dripping off her chin. A small duffel bag was in her right hand and a cell phone was in her left.

There was a fumbling noise at the front door. It pushed inward as Zach entered. He stopped cold when he saw Kelly and then Debbie with her duffel bag. He looked at Kelly and said, "Who the fuck are you?"

Kelly squared herself, facing Zach, and said, "I'm a friend of Debbie's and she and I are leaving."

"Where is Sammy?" Zach shouted.

"I sent him home," answered Kelly in her best cop voice.

Zach gave Kelly a wide birth and moved toward the couch. He was no closer to Debbie, but now there was no one between them. Kelly could intersect him if he made a move toward Debbie.

Zach looked at Debbie and spoke in a low and soothing voice. "Come on, Debbie, you don't need to be leaving with this woman. You're my girl and if you're upset, we can work it out. Why would you want to leave? I thought you were having fun. No more mommy telling you what to do. We were going to party with Sammy this afternoon. Shit, I'll take you shopping again. It's all good."

Debbie found her voice, "You low-life piece of shit. You only wanted someone to fuck and someone to suck that puny little cock of yours. All you tell are lies. You don't work, you don't go to school, and I know you want to share me with that fat bastard you call your friend. Well, I made a terrible mistake, and I paid for it. I don't want to ever see or hear from you again. Don't call, don't come around. I'm leaving and I'm never coming back. You took advantage of me and we're done."

Not sure if it was the puny little cock or the fat bastard friend that struck a nerve with Zach, but Kelly could see him swell up with rage. This was about to get ugly in a hurry.

Kelly looked at Debbie and said, "Walk behind me and go out the front door and wait at the curb. I'll be out in a few minutes."

Debbie did as she was told, moving quickly to and out the door. Zach stood transfixed and stunned as she left. The storm door slammed shut, bringing Zach out of his trance. "You fucking bitch. Who do you think you are coming into my house and fucking with me and my girlfriend? How about if I call Sammy back up here and you party with us this afternoon? I was getting a little tired of Debbie anyhow." *That's strike two, Zach*, Kelly thought.

Zach moved to a position, putting himself between Kelly and the front door. Then he advanced until they stood about an arm's length from each other. Zach looked closely at Kelly for the first time in the dim living room light. In his mind, he calculated and thought, *this broad is no kid. I bet she's older than I am. I'll bend her over a kitchen chair and teach her to mind her own business. Might even go get Debbie and let her watch.* His right hand exploded from his side, grabbing Kelly by her upper left arm with enough force to leave bruises. "I'll show you!" were the only words that he got out of his mouth.

Kelly's right hand shot across her chest, her hand coming to rest on top of his hand, pinching it together, rotating the wrist in a clockwise movement, peeling it off her arm. With one quick move, she performed a reverse wrist lock. Once on the floor, she placed her knee in the center of his upper back and used her left hand to force his face into the grimy carpet.

She now controlled him. He was pinned and she had his arm at such an angle that resistance would result in serious damage. She leaned down close to his right ear and said, "Don't embarrass yourself any further. A girl has put your face in this piss-smelling carpet and can snap your arm if you try to move. I can do this all day long. I'm taking Debbie home and if you ever come near her, call her, or cause any trouble for her or her family, I will come for you. Do you understand what I mean when I say I will come for you? If you do, just say, 'Yes, ma'am.'"

Zach's whimpering voice said, "Yes, ma'am."

Kelly stood up and backed off a couple of steps. "Get up," she ordered Zach. He struggled to rise, using only his left arm for support. Once standing, he saw Kelly pointing her cell phone at him. She turned it to face him, and he saw she had taken his picture. Kelly said, "I have a lot of friends in Sandpiper. All of them will have your picture by tomorrow. I will give anyone who sees you in Sandpiper five hundred dollars to call me and tell me where you are. You won't know it until it's too late, but remember my promise: I will come for you."

12

FEELING GOOD ABOUT MYSELF

The ride back to Sandpiper was long and difficult. Debbie was riding an emotional rollercoaster. She was gushing with thanks for having been saved one minute, while simultaneously filled with the guilt for making bad choices. She huddled in the front passenger seat, sometimes crying softly, and then spewing words of self-loathing.

After a while, Kelly tried to assure Debbie that the worst was behind her and she should not linger over what had occurred, but move forward with what lay ahead. She suggested Debbie apologize to her parents for what they had gone through and have a private discussion with her mother, answering as many questions as she could. Kelly suggested her mother need not know the very gritty details, but she did need to know Debbie now recognized the dangers of perceived adulthood.

Kelly told Debbie, "You still have a lot to learn about life and the nature of people you might meet in the future." Debbie vowed to double her efforts with her counselor in getting to the root of the problem of her self-doubting and insecurity.

Debbie said, "I need to develop tools and skills to deal with my issues." Kelly believed Debbie realized the near tragedy would help her see with clearer eyes in the future.

Debbie calmed down until they arrived at her home and she saw her parents. The reunion was joyous and very emotional for everyone. Kelly stood back from this very private moment for the Brightfields.

Ken Brightfield broke away from his wife and daughter and shook Kelly's hand and said, "Kelly, we are truly grateful for what you accomplished."

Kelly smiled and added, "You are welcome and I'm glad things worked out. I'll prepare an invoice for you outlining the hours and expenses incurred, including mileage and tolls. I believe you will have some money coming back to you."

Ken said, "You have no idea what you've done for this family. I don't want any money back. My wife and I talked and decided to give you a five-hundred-dollar bonus for your speed and proficiency in handling this matter." He handed her a check. Kelly tried to give it back, saying it was unnecessary, but he would not hear of it. When Kelly was leaving, she got hugs from the entire Brightfield family.

As Kelly walked to her car, she felt good about herself. She had helped a family in need and her first case as a PI had ended on a positive note. She was now twenty-five hundred dollars richer, minus expenses.

Kelly called Marie and said, "Well, Debbie is home and the Brightfields are happy and so am I." Marie was elated that Kelly had resolved her friend's problem so quickly. Kelly left out the portion about her parting words for Zach. She also kept the financial enumeration to herself. She was beginning to understand why they are called private investigators. Emphasis is on the private! Other than the thin file Kelly kept locked in her office, there was no record of anything ever happening. No reports were written, and Kelly enjoyed the freedom to talk to the bad guys in terms they would understand. *The private sector may be okay after all.*

13

NEED ANSWERS

The week after the confrontation with Zach was rather mundane. Kelly found herself with a folder full of subpoenas and summonses. All were routine and she was having great success, making money with every service. She sorted them out by location so she wouldn't be crisscrossing the county, wasting both time and gas.

She was in an area outside of Snow Hill that she didn't know well. That left her completely reliant on her GPS. The name on the summons was Raymond Bowker. The information sheet attached said he was sixty-three years old. MVA records report he owns a 2021 Ford pickup truck with Maryland tags. The address provided by the lawyer's office was 12528 West Chester Road, Snow Hill, Maryland.

Kelly found the address and turned into a long dirt and gravel driveway. It wound through a thin band of trees before opening to a flat stretch of ground. A one-story home with white siding, a dark roof, and a wide front porch marked the end of the driveway. Off to one side was an outbuilding, large enough to house a vehicle, but open and empty.

Kelly parked directly in front of the house and went to the front porch and knocked on the screen door. Television noises emanated from within but were quickly turned down. The brightly painted, red door opened and a woman, easily in her seventies, looked at Kelly with inquiring eyes. She couldn't be more than five-foot-one, with short, gray hair. She was wearing a dark blue dress that reached her shoes. Her face was tan and supported a pair of tortoise-shell glasses. For a very small woman, her voice was loud and clear. "Help you miss? If you're selling, I'm not buying."

"No, not selling anything," Kelly responded. "I'm looking for a gentleman named Raymond Bowker. Is he home?"

"Got the wrong place, missy. No one by that name lives here," the woman answered with a blank expression on her face. She began to close the door.

Kelly quickly said, "Do you know that name at all? I'm working for the court, and I have a summons for him."

The old woman responded, "My name is Deanna Teacher and I've lived here for thirty years. I've never heard of him."

Kelly pressed, "Think any of your neighbors might know him?"

Now irritated, the woman responded again, saying, "I keep to myself, and I don't know any of my neighbors anymore. I've got strangers living all around me. This used to be a place where neighbors came around to visit and maybe bring a cake or a pie. Not like that anymore. You're lucky if people will even give you a wave when you pass them on the road. God-damned country has gone to hell. Good luck finding your man." The door closed and the bolt rammed home. Conversation over.

Kelly returned to her vehicle and sat for a moment pondering her next move. *Hell, I'm in the neighborhood. Why not try a couple more neighbors? I don't think so, but maybe the old lady is hiding something.*

The next driveway was a quarter mile down the road. It turned out to be a lane suitable for moving livestock, but was barred with a gate. With the weeds growing around the gate, there was no sign a vehicle had passed that way in a long time.

Almost a mile later, another mailbox appeared, with a gravel driveway leading off to the right. There was no name on the mailbox. Kelly turned right and drove through a thick grove of trees. On the passenger side, she saw what she thought was a motion sensor attached to a tree at vehicle height. *Humph, you don't see that kind of thing in this area too often. Maybe there's some kind of mansion back here that warrants that kind of security.*

About five hundred feet further up the drive, a camera lens was partially hidden between two large branches of a tree, higher than the motion sensor, but pointed at the driveway. Like the old lady's place, the trees ended, and a modest two-story house came into view. It was painted white, neat and tidy, with a well-maintained front lawn. Kelly could see the backyard was enclosed with a three-rail fence, reinforced on the inside with chicken wire. A playground of plastic slides, swings, and small climbing walls occupied the center of the yard. Small bikes and push scooters leaned inside the fence, ready for action. Kids with dark hair ran back and forth, seeming to play some kind of tag or chase. All looked to be under six years of age. Mostly girls, but she saw one little boy try to kick a soccer ball, only to miss and fall on his bottom. Undeterred, he jumped up and pursued the rolling ball while laughing loudly. All seemed to be having a grand old time.

Shifting her gaze back to the home, she saw a rather large dark-haired, brown-skinned Hispanic-looking male standing in the yard a few feet from the porch watching her. He was dressed in bib overalls and a straw hat adorned his head. His dark eyes completed the picture. Although she hadn't seen him come through the door, Kelly assumed he had come from the house. *Had the sensor or camera alerted him to my pending arrival? Maybe the kids were the reason for the added security.* Kelly didn't remember seeing a sign announcing a daycare center, but maybe she missed it, so focused on the mailbox. That would explain the circumstances.

She stopped in the driveway a few yards from the man and exited her vehicle. Now out of the car, she could hear the children, voices loud and happy. She couldn't understand what they were saying. The children were yelling and speaking in Spanish. *Made sense, the guy looks Hispanic.*

"Hi, I'm Kelly Hart," she said. The man nodded but said nothing. Kelly started again. "Hi I'm Kelly. I'm looking for a man named Raymond Bowker. He's supposed to live here. Do you know him?"

With a thick Spanish accent, the man responded, "No, I don't. Nobody with that name lives here. Just me, Carlos, my wife, Rosa, and the kids, of course."

"How long have you lived here?" Kelly asked. "Do you know your neighbors?"

Carlos stared intently at her and said, "We've been here about three years and have never really met our neighbors. The closest neighbor is about a mile and a half away, an old lady down the road," pointing toward the Teacher's residence.

"Okay, like I said, my name is Kelly and I'm trying to serve a court summons on Mr. Bowker, but there must be some kind of mix-up on his address. Here's my business card, if you don't mind asking your wife if she's ever heard of Mr. Bowker."

Carlos nodded again, saying, "I'll talk to her and have her call you if she knows anything."

Striking out again, Kelly returned to her car and placed her file on the seat. As she looked up, she saw a young, brown-skinned woman moving among the children. She kicked the soccer ball and like a small herd, they all went after it, screaming with enthusiasm—seven, maybe eight kids. Kelly thought to herself, *I could never manage caring for that many kids. That woman's too young to have that many kids unless she birthed multiple twins. Knock it off, Kelly, I'm such a cynic. Shit, they may be doing a great thing by foster parenting half of those kids. Open borders! Am I a racist? Nothing to see here. Get back to work. This is Worcester County, Maryland, a long way from the Mexican border.* As she put her car in gear, she glanced back at the house. The man was standing in the same spot, still staring suspiciously at her. His stare was unnerving, but she was the one who came into his space, so maybe it was time to leave. And she did.

Kelly drove to the end of the driveway and looked around. No daycare signs. *Maybe illegal daycare? The kids were happy and laughing. Carlos was helpful. The young Hispanic woman was playing with the kids to their delight. Christ, Kelly, give it a break, not everybody is a wrongdoer. Sometimes things are as they appear.* She felt a nagging gut feeling telling her something wasn't right.

Kelly turned on West Chester Road and drove towards Berlin. *Why do I always need an answer to every question?*

14
TRIPWIRE

As Kelly drove towards Berlin, a phone rang in a real estate office in downtown Sandpiper. The office was fitted with high-end furniture and the walls were adorned with works by local artists. Every one depicted different water scenes of the Eastern Shore. A thick oriental area rug added rich colors to the room complimenting the art, while crown molding finished the successful look of the office.

The ringing phone was a vibrating burner phone in the pocket of Thomas Gordon. He pawed the inside pocket of his suit jacket hanging on a coat hanger behind his chair. The stylish clothes tree had been a recent addition to the office. He finally fished the phone out of his pocket and pushed the receiver button. This phone was to be used only in emergencies and it had never rung before. Only one person even had the number. *Why would Carlos be calling me in the middle of the day?* Gordon held it to his ear.

Gordon answered in a pre-determined manner, "Hey, what's up?"

Carlos responded, "You told me to call if anyone came

around. A woman private detective came to the house saying she is looking for a man named Raymond Bowker. She claimed to have a court summons for him. She said she might have the wrong address, but she may have been bullshitting me. The kids were outside playing in the yard and Rosa was with them. She saw the setup we have, but she didn't ask any questions about it. She left a business card. The name on the card is Kelly Hart, with a Berlin address and a single phone number. When she came down the driveway, it set off a trip wire I placed out there, designed to protect and alert us to impending danger."

Gordon made Carlos give him all the information on the card and told him to be especially watchful for any additional, unfamiliar vehicles or people in the area. He told him to check for drone activity in the area. He said, "This may be nothing, but we need to be careful. I'll check this woman out. You and Rosa need to stay alert. Call me if anything else happens. I will stay away from the farm for the next few days until we are sure this was just a wrong address."

Gordon slipped the phone back into his suit pocket and sat with his hands folded on his desk. Thomas Gordon was an impeccably dressed businessman. His neatly coiffed hair, Armani suit, and shoes symbolized the success of his public persona. His multi-million-dollar home in Snow Hill faced the Pocomoke River. He traveled in the best circles of movers and shakers in this part of the state, expressing conservative views, and donating to Republican candidates. People liked Gordon and sought his company on the golf course and at charity events. Gordon was single, but often had a woman attend events with him. He was the shiny prize that had women whispering to each other about whether he may be gay.

He had never been seen in the company of another man, but the women who occasionally accompanied him seemed more like arm candy. It was never the same woman twice. All were young and gorgeous, but just seemed to come and go. His private life was an intriguing mystery. The mystery was in truth; everything about Thomas Gordon was a façade. He was a chameleon who fit into every category of what was expected of the rich and conservative in this area of Maryland.

Thomas Gordon had a black heart. If friends and acquaintances knew who Gordon really was, they would fear for their lives and flee. A monster was walking among them.

Gordon was a licensed real estate broker, with offices in Sandpiper and Easton, and had eight agents working for him between the two offices. They were involved in the normal duties of a lawful real estate business. They had made Thomas Gordon a lot of money by aiding clients in buying and selling properties all over the Eastern Shore. What no one knew was that the bulk of his wealth did not come from his real estate dealings.

His affluence came from more sinister means. He sold lives on the internet. Through a dark web of contacts and smugglers in Mexico, children from three to five years old were being hand selected, culled from the thousands of migrants arriving daily at the US border. Gathered in small groups, they transported the kids across the country in vans driven by coyotes. Unlike some smuggling operations, this one took extra steps to see that the children arrived at their destination unmolested and in apparent good health. Their value lay in their cherub appearance. Once in Maryland, the smugglers met Carlos in the middle of the night at various secret locations where they transferred the children to the backseat of Carlos's pickup truck. They gave all the kids sleep-inducing medications to keep them malleable. When the children woke up, an overly friendly, Spanish-speaking woman, named Rosa, met them. Food, toys, and the companionship of kids their age kept everyone happy. They were given new clothes and allowed to play outside in a fenced yard filled with items far beyond the dreams of these little folks. Cartoons, toys, and Rosa reading stories kept them entertained on bad weather days. At that age, a missing playmate was easily explained and forgotten. Life was good for these little people—until it wasn't.

In the room where the girls slept, there was a closet. On a rod far out of their reach, hung numerous princess dresses. The dresses were in a variety of colors; a little girl's dream just out of reach. Of course, they all wanted to wear them.

Rosa collected the girls and shared, "Girls, the one with the best behavior each day will be allowed to wear the dress of her choice on the next day. Doesn't that sound great?"

The next morning Rosa called to the girls, "Gather round, I have selected a winner."

The girls yelled out, "Pick me, pick me, pick me."

Rosa said, "Terrassa, you are the winner. I am going to help you bathe and do your hair into fancy curls so you will look pretty in your new dress. Let's go, baby." Rosa selected the undergarments and then the little girl picked the dress she wanted to wear. All the dresses were about the same size, matching the selection process at the border—all very frilly and short.

After Terrassa was dressed, Rosa said, "You are beautiful and we need to take pictures to preserve the occasion." Rosa posed Terrassa in alluring poses, nothing pornographic, but suggestive to a certain audience of viewers. Videotaping was done during the entire process, including while the child bathed and dressed.

Videos were available on the dark web as a possible inducement to a prospective buyer. If he or she was willing to pay extra they could download the video before making a final decision. This turned out to be very lucrative as some customers would pay exorbitant fees just to get the videos. Rosa always wore a Covid mask and kept her face averted from the cameras while performing these rituals. The girls got to keep their party dress and their first name was put on a tag and sewn into the fabric of the dress.

The boys went through a similar process based on their behavior. They would be bathed and dressed in shorts, little blazers, ties, and shiny shoes, videoed, posed, and photographed. The best behaved would then receive a soccer ball with their name on it in a black magic marker. The boys were anxious to get out of their costumes as soon as the photography was over. Their videos sold as well as the girls' videos did. The kids never realized there was a new winner every day until everyone had a dress or a ball. When someone disappeared, their dress or ball would also be gone. An unending supply of dresses and balls were stored in the house's attic.

Gordon understood the level of depravity in this land of the free and home of the brave. He was making money meeting their deviant needs. He never met them nor knew their real names. Everything was done on the dark web. Photos were posted, videos were available, selections were made and bidding wars occurred. A winning bid was announced and money was sent directly to numbered offshore accounts. The children were delivered to their owners by methods selected by the buyer. Gordon and Carlos hid below multiple levels of deception. Neither had ever attended an actual handoff. The person surrendering the child to its owner was paid handsomely for not knowing where the child came from or where they were going. Gordon suspected the buyers also were seldom, if ever, at the site of the transfer. Gordon never knew what happened to these children after the sale. He didn't care and still slept soundly at night. This was just business. If not for him, someone else would prosper from this enterprise.

When Gordon's office was designed, he had a soundproof inner door installed. It was on a remote switch so he could lock and unlock it from his desk. The construction workers were intentionally hand-picked illegal immigrants from the Washington, D.C. area. Only one of them spoke English. Gordon knew better than to allow locals to do the work. A handgun was concealed under his desk as his final line of defense. He proclaimed to anyone who would listen that he was a second amendment advocate, practicing frequently at a nearby range. A small camera in his lobby and the monitor on his desk allowed him to view all visitors. His own safety was paramount. A bookcase concealed a secret exit from the building. People observing the outside would see only a large vent secured by many screws and a large padlock. This entire arrangement swung out into the alley when a lever was turned from the inside which allowed him to exit the building.

His secretary, April, had never worked in a real estate office. Gordon told her that sometimes emotions run high when someone loses a house to a higher bidder or when things fall apart at the settlement table. He explained to his secretary that the soundproof inner door was a security feature and prevented anyone from barging into his office. He quelled her curiosity by having a silent alarm button placed under her desk as well. He told her that at the slightest problem, she should push the button and he would come to her aid after he dialed 911. This was just another layer of protection for him. He had no intention of calling 911 or coming to her aid.

Thomas Gordon had many secrets. There was a safe deposit box in a bank in Snow Hill. The key to the box was hanging around his neck on a two-thousand-dollar gold chain. He never took the chain off. It was more than just a key to a safe deposit box. It was his key to freedom. The box held Gordon's darkest secrets. It contained journals documenting the children by first name, photo, account number to which the money was sent, date of sale, and date of transfer to the owner using only the bidder's number. A brown leather file contained a complete portfolio, creating a new identity. His picture was on these documents, but his personal information was replaced with a new name, social security number, and driver's license from a nearby state. Counted and stacked in the box was one hundred thousand dollars in unmarked cash. In a small white envelope was a yellowing newspaper clipping, dated four years earlier. It described the shooting death of a California real estate broker, Edward Russo. The police were seeking help from the public because they had no known motive, persons of interest, or actionable leads. The weapon was a 9mm, but was not found at the scene. The article didn't mention the numerous documents stolen at the time of the murder. No one knew the documents were the motive and formed the foundation for Gordon to recreate himself into a real estate broker in Maryland.

If Gordon could reach this bank and his storage unit just outside of Snow Hill, he could disappear into the fabric of America, only to resurface somewhere else and begin again. He had done it before. The storage unit held a car that Gordon never drove. It had been there for three years. He visited the storage unit once a month to start the car and guarantee it was in working order. It was on temporary jacks so that the tires would not deflate. Occasionally, he would bring fresh gas and add it to the car's tank. This dark blue Chevrolet Camaro muscle car was his getaway vehicle. The registration and tags on the car were current; and listed and insured to an LLC in Delaware.

Carlos and Rosa were like the rest of the people on the Eastern Shore. They knew him only as Thomas Gordon. They were expendable. There were plenty of Hispanic men and women willing to look the other way to make money. The dark web allowed this operation to be run from anywhere in the world. The US just happened to offer the most rights to protect the guilty.

Gordon considered the situation. *This Kelly Hart woman may be a problem. She is the first stranger to be on the farm property in over three years.* He made a phone call and verified her authenticity without bringing attention to himself. *Kelly Hart is not going to fuck up what I've got going. There is too much at stake. If necessary, I will personally remove her from the playing field. Carlos has a backhoe and plenty of land to work with.*

15

WHITE RUBBER BOOTS

It was 4:30 p.m. as Brogan cruised the lower end of Sandpiper. He was thinking about heading home after being in his office since 7:30 that morning and was all caught up on his reports and administrative duties. It had been a quiet day. *Maybe too quiet.*

The PCO called Patrol Car 12, "We have another call. Are you still 10-6 (Busy)? Officer Barringer responded by saying he would be clear in about five to ten minutes. The PCO said, "We have a report of a bar fight at the Friendly Tavern on 2nd Street."

Brogan broke in on the radio and said, "Car 3 to Headquarters. I'm only one street away. I'll check it out and wait until you can get a uniform on the scene. Mark me 10-7 at Friendly's." That was the police Ten Code communication system that meant, out of service, leaving the air.

Brogan double-parked in front of the tavern, left his car with the emergency lights flashing, crossed the sidewalk, and entered the bar. The sound of breaking glass and angry words greeted him. He saw two enormous men squared off as if they were in a boxing ring. Both were bleeding from cuts on their faces, most likely the result of punches delivered by the fists of their opponent. Both were wearing plaid shirts, jeans, and the watermen's traditional calf-high white rubber boots well known in this Chesapeake region. Gail, the dark-haired female bartender, screamed at them, "Stop!" She was holding a Billy club in her hand and would bust their heads if she got a chance. She stayed behind the bar, protecting all the liquor bottles on the shelves behind her.

Brogan stood calmly just inside the door as the two combatants exchanged punches that landed harmlessly on the shoulders of each other. Both displayed a weakening of arms and punches. Both were beefy built, obviously watermen strong, but not accustomed to throwing punches. Watermen as a whole are pretty much good ole' boys. This fight was winding down, and to their credit, neither sought to elevate the fight with a weapon.

Brogan pulled his jacket back, displaying both his badge and his gun. "Are you guys about done?" Both fighters glanced over at the stranger who had entered their fight. One fighter immediately stepped back and raised his hands signaling he was done. The other saw this as an opportunity to take a cheap shot and stepped in and punched the guy in the face, knocking him to the floor.

Brogan took that move as a crossing of the line. Fighting was one thing. Sucker punching a guy who had raised his hands in front of a cop was laying down a challenge to the authority of the badge. Without further comment, Brogan moved in on the guy still standing and put his hand on his shoulder, and said, "You, my friend, are under arrest."

The brute of a waterman made a bad decision and took a

swing at Brogan, who easily ducked the wild haymaker. Brogan blocked the arm that was coming toward him. He immediately captured the wrist and above the elbow. He applied pressure to the joint of the wrist, simultaneously pushing down on the elbow and up on the arm, pointing the hand to the ceiling, and drove the guy to his knees. The big guy had a choice to make and he chose wisely. It was either have your arm snapped at the elbow or go with the momentum Brogan created. He made no attempt to get up.

Brogan's lifetime of martial arts training and workouts had prevailed once again. There was nothing braggadocios about Brogan. There was no speech about kicking ass and taking names. His quiet demeanor was itself a signal of unleashed violence. He quickly gained the respect of two more citizens of the town he protected.

Both watermen were on the floor looking up at a well-dressed cop who could obviously handle himself. The fight had been knocked out of both men. Brogan stared down at them, fully prepared if either man decided he wanted more.

The front door banged open, and Officer Anderson and Officer Thurlow entered the bar and immediately saw Brogan had the situation well in hand. They moved forward ordering both men on the floor to roll onto their stomachs. Their arms were handcuffed to the rear and then assisted to their feet. They were quickly patted down and no weapons were found. Both were led to chairs and ordered to sit. The arrestees had become very compliant, sobering with the thoughts of what lay ahead for them. They were identified as Glen Schultz and Dick Dorsey.

Anderson watched over the two detainees, while Brogan and Thurlow spoke with Gail. She said, "Both those guys are regulars and work together on the fishing boats. They came in here today and were all friendly until they started doing shots and arguing over the football game on the television. Next thing I know, they're up duking it out and breaking shit. I couldn't get them to stop, so I called you guys."

Brogan asked, "Do you want to press charges?"

Gail said, "The owner, Dutch, doesn't usually press charges if they're willing to pay for damages and they are banned for the next thirty days. I called him and he said he'd be okay with that arrangement. I saw that one guy swing at you, so that changes everything. We'll press charges if it's what you want."

Brogan responded, "Let me talk to these guys and explain what might be in store for them."

Brogan approached Shultz and Dorsey and said, "Dutch says he won't press charges if you pay for the damages and stay out of his place for the next month."

Both nodded in agreement with that arrangement. Brogan squared with Schultz, who had swung at him. "You ever swing at another cop in this town, I'll see you spend some time in the county jail. Do you understand?"

The brute with the clumsy haymaker said, "Yes sir, and I apologize. I was acting stupid, and my family can't do without my income for a month. I'll stay out of this place, and I won't be drinking any more shots." He turned to his compaion and said, "I also apologize to you for that cheap shot. Are you and I okay?"

His companion responded, "Yeah, you always were a dumb fuck."

Brogan told Anderson and Thurlow to take them to the PD and write them a summons for disorderly conduct and have someone sober come and pick them up. "Give them the phone number of the owner and tell them to square away the damages," he said.

Brogan turned to Gail and explained what was going to happen. He told her he wanted a fair assessment of the damage and said Dutch needed to not capitalize on these two oafs.

Gail said, "I understand, and I will pass the message to him. Only one chair is broken and a couple of drinking glasses, so it shouldn't be much."

Satisfied that all bases had been covered, he shook hands with Anderson and Thurlow and asked if they needed further assistance. They said no, and they all walked out together. Two patrol cars sat in the street behind Brogan's car. Shultz and Dorsey were placed in the backseat of a patrol car and were now ready for transport. Anderson and Thurlow go 10-8, (In service, Subject to call) with two 10-95s, (Prisoner/ subject in custody) and 10-19 (Return/returning to station). Brogan calls 10-8 and heads home. *Just another day in the life of a cop.*

16
FAMILIAR GROUND

Over the next few weeks, Kelly stayed busy. *I've added four attorneys that are feeding me process work. I'm making money by running my ass off every day. My reputation for making the serves, plus my ability to find those avoiding service, are paying great dividends.*

Kelly decided to knock off from work around 5 p.m. three days in a row. She perched herself on the same bar stool in the same restaurant where she had encountered Mr. Tall, Dark, and Handsome. She sipped her wine and ate an appetizer. He never reappeared. Disappointed, and feeling foolish for setting up a romantic ambush that never happened, she considered her options. On the first evening, she returned to the restaurant and found the same bartender working. Kelly learned his name was Anthony, but she resisted inquiring about information on the mysterious Brogan. She knew the bartender would reach out and put him on notice. She didn't want him to think she was stalking him.

She thought, *I just need to be patient.* More than once, 'Brogan' played a role in her dreams. She awoke each time with beads of sweat between her breasts and with an unexplainable glow. She tried to regain details of the dream, but they always eluded her. *My mother had a name for this kind of guy: DREAM-BOAT.* Kelly thought she finally understood what her mother meant—after all these years. *I'm dreaming about a guy I know nothing about, chasing a ghost and a fantasy. I think that bullet in my arm fucked up my brain!*

On Sunday, the third day of her failed ambush, she was finishing up her meal when her cell phone buzzed. She retrieved it from her purse and placed the phone against her ear and said, "Hart."

"Hi, this is Ricky Morris," the voice on the phone responded. "I'm a retired Baltimore County cop. I have my own PI firm here in Baltimore County. Gretchen Miles recommended I give you a call. I have a high-profile, low-risk client who will be traveling to Sandpiper on Friday of this week. It's short notice, but I was hoping you could help me out with a two-day executive protection detail. I'm having one of my employees drive the client to the beach and would like to have someone with local knowledge and connections help him out. They will arrive around 5 p.m. on Friday and are staying at the Sandpiper Suites Hotel in downtown Sandpiper. The Principal will be dining alone in the hotel's Hightop restaurant and then retiring for the evening. I just need you to do the advance work at the hotel and stay with them until he's tucked in for the night. The next day there is a program at the Sandpiper Arts Gallery on 54th Street, with wine, cheese, and promised donations. It's a lot of glad-handing for a good cause. The event starts at 1 p.m. and should be over by 4 p.m. Again, I need the advance done at the gallery location and for you to stay with my guy and the Principal until they are back in the car headed to Baltimore. The detail pays five hundred dollars a day."

Before Kelly could respond, Morris continued, "My guy is a retired state trooper named Alan St. Clair. He's trained in executive protection and has worked the principal in the past. There are no current threats or expected trouble. It's doubtful he'll even be recognized outside of Baltimore unless you bump into someone who's heavily into the arts. We just want to cover the bases. The Principal likes the appearance of wealth and influence."

Kelly's said, "That sounds interesting."

Morris went on to say "He's a nice guy and easy to work with so we don't expect any problems during this detail. If you're interested, I'll give you Alan's cell phone number so you can call him and discuss the details and come up with a plan. Once they arrive in Sandpiper, we expect the Principal to be in his room for at least an hour before dinner. Alan can meet with you and you can give him the setup, and you can brief him on your advance. Gretchen said you have her number and you can call her to verify all of this is legit. Can you help us?"

Keeping a professional tone, hoping to disguise her excitement, Kelly said, "Give me your number, Ricky. I'll call Gretchen and then give you a call right back. If she says you're good with her, then you're good with me and I'd be happy to help you."

Kelly recognized Gretchen as one of the women she worked with in the Dignitary Protection Unit, and called her phone number. While the phone was ringing, she thought, *this is a true gift. I'm getting to do what I loved during my police career. The money's right and the detail seemed pretty straight-*

forward. I don't have any commitments for Friday or Saturday. If Gretchen verifies this guy is who he says he is, I'm definitely in.

Gretchen answered on the second ring, and she jumped right into the vetting. "Ricky is a good guy and easy to work with. He pays at the end of each assignment, so you don't have to chase your money." Kelly spent a couple of minutes chatting with Gretchen, thanking her for the referral before signing off.

She called Ricky and got Alan's phone number. Alan seemed to be waiting for Kelly's call. They discussed the upcoming detail, how they would identify each other, and a time and location to meet at the hotel. Alan told Kelly that the Principal would be dining alone and liked to sit at a table where he could observe the bar and other people dining. A view of the water would be a big plus.

Alan said, "We need a second table from where we can observe, but not intrude on the privacy of the Principal. I've captured your phone number and will call you when we are about thirty minutes out for any updates. Be prepared to eat a meal, all expenses will be covered by the client."

Alan continued, "If things go well, the Principal takes great pride in over-tipping the restaurant staff. I have a carry permit and will be armed. Do you have a carry permit?"

Kelly responded, "I'll be carrying."

Alan concluded by saying, "The Principal's name is Ray Hiltzberger. Google him to get his background. There are pictures of him, so you'll know what he looks like. I also heard good things about you when you were with Baltimore County PD. I Googled you and I'm impressed with your story. It sucks that your good work led to you having to leave police work."

Kelly said, "Thanks for the compliment. I'm sure we'll

work well together. I'm looking forward to it and I'll cover all the bases down here. Call me if anything changes or if you have any questions or concerns. See you Friday."

Kelly smiled as she hung up. *Wow, I'm back on familiar ground. I can't wait to get into this detail and make it come off seamlessly.* A small voice in the back of her mind reminded her that the last time she worked a detail, it did not end well. All the preparation in the world did not prevent an unexpected and violent attack. She unconsciously massaged her right arm along the scar made by the bullet meant to kill her.

17

How To Make It Seamless

Early Tuesday morning Kelly got a text from Alan advising that there had been a slight change in plans. The Principal was going to be joined for dinner by the director of the Sandpiper Art Gallery and the mayor of Sandpiper, making it a party of three for 6 p.m. Everything else remained the same. Kelly acknowledged the text with a two-word response, "No problem."

Kelly's mind was swirling as she contemplated her assignment. *Wow, it's been a year since the shooting and working a protection detail.* Kelly knew she must prepare for every possible scenario. Kelly would always create a checklist that she followed that assured every detail had been addressed.

After receiving Alan's text, Kelly went directly to the Sandpiper Suites Hotel. Kelly had met the restaurant manager during prior visits to the restaurant for dinners of her own. She was confident he would help her in making the dignitaries' visit to his restaurant memorable. Kelly hoped that Kathie, the bar manager, would be there too.

The restaurant was appropriately named, The Hightop, as it sat on the very top of the hotel. It offered spectacular views from both the outside deck and the glassed-in dining room and bar. Diners looked down upon the entrance to Assawoman Bay and the bridge into Sandpiper. The land sat on what was previously a concrete company and was a striking addition to the Sandpiper skyline. Kelly took the elevator to the restaurant and saw the restaurant staff was busy setting up for the day. She approached the bar only to find Kathie, the lovely bar manager, working that day.

"Hi, Kathie, I'm looking for Paul, is he around?"

Kathie smiled and answered, "Yeah, he's here somewhere, probably in the kitchen. I'll get him for you." Kathie put down the glass she had been wiping dry and went through two swinging doors just off the bar and disappeared. Moments later the doors swung the other way and Paul came into the bar area. His face lit up when he saw Kelly waiting. He recognized her as one of his frequent customers.

"Good morning. How can I help you?" Paul asked in a warm greeting.

"Hi, Paul, I'm Kelly Hart. I'm working a dignitary protection detail." She presented her PI credentials, including a flash of her badge. Paul seemed duly impressed as he automatically stood a little straighter acknowledging her importance.

Kelly continued, "I need your help arranging dinner for a VIP who will be visiting your hotel and restaurant this Friday. Do you have time to talk to me?" The use of the term VIP got Paul's attention and he pointed her to an empty table and they sat across from each other.

"Tell me what you need. I'm sure our staff will do whatever it takes to make your VIP feel welcome."

Kelly said, "The VIP is a very wealthy businessman and benefactor to the arts. He has chosen your hotel and your restaurant to meet with the director of Sandpiper Art Gallery and your mayor. I was thinking the small glassed-in nook you have overlooking the water would be the perfect place to have a private dinner for these important folks. I would need a second table for myself and another protection specialist where we would be close but not intrusive."

Kelly pointed to a table near the entrance to the nook. "The walls are glass, so observing the Principal is not an issue. We will need to keep a protective eye on them while they dine. The party will be arriving for dinner at 6:00 p.m. If all of this is workable, I can make the reservation right now. We will expect of course, the highest level of attention to all the details of the meals and service. Hopefully, you will be here that evening to greet the guests and show them to their table. Your personal discretion and attention are expected. I will share the VIP's name with you on Friday so you will be able to properly greet him. I'm sure you know the name of your mayor and the head of the Sandpiper Art Gallery."

Kelly pushed her business card across the table to Paul. A hundred-dollar bill was peeking out from under the card. Paul placed his hand over the card and the cash and pulled it to himself. "Your every need will be taken care of. You have my word on that." Paul smiled as he pushed one of his business cards to her. Kelly picked up Paul's card and, for the first time, she knew his last name: Geppi. She stood and extended her hand across the table to Paul. As he shook her hand, he placed his other hand on top showing her she could count on him.

She smiled and said, "I'll see you Friday. I'll be here early to see if everything is in order. Please call me if you have any concerns at all. Thank you for your help. I'm sure everything will be wonderful with you making the arrangements." Paul nodded his head in response.

After her meeting, she explored the entire hotel checking for emergency exits, cameras, and lighting. She walked the two available staircases should the public elevators be unavailable. She searched and found a service elevator near a back-delivery entrance to the hotel. The elevator was marked for staff and delivery only. Kelly pushed the up button and the elevator door opened. She got in and pushed the button for the top floor. When the door opened, she found herself in a small service area with two doors, one single and one double. She opened the single door and found a small hallway leading to the dining room. Kelly retraced her steps and entered the double doors. They opened into a storage room that then led directly into the kitchen. It was busy with people prepping food. No one paid her any attention as she passed through and out the double doors Paul had used to enter the bar area. Kelly was concerned with the lack of visible security, unlocked doors, and no one challenging a stranger walking in areas that were marked employee-only.

Kelly returned to the ground floor and went to the reception desk. She spoke to the clerk attending the desk. "Hi, may I speak to someone from your security staff?"

Taken aback, the clerk said, "Okay, is it something I can help you with?"

Kelly said, "No, this is strictly a security issue. Is there anyone I can speak to?"

"Yes, I'll call her now." The clerk called for someone on the handheld radio.

"Hey Robin, can you come to the main desk and meet with someone?" A female voice responded, "Sure, be there in a minute."

About two minutes later, a professionally dressed,

middle-aged White woman came across the lobby. She had brown hair, freshly pressed white blouse, and dark navy pants. The woman carried a small handheld radio. Since Kelly was the only person standing at the desk, the woman looked at her and said, "I'm Robin Love, chief of security for the hotel. Is there a problem I can help you with?"

"No ma'am, no problem. I'm Kelly Hart and I'm part of an executive protection detail. Could I talk with you privately? I'll explain why I'm here." Kelly handed her a business card that Love examined closely.

"Can I see some credentials?" Love asked.

Kelly said, "Sure, actually I'm glad you asked. May I call you Robin?" Robin nodded her head yes. "Then please call me Kelly."

Robin said, "Please follow me." Robin led Kelly down a hallway to a small office with a placard announcing Hotel Security. Robin gestured to her to have a seat in the chair facing her desk and asked, "What's going on?"

Kelly explained what was occurring Friday, including her meeting with the restaurant manager.

Kelly delicately told Robin, "I don't want to seem critical, but I'm charged with the job of doing the advance work on any venue where we will be taking our Principal. I have just explored your hotel, including staircases and service elevator. Not one person challenged me or gave me a second look. I passed through doors that I was surprised were unlocked, and until I met you, I saw no one who appeared to be performing security for the hotel."

Robin sighed. "Security is always on the short end of the stick when it comes to personnel and a proper budget. Training of all the employees on the issues of safety and security is an ongoing and mostly an ignored problem."

Robin stood and motioned for Kelly to follow her into an adjoining office. The room contained a large bank of TV monitors and recording equipment. Kelly counted twenty small monitors that captured the lobby, parking lots, all exits, stairwells, hallways and even the elevators. In front of the monitors was an empty chair.

Robin said, "That's where Dennis Dewy sits when he's not making his rounds. It's only the two of us during most day shifts and we have two security people for each of the evening shifts. All are unarmed and equipped with a radio and a canister of pepper spray."

Robin pointed to one of the monitors that displayed the image of a White male with thinning gray hair, wearing a white polo-style shirt walking around the parking lot. "That's Dennis. It takes him about twenty minutes to walk the entire hotel complex. I try to watch the monitors while he walks, but I confess that I am frequently distracted by all my other duties. The chance of you running into Dennis during one of his tours is hit-and-miss at best.

"As you can see, we rely heavily on video surveillance to supplement our lack of people. Everything is recorded, so we have an excellent picture of everything that has happened, but virtually nothing to prevent something from happening."

Kelly nodded her head, thinking to herself, *I know Robin's explanation to be so true. She does the best she can with what they give her. I don't envy her job.*

Robin stepped up and said, "I'll work later Friday evening and make sure security is buttoned up during the hours in question. I'm sure I can get some overtime approved by the hotel management once I explain to them who will be present. I wouldn't be surprised to see a member of the hotel's upper echelon hang around and try to make an impression on the VIP guests if that wouldn't be a problem."

Kelly said, "Not a problem. Special attention from management is welcome. Can we expect a parking space near the entrance?"

Robin nodded. "I'll see that you have slot one right next to the front door. I'll have it coned off and you can move the cone out of the way when they arrive. Any problems, just call me."

She handed Kelly her business card. Kelly and Robin shook hands and Kelly left Robin's office and headed towards the exit to go on with her checklist.

Kelly pulled from the hotel parking lot. *I just put out a hundred dollars for this gig. I hope Alan is prepared to make that right when we get together. When you need special treatment, you have to build a close rapport with those giving the treatment. Money is the universal language of special treatment.*

The next stop was the Sandpiper Art Gallery. Kelly entered the two-story building on 54th Street for the first time in her life. She was delighted to see a brightly lit lobby and gift center. *Maybe I should put a little art into my life. I might meet more insightful and cultured people.* Kelly approached the front counter, "Hello," she said in her most cultured voice, "Is the head of the gallery here, and would they have a moment to speak with me?"

"Do you have an appointment with her?" the receptionist inquired.

"No, sorry I don't, but it's important I speak with her regarding events she will be attending this Friday and Saturday. I'm part of an executive protection detail and would like to chat about the events. Her input and cooperation are imperative." Kelly laid her business card on the reception desk.

One phone call and about three minutes later, Kelly saw a woman exiting a door near the staircase. She came directly to Kelly and said, "I'm Cynthia Abbott, the Director of the gallery. Is there a current threat to this location or the staff working here?"

Kelly quickly responded, "Absolutely none that I'm aware of. My purpose for being here is to make you aware of who I am and the fact I that will be attending your Friday night dinner with the mayor and Mr. Ray Hiltzberger. Mr. Hiltzberger travels with an executive protection detail, and I have been hired to be part of his security while he is in Sandpiper. There is no known threat or anticipated problem concerning Mr. Hiltzberger, the mayor, or you. I need to conduct an advance, which is a term that means I have to gather information as well as make arrangements for Mr. Hiltzberger. I have been told you will be dining at the Hightop, the restaurant at the Sandpiper Suites Hotel, at 6 p.m. on Friday and you will meet with him again at an event here at the gallery at 1 p.m. on Saturday. Can you confirm your attendance?"

Abbott said, "Yes, that's all true, but I've never been involved with a protection detail. What's going to happen and is there anything special I need to know or do?"

Kelly smiled reassuringly and said, "I've been to the hotel and all arrangements have been made. You just need to show up and enjoy your meal. I will be there with another protection specialist, and we will be dining at a nearby table in case any problems arise. In the current world we live in, you can't take anything for granted and Mr. Hiltzberger goes out of his way to be sure things go smoothly. Because you're in charge of this gallery, I'd like you to assist me in doing my advance here. It's simply touring the building and making sure I know where all the exits are, and where I would move my Principal should an emergency occur. Do you have any security of your own here or do you have cameras covering the different areas of the gallery?"

Abbott answered, "We have no people performing security, but we do have cameras that cover the critical areas. The taped videos are rotated every month and reused after three months. We call Sandpiper PD if we have a problem. They are very efficient and professional. Do I need to call them and let them know about this?"

"No, I'll notify them on the day of the events so that their patrol supervisors are aware of who we are and what's going on. Oh, by the way, is this event open to the public?"

"No this is by invitation only; we are expecting approximately seventy-five guests."

Kelly assured Abbott the secret to a good protection agent is to do whatever is called for, including remaining invisible, blending in, and playing the role of a guest or staff member. The time of no-neck bodyguards with low IQs was pretty much over. The liabilities were too great. Walking around with hulk-like figures draws other hulk-like figures wanting to test their muscle. A perfect detail happens without people even noticing or knowing protection was in place. Kelly concluded, "Cynthia, please have a relaxing and wonderful dinner Friday night and enjoy your program on Saturday. Call with any concerns."

After Kelly made a quick tour of the building and recorded

the necessary notes, assuring herself this would be a pretty hard target, she departed. She then drove the distance from the gallery to the hotel so she would know how long the drive took. She explored alternate routes, and the times to traverse the distances. She also checked the distances to the closest hospital, airport, and police station. She obtained the phone numbers and names of the people in charge of each of these locations. She would share all this information verbally and in written form with Alan when he arrived.

By mid-day on Wednesday, Kelly felt confident she had completed her advance of the venues to be visited by the VIP. Kelly returned to her office and prepared a report for Alan. The report was not requested, nor a mandatory part of the advance, but she had done it for two reasons—one was to brief Alan on her preparation of the detail, and two was to review her check-off list to be sure she had missed nothing. She looked at the checklist before her and found two items yet to be addressed.

- Interview hotel security ✓
- Interview the restaurant manager ✓
- Identify emergency exits ✓
- Identify parking ✓
- Inspection of the hotel & room
- Identify the hotel room ✓
- Drive the route to identify the time and distance to the gallery building ✓
- Meet gallery director ✓
- Walk the gallery building ✓

- Identify emergency exits ✓
- Identify if the event was open to the public, and look at the parking ✓
- Get the phone number for the director of the gallery ✓
- Contact the mayor's office to see if he had security ✓
- Call Sandpiper PD desk SGT & put him on notice for both Fri. and Sat. ✓
- Re-contact PD on Sat. Ensure that info was passed on to the on-duty SGT
- Find locations of the closest police building ✓
- Find location of closest hospital ✓
- Find location of closest airport ✓

The plan was now in writing. The only problem was the well-known expression: "No plan lasts beyond the first contact with the enemy."

18

FIRST THROUGH THE DOOR

She was folding her one-page report into an envelope when she heard the alley door open. No one had ever come through that door since Kelly set up her business. A White male in his mid-forties, with a brown receding hairline, entered her office door. He was dressed casually in slacks and a collared shirt. Bright white tennis shoes completed his attire. He appeared hesitant, but stepped inside Kelly's office and said, "Are you, Kelly Hart?"

Kelly smiled and said, "Yes, I am. How can I help you?"

In a soft voice, he said, "My name is Tom Shelby. I think my wife is cheating on me and I need some help proving it. My attorney, James Ewing, told me I should consider hiring a PI to watch her and see if my suspicions are valid."

Kelly pointed to one of two chairs in front of her desk. "Please sit down, Mr. Shelby. I need to hear a little bit more before I can make a decision." Kelly moved from her chair to her office door and quietly closed it to add a level of privacy to the conversation that was about to follow.

Tom Shelby told Kelly that he had suspected for some

time that his wife, Ava, may be having an affair. Shelby explained that he was in sales, which required quite a bit of out-of-town travel overnights during the week. He said he was always home on weekends and spends as much time as possible with his wife. They go to dinner or the movies, and pretty much do anything she likes to do. He further explained that they had been married for four years and everything seemed to be great until about four months ago.

"I feel bad for being gone so much, but when she married me I was already a salesman, so she knew what it would be like. We even lived together for seven months before we got married."

As he told his story, Kelly could see frustration and anger growing in his delivery of the information.

Shelby continued, "My wife works as a physical therapist and I know that she has her hands on people all day long. Some of these people are men and I fear one of them has come on to her and she has bent to his advances."

Kelly questioned, "Do you know of any other location where she might have met a man?"

Shelby replied, "No, I can't imagine her going to a bar alone and she has no girlfriends to hang out with."

Kelly said, "Mr. Shelby, I've heard you speak of feelings and suspicions. Can you be more specific or describe what has happened to make you think she is cheating? Have you talked to your wife about your feelings?" Before he could answer, Kelly offered him a soda or water from her small refrigerator in the corner of her office. He accepted and greedily drank down a sugary soda which seemed to temporarily settle him down.

"When I'm on the road, I call my wife every night at 10

p.m. to check on her and say good night. We have no children, so talking to each other every night has helped us deal with the loneliness of separation while on the road. About three weeks ago, I called her and everything seemed fine and we said good night. At 10:30 p.m. I remembered I hadn't told her that I had found a bracelet I thought she would love, and I wanted to send her a pic to see if she liked it. The phone rang and rang and went to voice mail. Thinking she was in the shower, I called again at 11 with the same result. I figured she was asleep and just couldn't hear the phone, so I gave up.

"The next day when I got home, I told her that I had tried to call her about the bracelet and she said she hadn't heard the phone. She told me 'I was stiff and sore from work, and I took an extra-long soak in the tub to ease my muscles.'

"Later that same day, she got a phone call. She walked out of the living room into the kitchen to take it. When she came back into the living room a couple of minutes later, she said, 'That was a telephone solicitor calling and I asked him to take my name off his call list.' It may be my paranoia, but her actions just seemed nervous, as if she knew she had to explain herself. It was not Ava's normal behavior."

Shelby looked down at his feet before he continued. "It's embarrassing to talk about, but our sex life has changed. It seemed to fall off about four months ago. She and I have always been quite active in that area. When alone, we can hardly keep our hands off each other. Our personal display of affection is sometimes mocked by our friends teasing us and saying we act like high-school kids when they first experienced sex. She is not only a willing partner, but one that is willing to be a little bit on the wild side. I always loved that about her. I'd come home and find her naked or dressed seductively. She would turn the television to channels that aired porn and we'd end up having sex on the couch or the floor in front of the TV. She would suggest we go to hotels and have sex like we did when we first met."

Kelly asked, "How did things change?"

"Four months ago, she started making up excuses why she didn't feel like having sex. She had a headache, she was tired. Sometimes I'd come home, and she had already gone to bed wearing nightgowns I'd never seen before. I knew something was fucked up and I told her so. She said I was imagining things and everybody's marriage slows down sexually after a few years. I've never been married before, but she was married when I met her and was in the middle of a divorce. She was cheating on her husband with me when we first started having sex."

"Have you ever cheated on her?" Kelly inquired.

"I told her when we decided to get married that I wasn't like her first husband. I told her I would never stray and would expect the same of her. I stressed to her I couldn't stand for that to happen—and I'd kill her if I found out she was cheating. She laughed at me. I guess I did sound a little overdramatic at the time. Now that I'm faced with the possibility that she is cheating, I'm trying to handle this the right way. I'd like you to watch her when I'm away and find out what—if anything—she's doing. I'm hoping it's just me being suspicious, but I don't think so. Can you help me?"

Kelly decided, "Yes, I will take your case. I charge eighty-five dollars an hour plus any documented expenses, and I require a thousand-dollar retainer that may need to be replenished, depending on the length and findings of my investigation. The only other condition is that I will submit all my reports to your attorney. It would then be the attorney's decision on any continuing action." Kelly did not tell him what she was thinking. *Divorce cases are very sensitive and can be highly volatile if not handled properly.*

"Tom, you're doing the right thing by going to an attorney and seeking a neutral party to investigate. Try to keep your emotions under control as we go forward. I will need your wife's full name and description, the tag number for her car, her cell phone number, the days you'll be out of town, and a check or cash for the thousand dollars. Also, the name, address, and phone number of your attorney."

"When can you start," Shelby asked as he pulled out his checkbook.

"When are you going out of town on business next?" Kelly asked.

"Next Monday. I leave and won't be home until Wednesday afternoon."

Kelly told him to call if anything changed, otherwise, she would be checking on his wife Monday and Tuesday night.

"Oh, there's one other thing," Shelby said while stabbing his hand in his front pocket and pulling out a tattered piece of paper. "I took out the garbage a couple of weeks ago and when I dumped the pail from the bathroom, this fell out on top. It's an address with just the house number and the street name, but no town, zip, or name with it. I checked and found there's a street in Tall Pines with that street name. The house number matches a house there, but there is no name on the mailbox, and I didn't see a car there on the two occasions I drove by. I don't know who lives there. And I checked our phone directory in the kitchen and our Christmas card list and found nothing matching."

"Did you ask your wife?"

"No, I think I was afraid she wouldn't tell me the truth. I couldn't stand it if I found out later that she lied."

"Okay," Kelly responded as she took a scrap of paper and waved it at Shelby. "Tom, do you recognize the handwriting?"

"No, I don't."

Kelly told him, "Stop conducting your own investigation. That's why you're paying me. Stay away from this address."

As Shelby headed out the door, curiosity got the better of Kelly. "How did you find me?"

Shelby stopped in the doorway and turned around. "My wife and I were at a house party last weekend and a couple was raving over a PI they had hired to help them in a serious situation. We were standing close enough that I could eavesdrop on some of their conversations. Not sure what you did for them, but they had nothing but good things to say about Kelly Hart. I asked somebody later at the party who the couple was that I was standing near. They told me their name was Brightfield—do you know them?"

"Not sure I do," Kelly said while holding a smile and slowly closing the door. "I'll be in touch."

19
FRIDAY HANDLED

Friday rolled around quickly. Kelly felt she was ready for the upcoming protection detail. She reviewed all the steps she had taken. She learned Mayor Stanley Wells had no personal security and normally drove himself to all events, as was expected for his scheduled dinner Friday night. Kelly spoke briefly with his administrative assistant, Peggy, identifying herself and Alan St. Clair as the EP team for the protection detail on Friday evening and Saturday afternoon. Peggy thanked Kelly and said she appreciated the heads-up and would make the mayor aware of the situation. Kelly emphasized that there was no reason to believe there was any threat.

Kelly also spoke with the chief of Sandpiper PD, Elwood Richards, and provided him with the same information.

He said, "If things are quiet, I will have one of my people stop by the gallery on Saturday just to show local support for the organization. Thanks for the call, Kelly."

Chief Richards asked his deputy chief, Barry Trout, to step into his office—he brought him up to date and asked him to handle the Saturday assignment if he had the manpower.

"Barry, you might want to let Brogan know about this, just in case. I don't think he necessarily has to do anything, but let him know."

Trout responded, "Will do, Chief."

At 3:00 p.m. Kelly walked into the lobby of the Sandpiper Suites Hotel. She looked sharp in her navy pantsuit with a starched button-down blouse underneath the jacket that was tailored to fit her concealed weapon. The black kitten pump heels completed her outfit. Kelly's favorite seven-shot 380, stainless steel Sig Sauer P230 with rosewood grips was in her waistband. The clip was full of hollow point bullets with one already in the pipe. Two hours before the arrival of the Principal, there was still work to do.

Kelly called Robin Love and told her she would be there at 3:00. Robin did not disappoint and was waiting for Kelly in the lobby. The hotel reservations had already been made by Mr. Hiltzberger's office.

Kelly greeted Robin and asked, "Can you show me the accommodations for Mr. Hiltzberger?"

They went together to a room on the top floor of the hotel. Robin opened the door and Kelly toured the space. It was well-appointed with furnishings of a higher quality hotel and recently cleaned. Kelly smiled as she toured the room. All surfaces were free of dust and sparkled with the sun shining through the patio doors.

Kelly was finalizing her checklist anticipating there would be no issues. She began at the bed, it was made and dressed with clean, ironed white sheets. The bathroom was spotless and stocked with towels and the normal hotel offerings of personal care items. A hairdryer was present and Kelly tested it and found it in working order. There was a large television mounted on the wall over a dark dresser. Kelly tested the remote to verify it was operational. The carpet had been recently vacuumed and showed no stains. The clean glass sliding door allowed access to a deck that hangs off the side of the building. The ironwork was clean and freshly painted and four chairs and a small table occupied the space. The view was spectacular from the room and was pretty much the same view the Principal would have from his dining location. A complimentary bottle of champagne sat in a silver ice bucket. The suite refrigerator was stocked with beer, miniatures, soda and water. There was ice in the freezer. As tedious as this sounds, this was Kelly's job. Her checklist was finally complete.

Kelly was impressed. *This should be everyone's expectation when checking into a hotel—not just the wealthy.* Even more impressive was the information Robin shared with her. "There are only two suites on this level, and we did not have the second one booked, so we are giving it to the protection specialist traveling with your VIP at a normal room rate. I think the higher-ups are trying to distinguish themselves and the hotel, hoping for continued visits or referrals. Kelly, I took the liberty to obtain the keys for both rooms now. This will eliminate you having to stop at the front desk at the time of arrival."

Robin handed Kelly the keys in separate key holders with the suite numbers written on them. "I'll be in the lobby at 5 p.m. and if you let me know, I'll pull the orange cone out of the parking space when they enter the parking lot." Kelly could tell that Robin was engaged and getting into the rhythm and flow of the detail.

"Great, that will be very helpful, and Mr. Hiltzberger will

be impressed," Kelly said. She quickly checked the other suite and found the same conditions. Kelly took possession of both keys. When they reached the elevator, Kelly said, "Oh, there was one more thing I wanted to check. Can I meet you in the lobby?"

Robin responded, "Sure, I'll meet you down there," as she stepped into the elevator and pushed the down button.

Kelly didn't need to check anything, but she sealed both of the suites with a small piece of tape in the upper right-hand corner of each door. Kelly withheld this information from Robin as this was a level of security known only to the agents working the detail. There was a small private hallway that led to a door that could be opened only with a key card matching the two suites. The door exited into a public lobby area near the elevators. The door was not marked, which gave the guests in the suites another level of anonymity and security.

Kelly met again with Paul in the restaurant. He reassured her that everything was in order for the dinner and that he would be present to meet and seat the guests. Kelly told Paul, "The VIP is Ray Hiltzberger and he's a wealthy businessman and supporter of the arts. I'm sure he will be impressed with your hotel and restaurant. Call me if you need anything before 6 p.m. I'll be here when you meet Mr. Hiltzberger, the mayor, and the director of the gallery."

Paul acknowledged the information and said to Kelly, "Every detail of the dinner has been addressed and the senior hotel manager, Gail Harford, will be present to help seat the guests."

At 4:30, Kelly's cell phone buzzed in her pocket. She answered it on the second ring and as expected, it was Alan St. Clair.

He said, "We're thirty minutes out. All good?"

Kelly responded, "All good, pull right up to the front door. Someone will remove the parking cones and you will have the slot closest to the door. I will meet you at the car and walk you directly to the elevators. One will be locked open for you and Mr. Hiltzberger. I'll accompany you into the elevator and walk you to the door of Mr. Hiltzberger's suite. I'll give you the key so you can take him in. The next door down the hall is yours and is a duplicate of Mr. Hiltzberger's room. Don't worry; the hotel is giving you the suite for the price of a regular room. I thought you'd like to be close if needed. Both rooms have been advanced and sealed. Check for a small piece of tape in the upper right-hand corner before opening the door. I'll be right there with you if you need anything. This hotel does not normally have bellmen, but they have assigned one of their check-in staff to handle those duties for us today. Dinner reservation is confirmed for 6 p.m. and the restaurant manager will seat Mr. Hiltzberger and his guests. Any questions?"

"Sounds like you've knocked it out of the park, Kelly. I'm anxious to meet this one-person advance team who's thought of everything. You're going to make us look good. Thanks. We're in a black Chevrolet Suburban. I'll flash my lights as I approach the building."

At precisely 5 p.m. a black Suburban with tinted windows rolled smoothly onto the parking lot of the hotel. The headlights flashed once as it proceeded toward the front of the hotel. Robin removed a single orange cone from the parking slot and placed it off to the side. The man assigned to act as bellman stood in coat and tie with his arms crossed behind his back in anticipation of moving forward when the car stopped. A luggage cart stood at the ready.

Kelly stood just feet away, observing the approaching vehicle and the rest of the parking lot. There was no activity that gave her concern. She would allow Alan to open the door for the Principal and keep an eye out for any potential threat. She would observe the handling of the luggage and then accompany Alan and the Principal through the lobby. Robin had retreated into the hotel and was now positioned next to the elevator door, awaiting their arrival. Other guests would be directed to use the other elevator. Fortunately, at this moment in time, no competitors were looking for an elevator ride.

The Suburban pulled into the slot and the driver's door opened immediately. Alan walked to Kelly, who had moved next to the car. He shook her hand, smiled, and said, "Looks like you may have done this a few times before. Nice to meet a professional." The exchange took only seconds and Alan continued around the rear of the car to the back-passenger door, opening it while gazing out over the parking lot, scanning for potential problems. He saw none.

The Principal emerged from the car, standing with a watchful eye. He was a tall, light-skinned Black man with a willowy frame, full head of hair, and coffee-brown eyes peeking from his Silhouette glasses. He looked to be in his seventies, wearing a well-tailored suit and black shoes that glistened in the sun, and he carried a soft-brown leather briefcase. As he walked to the rear of the car to prepare for the removal of the luggage, he saw Kelly and walked up to her, extending his hand. "You must be Kelly Hart," he said. "I've heard favorable comments about you from Alan and some of my friends in the Baltimore County Police Department. It's a pleasure to meet you and have you working with me over the next couple of days. Please call me Ray while we're together." He chuckled quietly and leaned in. "I love all this attention. You guys choreograph these events so well; I sometimes forget I'm just a simple man. This will be fun."

Kelly shook Mr. Hiltzberger's hand and was taken aback by his warm greeting. *Is he kidding me? Is this a test?* She looked to Alan for some kind of sign. He just smiled and winked at her.

Alan indicated the bags that needed to be removed from the car and the newly appointed bellman worked like he'd been doing this all his life. Soon the luggage cart was loaded and the entourage was moving into the hotel, across the lobby, and into the open elevator. The bellman stopped short of entering the elevator. He would follow in the next elevator, accompanied by the head of security.

As the elevator doors closed, Kelly handed Alan two plastic key cards. One was marked "Hiltzberger" with the suite number, and the other was marked "St. Clair" with his suite number. Out of the elevator, straight to the unmarked door, Kelly told Alan to use his card, this signaled Alan she had added an additional step of security into play. He did so and it flashed green, allowing entrance to the short hall and the doors to the suites.

They arrived at the door for Mr. Hiltzberger. Alan checked the security tape and saw it was still in place. Using the appropriate key card, Alan entered the suite first; confident Kelly had done her work. He found it secure. Alan told Hiltzberger it was safe to enter and he did, dropping his briefcase on a chair and walking to the sliding glass door admiring the view. His eyes took in the rest of the accommodation and he remarked, "Very nice. I like this place a lot."

A knock on the door announced the arrival of the luggage. Alan removed the pieces for Mr. Hiltzberger and placed them on the luggage rack and a spacious dresser. He tipped the bellman and asked Mr. Hiltzberger if he needed anything further. Hiltzberger responded, "No, thank you. Please come to my door at 5:45 and we'll walk to dinner together."

"Yes sir," Alan said and he closed the door and stepped into the hallway.

Kelly had heard the conversation and told Alan, "Go do what you have to do. I'm going to the restaurant now and will greet the other guests if they show up early. I'll make sure everything is as it should be. Glad he likes the room. What's the deal with him telling me to call him Ray?"

Alan said, "I told you he was easy to work with. He's just a laid-back rich guy who likes to make an appearance when he goes anywhere. He enjoys being pampered, but never complains when things don't go quite right. So far, I would say he is happy with his treatment and what you have done to make it happen."

Kelly nodded, "Okay, let's keep it rolling then. Doubt I'll be calling him Ray, though. That's a little over the top for me."

Alan laughed and said, "I get it. I still call him Mr. Hiltzberger myself and he tells me every detail I can call him Ray. Guess our training just won't let that happen. See you in about forty-five minutes."

Kelly went into the restaurant at 5:30. She saw the *Reserved* signs on the table in the glass nook and on the table for Alan and herself. She checked out both tables and found them dressed in white tablecloths, with silverware and glasses gleaming. Paul Geppi was standing behind the bar and nodded at Kelly. She returned his gesture with a thumbs-up.

"Please let me know if there is anything else we need to do to make this an enjoyable evening for these VIP guests," Paul said.

Kelly told him, "Just make sure the meals are done properly and come out hot and I think we'll have a winner!"

Paul gave Kelly his brightest smile and said, "We can do that."

Kelly checked out the bar and saw there were three couples having drinks. Near the end of the bar that was closest to where Kelly and Alan would sit was a lone individual who didn't seem to fit in. The man was a little loud and appeared to have indulged a few too many. This big guy was disheveled and about six foot one, probably 245 pounds, and in desperate need of a shave. He was wearing a lightweight jacket over a plaid shirt and khaki cargo pants. The pockets were flat against his legs so they didn't appear to hold any items that may be of concern. Kelly saw a utility knife in a leather sheath on his belt when he reached across the bar for a cocktail napkin to mop up a small spill he had created on the bar. With a beer and a mixed drink in front of him, the big guy was talking to Kathie, the bartender, but she seemed to be ignoring most of what he said and only responded when he raised his voice or ended his comments with a question mark.

Kelly had seen it all before. This guy was already on the edge of being a problem. He was slurring some of his words, but right now he was reasonably in control of himself. If he did not leave before the arrival of Mr. Hiltzberger and his guests, he would bear close watch. Kelly began to generate a plan in her mind to deal with this potential trouble.

Ten minutes before six, the mayor and gallery director entered the restaurant together and were immediately recognized and greeted by Paul and the senior manager of the hotel. They were guided through the bar area into the private dining nook. Kelly swung into action, introducing herself to Mayor Stanley Wells while saying hello to the director, Cynthia Abbott. At their table, Kelly suggested a particular seat be saved for Mr. Hiltzberger, so that he could observe the bar area and the water view simultaneously. The mayor and director readily agreed and took seats that would flank him on either side.

While they waited, a server handed the wine list to them as he placed glasses of water on the table for all three guests. They were still settling in when Mr. Hiltzberger and Alan entered and approached the nook. Paul greeted them enthusiastically with a wide smile and gestured them to the designated table.

Kelly had withdrawn to stand in the doorway entering the nook. Mr. Hiltzberger stopped at the doorway and shook hands with Kelly, thanking her again for her presence and seeing to his guests. Alan stepped slightly back and let Paul and the hotel manager take over for the last few steps to the table. Both the mayor and director rose to their feet and exchanged handshakes and welcomed Mr. Hiltzberger to Sandpiper. Hiltzberger motioned for them to return to their seats and he took the seat Kelly had selected for him. He looked around taking it all in and gave a small quick nod at Kelly, indicating he was pleased with everything.

Alan and Kelly exited the nook and went to the table where they would dine. Kelly checked out the big guy at the bar and was disturbed when she saw his gaze had settled on the party in the nook. She hoped it is only because of all the fuss made over them when they had entered the restaurant.

She told Alan, "Don't look over your shoulder, but there's a big guy sitting by himself at the bar. Appears to be in his cups and has a utility knife on his right hip. He's been a little loud so far, but nothing else. He's eyeballing our people. I'll be watching him, especially if he gets off that barstool."

The nook provided an area of complete privacy and their conversations were muted. All three in the nook appeared to be enjoying each other's company while they awaited their meals. Kelly and Alan had ordered the cheapest and easiest thing to eat on the menu. They weren't there to have a grand meal. They were there to fit in and stay alert.

Everyone's meals had been served. Chef Hammond came out of the kitchen with Paul and made sure everyone's plate met their expectations. Mr. Hiltzberger was beaming at all the attention and care being given to him and his guests.

At the bar, the big guy leaned over and spoke to Kathie in what he thought was a low voice. Alcohol sometimes removes the ability to whisper. "Is that the mayor over there having dinner?" he asked while pointing at the nook.

Kathie leaned to the side to see around him and said, "Yeah, that's him."

The big guy tried to whisper, "I need to talk to him. I've been trying to get a stop sign at the intersection where I live before somebody runs over my daughter and her playmates. They don't play in the road, but cars go through there at forty miles an hour because there's no stop sign. It's just plain dangerous and nobody is doing a fucking thing about it. I'm going face-to-face with him right now so he knows he needs to do something. Don't dump my drinks. I'll be right back."

Kathie said, "Jesse, I don't think that's a good idea." Her comment had no influence on him as he spun his barstool and took his first step toward the nook, completely oblivious to Kelly and Alan.

"This is between me and the mayor."

Kelly whispered to Alan. "Be ready, but I think I got this." She stood up and eased herself into the path to the nook. The big guy was only halfway to his destination when Kelly said, "Hey Jesse, what are you doing here? Haven't seen you in a long time. How have you been?" Jesse came to a dead stop and looked with confusion at the woman who had just addressed him. Kelly could almost hear the gears of his brain spin trying to gain recognition.

Kelly moved forward and folded him into a friendly hug and then backed up with a look of expectancy on her face. Jesse's face reddened with embarrassment. He stuttered, "Hi, I'm sorry. I can't remember your name."

"I'm Kelly! Don't you remember me?"

"Kelly? Where do I know you from?"

"School," she responded.

"Pocomoke High?" Jesse asked.

"Yep, I was a couple of years behind you."

"Sorry, guess I'm getting old and can't remember everybody."

Kelly looked at him and said, "That's okay. Where were you going?"

"I was headed in there to talk to the mayor. He needs to listen to me and take some action!"

"Maybe I can help you with that. I work with the mayor," Kelly said, trying to move Jesse away from the table. "He's in a private meeting right now, and if you go in there, you won't accomplish shit. Walk back over to the bar with me and I'll listen to you. I'll guarantee you I can get you the attention you need. Does that seem fair?"

"Thanks, yeah it does. Guess it pays to know people," Jesse said, slightly confused.

Kelly walked towards the bar, and Jesse turned on his heel and followed her back to his stool. Alan watched and listened to the entire interaction with a sense of awe. Kelly was talking to the giant of a man, and a few minutes later she shook his hand and walked back to her table and sat down. Alan watched the big guy pay his bill and head out the door, leaving his unfinished drinks on the bar

"What the hell did you tell him? I thought we were going to have a real problem."

"I told him I worked with the mayor. He said he needed to talk to him about a stop sign, and I promised I would use my influence to have someone on the mayor's staff call him personally to discuss his problem and come up with a solution. I also told him his little daughter was home right now, waiting for her daddy. That did the trick. He said he had to go, paid his bill, shook my hand and left."

"How well did you know him in school?"

Kelly smiled and said, "We went to different schools. I've never seen the guy before tonight, and he's never seen me. I just planted the seed, and he went with it. He's one of those gentle giants who, when sober, is a good guy. A few drinks and he starts to drift toward a line he shouldn't cross. Tonight, he pulled back and did the right thing. I'll talk to the mayor before he leaves and give him the guy's name and phone number. I'll suggest strongly this guy should be called before someone gets hurt, children or adults." Kelly unfolded a cocktail napkin with a name and phone number on it. She also produced a utility knife and laid it on top of the napkin.

"Did he give you that?" Alan inquired.

"Sort of. He let me hug him." Kelly grinned despite herself. She looked into the nook and Hiltzberger was staring straight at her. He gave her a knowing smile and returned to the conversation with his guests. The situation was handled with a little bit of verbal judo.

The rest of the meal went without issue or incident and all parties retired happy and filled with good food. Kelly took the mayor aside for a few seconds and gave him the napkin. As she exited the bar, she handed Kathie the utility knife and said, "Jesse dropped this when he was leaving. Please return it to him. Tell him Kelly found it and was glad to see him again."

Kelly followed up by contacting Paul and Robin and thanked them for their help during the protection detail. Paul said, "Mr. Hiltzberger was very complimentary of the hotel and our staff. He tipped lavishly and will always be a welcome guest at Sandpiper Suites."

Jesse spent the next three days looking at old yearbooks, but never found a Kelly that looked like the woman in the bar. He spent the rest of his time looking all over his house and truck for his lost utility knife. He was happy, though. The mayor's office called him, and he was getting a stop sign.

20

SATURDAY'S SURPRISE ENCOUNTER

Friday night, after tucking Mr. Hiltzberger in his suite for the night and sealing his door, Alan told Kelly that Mr. Hiltzberger was going to take breakfast in his room in the morning and they would be leaving for the gallery at 12:45. He asked if she could be at the gallery when they arrived to assist in parking and bringing Mr. Hiltzberger into the building. Kelly assured Alan the venue would be ready when they arrived.

Alan shared with Kelly, "Mr. Hiltzberger was extremely impressed with you and your attention to detail. He asked me about the big guy and I promised to tell him the story on the ride back to Baltimore. Mr. Hiltzberger said he knew something had happened and was anxious to know the details."

Alan asked, "Did you incur any out-of-pocket expenses while setting up the restaurant and hotel?"

She said, "I tipped Paul, the restaurant manager, a hundred dollars on the first day I met with him."

Alan pulled out a wad of money and peeled off a hundred-dollar bill. "Anything else?"

Kelly answered, "Not so far."

"See you tomorrow at the gallery," Alan said. "Have a good night."

Kelly went home to her parent's place and fell asleep almost immediately. Protective details seldom have extreme physical activity, but mentally they are exhausting; always on edge, wondering where the next problem would arise. Sleep took her away with thoughts of how she had played Jesse for his own good and how she had no other hiccups during the detail.

Kelly awoke at 5 a.m. to the sound of her alarm. The sun was coming up and it looked like a perfect day to sleep in, but that wasn't happening. Out of bed and off to the gym for a quick workout and then a short jog on the beach. Someone had mentioned to her the dangers of running alone on the beach. Kelly was confident she could handle herself should the need arise. The flick-knife she had tucked in her waistband would hopefully turn the odds in her favor. She returned to the condo sweating like it was mid-summer. A run through the shower, clean hair, light make-up, and another impressive pantsuit would start her day. She felt like a million dollars. At 11 a.m. she was out the door and on her way to the gallery. *This should be an easy day, but you could never be sure and should always have your head on a swivel.*

The gallery was bristling with activity and preparation for the upcoming gathering of art lovers and members of the gallery. Several artists who currently had their work on display would also be present. If any of their pieces sold, they would be there to personally thank the buyer and chat with them about the history and story behind the piece purchased. Sort of like a book signing for an author, but much more expensive.

Kelly walked the entire building, admiring the many paintings of different media—watercolor, oil and acrylic, not to mention the pottery and sculptures she saw. She knew she could afford none of them. For the time being, she would remain a HomeGoods kind of girl. Kelly did take a special liking to a jewelry collection by Sunshine & Goldie. The collection consisted of hand-wrapped gemstone pendants in precious metals. She found the intricate wrap to be unique and appealing.

Kelly met with Cynthia Abbott and said, "I had a delightful meal with Mr. Hiltzberger. He is a very intelligent man with a true interest and devotion to the arts of every genre. I am excited about showing him the Sandpiper Art Gallery and its offerings."

Abbott had the best parking slot coned off for Mr. Hiltzberger. The catering service, paid for by a local contributor, set up trays of food for the guests to enjoy as they mingled. There was a cash bar with all proceeds going to the gallery. Everyone seemed excited that this event was happening. Mr. Hiltzberger was to be the guest of honor and would make some remarks around 3 p.m. He would not only write a check to the gallery, but he would urge participants to dig deep to benefit this worthy cause.

The doors remained locked until 1 p.m. and early arriving guests mingled on the front patio. The early fall weather was near perfect for the occasion. At 12:50 p.m., Mr. Hiltzberger arrived and parked in the designated slot after Kelly removed the last cone. Alan saw Kelly and scanned the crowd. She gave him a nod to signal everything was okay. Alan opened the rear passenger door and Mr. Hiltzberger exited the car. He was met at the curb by Cynthia who was aglow at the opportunity to greet him. They walked together into the crowd of guests with an almost celebrity presence. This man from Baltimore was well known to this crowd. They loved him. Alan was right beside him—vetting the attendees as he went; close, but not intrusive.

Over seventy-five people attended the fundraiser and the building was not overly large. It consisted of two floors with exhibits and art on both levels. The crowd spread out on its own and soon the guests mingled in the exhibit rooms and hallways. Caterers served drinks on trays they carried throughout the venue, with multiple food stations spread out so finger foods were easily available to the attendees. Quiet conversations and laughter drifted throughout. The attendees examined and commented upon the pieces of art. The atmosphere was quite uplifting if you were into the arts.

Kelly had visited previously and was not uplifted, but acted the part. Alan handled the close-in coverage with his Principal while she continued sweeping the rooms, examining faces and postures to see if anyone looked out of place or threatening. She found only warm. and possibly artificial, smiles all around.

Cynthia Abbott stayed at the side of Mr. Hiltzberger. She seemed to know everyone present and was introducing her special guest to each attendee. Mr. Hiltzberger seemed very relaxed and comfortable with the setting and his role in making this a special get-together.

At one point, Abbott, Mr. Hiltzberger and Alan entered the small elevator alone and went to the second floor. Kelly immediately took the stairs to the second floor and arrived just moments after the elevator door had opened, disgorging its passengers. She had a clear view of her responsibility and resumed scanning the faces and hands of those on the second floor. The second-floor railing was constructed of clear glass panels topped with a wooden handrail. It allowed everyone to see both floors and the people occupying the spaces above or below.

The tiny hairs on the back of Kelly's neck went up, warning her that something had changed. A sixth sense sent alarms to her other senses. *Where's the threat?* The volume and tone of the crowd were the same. People still laughed, mingled, and seemed to be enjoying every moment of the occasion.

With practiced stealth, Kelly moved closer to a solid wall and turned slowly, but naturally, to observe her entire surroundings. Behind her, a man stood watching her. Kelly noticed the man was around five foot eleven with gray hair and a smooth tan complexion. It was hard to estimate his age. Somewhere between 60 and 70 would be Kelly's guess.

Her eyes met his and, without hesitation, he moved toward her. When within reach, he extended his hand and said, "Hello, I'm Thomas Gordon. I don't believe we've met. I thought I knew everyone here, but I don't know you."

Kelly quickly recovered from this unexpected circumstance and said, "Hi, I'm Kelly Hart. I know Mr. Hiltzberger and was invited to be here today. I recently moved to the area, so I don't know many of the local people yet. Actually, it is my first time at the gallery."

"Well you've met a local now," Gordon responded, as he released her hand. "I'm in the real estate business and have an office right here in town. How about you?"

"I'm in the security industry," Kelly said. "I have an office in Berlin, but live here in Sandpiper. It's nice to meet you and thanks for taking the time to introduce yourself."

Kelly was still weighing in her mind the warning signals

her body had sent out and compared them to the approach of this total stranger. *Was he just being nice or was he trying to find out who I was and why I was here?*

At that moment, Mr. Hiltzberger, Cynthia Abbott and Alan made their way to Kelly's location. Abbott knew and introduced Thomas Gordon to Mr. Hiltzberger. Mr. Hiltzberger turned and said, "Good to see you, Kelly. Are you enjoying yourself?"

"Yes, Ray I am. Thank you for asking. This is a wonderful event."

At the use of his first name, Mr. Hiltzberger smiled widely and began moving further down the aisle, meeting still other guests. He had played his role perfectly. *No wonder Alan liked this guy.*

Kelly had moved away with Mr. Hiltzberger, leaving Thomas Gordon standing alone. Kelly had the eerie feeling he was still watching her with an unhealthy interest. Kelly thought, *God damn, I'm getting paranoid. It's like he was sizing me up. Not flirtatious, but in a creepy way. Maybe I'll find out a little bit more about Mr. Gordon.*

At 3 p.m., Mr. Hiltzberger gave his remarks from the railing of the second floor. A sound system and microphone allowed him to speak to the entire gathering. As Kelly looked down upon the crowd on the first floor, she saw a familiar face. It was the mayor. He saw her and gave her a little smile. The man he had been talking with turned to the voice of Mr. Hiltzberger's address.

Kelly couldn't believe it. It was him. It was dreamboat. It was Brogan! He didn't seem to notice her, and he began moving away from the mayor towards the entrance to the gallery. *Oh, shit.* He was leaving her again. Without being obvious,

Kelly descended the stairs and worked her way through the crowd toward the entrance. At one point, she thought she could see him above the heads of the other guests. She pushed through the entrance doors onto the patio. She scanned the parking area and saw no one. She looked toward Coastal Highway and caught a glimpse of a dark sedan turning right; too far away to see its occupants. *Was that him? Was he gone again? Maybe one more clue. Perhaps he drove a dark sedan.* She would remember it because it looked like a police car; the kind she used to drive. Her mind raced with all these thoughts. *Time to get back to work.* Back inside, Mr. Hiltzberger was wrapping up his address to a rousing round of applause.

Abbott, Hiltzberger, and Alan positioned themselves near the door as guests began leaving. Nearly everyone had a check in hand that they dropped in a decorated box placed near the door for just this occasion. A few apologized for not having a check with them, but pledged to send one as soon as they got home. It would not go unnoticed if their checks did not arrive in quick order. Abbott's assistant was writing down the names of those without checks in hand. It would be in very bad form to be on that list and not contribute. The art world of the Eastern Shore was an intimidating group and no one wanted to be on the wrong list.

Eventually, everyone was gone and Abbott said, "Mr. Hiltzberger, thank you for coming and speaking to the guests. I can't tell you how much your visit meant to the gallery."

"I was honored and I look forward to visiting again in the future. I urge you to continue your good work for Sandpiper Art Gallery." Mr. Hiltzberger's final act as he left was to place his check in the box.

Kelly and Alan walked with Mr. Hiltzberger to the car and

secured him in the backseat, but not before he again shook Kelly's hand. "Thank you for your help over the last two days. I told Alan to give you one of my business cards with my personal cell phone number should I ever be able to help you in any way." Alan then closed the car door.

Alan turned to Kelly and shook her hand. He then placed in her hand a neatly folded paper. He said, "Kelly, you did a fantastic job and I'll be sure to let my boss know to call you if we have any future business on the Shore. In your hand is our check for a thousand dollars." Alan reached for her other hand and placed some folded cash and said, "Mr. Hiltzberger was so impressed he has given you a bonus of five hundred dollars in cash. I hope to see you again." And with that, they were gone.

The detail was officially over for Kelly. She didn't open her hand until she reached her car, but when she did the check and cash made her glad her work was appreciated.

The next day was Sunday and she planned to take the day off. Monday, she would begin work on the domestic case that had walked in her door. Kelly pondered. *I hope it goes as smoothly as this assignment. I hate domestic cases. They are potentially explosive and, as an investigator, I'm inserting myself right in the middle of the situation. Careful is the watchword.*

21

JUST BROGAN

The black Ford sedan turned right into the parking lot. The driver guided the car into a parking spot near the entrance of the building. A small white sign with black lettering indicated the slot belonged to DET. BROGAN. He was now at his workplace.

Over the years, much to his mother's chagrin, the name William had fallen away, and everyone—both friend and foe—just called him Brogan. Baltimore's mayor and chief of police really had not wanted to lose him, but they bowed to political pressure. They felt it was unfair and when they'd had the opportunity, they strongly endorsed Brogan for a position with Sandpiper PD.

Brogan was forty-five years old and religiously maintained his strong stature through diligent workouts and martial arts. He was six-foot-two with a full head of dark hair and just enough silver running through it to show he had been around the block a time or two. Brogan was often described as ruggedly handsome; sometimes described as a lady's man. He was quiet and unassuming, often aloof, but always had an easy smile. He had won the affection of many women over the years. He even tried marriage once, but it didn't work out. Now he lived by one firm rule: no long-term commitments.

He once had a fairly regular relationship with a television reporter named Lynn Murphy, but there was a little trouble in Sandpiper last year and some women died. Lynn thought she knew about police work, but on that occasion, she got too close to the fire. She still visited a psychologist regularly and she and Brogan had drifted apart.

22
COULD USE A LITTLE HELP

Sunday and Monday passed quietly into history. Tuesday morning, Brogan arrived at Sandpiper PD carrying his standard hot, black coffee. As was his norm, he headed for his desk to review the reports submitted covering the activities from the night before. The reports gave him a thumbnail sketch to determine whether detectives would conduct follow-up, or just lend a hand to a patrol officer's investigation.

Passing through the communications section of the office, he stopped to say hello to Police Communications Officer (PCO), Maggie Scott. She had more time on the job than Brogan and was the backbone of the office when the shit hit the fan on the street. Cool under the most strenuous situations, she often guided young police officers facing dangers and complicated conditions. All of Sandpiper's PCOs were more than competent, but Scott was the best at supervising and scheduling the rest of her colleagues, and at manning the radios for the PD.

"Quiet night, I hope," said Brogan as he stopped at her desk and scooped up a pile of recently submitted reports from the detective's inbox.

Scott replied, "Quiet in Sandpiper, but Tall Pines, not so much. They had a triple-fatal shooting. I don't know the details, but from what I gather, it's a domestic situation that turned into multiple homicides, and then a shoot-out that left the killer dead and his shooter in custody."

"What are you saying? Did someone kill the killer? Who killed the killer?"

Scott shrugged her shoulders. "Best I could make out from the radio chatter is there was a PI involved, and the PI is now in custody while Tall Pines PD is trying to figure it all out."

"Have you heard from the Tall Pines Chief of Police? Do they need help from us?" Brogan asked.

"Haven't heard anything from them, but you've got to believe it's a cluster fuck over there. I heard Detective Sergeant Jerry Harbour on the radio, so I suspect the entire night and day shifts are involved and all the detectives available are on the scene. I know the medical examiner and the forensic investigator are there as well. Ambulances dispatched to the scene have been told to clear, as there are no hospital transports. They haven't requested help or backup on anything yet, but the sheriff's office may be helping them out. Give Jerry a call on his cell phone and see if he needs any help. Our night shift has knocked off, but the day shift is on patrol and our forensic guy is available if needed. You've got all your detectives working today."

Brogan called Detective Sergeant Harbour, who answered on the first ring. "Hey Brogan, I'm up to my ass in alligators. Have you heard what's going on?"

"Only that you've got three dead people and a PI in custody. What am I missing?"

"Well, it appears an irate husband found his wife in bed

with her boyfriend at her boyfriend's house. He shot and killed both of them. Then a PI burst into the house trying to save lives and the shooter pointed the gun at her and she put two shots center mass and he's DOA."

Brogan listened, and then asked, "Did you say the PI is a female? What's her name? How did she happen to show up at the scene?"

"Initial report from officers first on the scene is that she was hired by the shooter to find out if his wife was cheating on him," Harbour said. "She was staked out at the boyfriend's house and saw the wife enter. She was waiting to give them time to start doing the nasty when she sees somebody cross the backyard, kick the back door in, and then shots are fired in the house. She called 911 and went into the house to see if anyone was shot and if she could render first aid until help arrived on the scene. She was working alone and had no back-up."

Harbour paused, and when Brogan remained quiet, continued. "She said the shooter turned the gun on her and she shot first. Turned out the shooter was the guy who hired her. Guess he couldn't wait to get the report from his investigator and decided to take matters into his own hands. The scene was pretty gruesome with two naked dead people on a bed and the husband slumped against a wall in the bedroom. PI was sitting on the back steps when our people got there. She's lawyered up now. Marie Barnett."

"That's pretty intense. Who's this PI? Is she legit? Licensed and with carry permit?" Brogan asked.

"Her name is Kelly Hart. She has the proper PI license and permit and is a retired cop from Baltimore County PD. Somewhat of a hero, I've been told. She's the one who shot and killed the guy who was trying to kill the county executive about a year ago. She got shot herself during the shootout and had to take a medical because of her gunshot wound. She's moved here to Worcester County and set up shop in Barnett's office in Berlin. That's about all I know. I was fixin' to interview her in the next few minutes. I've handled a few murders before, but this one is such a mess I would feel better if I had a second guy in the room with me to make sure I don't miss anything. You have jurisdiction. Are you available?"

Brogan thought a moment before responding. "I'll be there in fifteen minutes to sit in with you. Does that work?"

"Hell yeah. Thanks, Brogan. I'll owe you one."

"Offer Hart and Barnett a soda or coffee if you have it and tell them you'll get to them in about fifteen minutes after you check on a few things. I'm on my way," Brogan declared.

Brogan turned to PCO Scott. "Tell the chief what's going on when he gets here and let him know I'm with Harbour interviewing a person of interest in a triple shooting with three dead that occurred in Tall Pines. I'll brief him when I'm done."

Brogan was out the door and in his car. *What is going on? This county is getting to be like Baltimore City. Homicide rate is out of sight. People will be afraid to come here for vacation. It took balls for that PI to go into that house with no backup. I'm interested in meeting this superwoman. Damn, two-center mass! This is serious shit.*

23

RECOGNITION IN THE AFTERMATH

Brogan made the trip to Tall Pines PD in ten minutes, parked in a visitor slot, and went through the front door. Brogan noticed the PD had recently been remodeled and looked modern and well-kept, unlike many police stations he had been in. The PCO recognized Brogan and buzzed him into the inner sanctum. He walked to Harbour's office and found him sitting at his desk writing points he wanted to cover in the ensuing interview. "Hey Jerry, we ready to go in?" Brogan asked.

"Yeah, I think I'm ready. How about you?" Harbour asked.

"Always ready," Brogan joked. "I'll follow your lead and take a few notes as we go through this. Best to let this PI do most of the talking if she's willing and if her lawyer will let her tell her story."

"I agree," Harbour said, rising from his desk. Grabbing up his notes, he led the way to the interview room.

Brogan knew they had also refurbished the interview room during the remodel, and he considered it profession-al looking. It contained a table, four chairs, a camera, and a sound system to record interviews. They had soundproofed the room to prevent eavesdropping from anyone outside the room and installed one-way glass in the adjoining office so the interview could be viewed by others authorized to do so.

Harbour led Brogan right to the interview room. The door swung inward and Harbour entered first, blocking Brogan's view of the attorney and the PI. As he moved toward one of two chairs facing the interviewee, Brogan got his first look at the two women seated across the table. He recognized Barnett immediately from previous court appearances. Then his eyes shift slightly, and he was momentarily stunned and speechless at the same time.

He looked into the eyes and face of the girl from the restaurant and the gallery. She was somber looking now, but still beautiful. Brogan was seldom shocked by anything that happened in his world of policing, but this set him back. *She's a retired cop? She's a PI? And she's killed two people in just over a year?* He thought he was a master at drawing trouble, but here sat a competitor for that honor. His interest in this young woman ratcheted up about five notches. *God, I hope she's not a murderer!*

On the other side of the table, Kelly's mouth fell open slightly. *Dreamboat is here to save me! No, why is he here?* His penetrating blue eyes scanned her and she felt her body temperature escalate. Her mind raced to figure it out, but she had no answers. Marie didn't seem surprised or shocked to see either of these two men. *Keep your mouth shut,* she thought.

"Hi, I'm Detective Sergeant Jerry Harbour and this is Sandpiper PD's lead detective, William Brogan. Detective Brogan has county-wide jurisdiction and a wealth of experience in death investigations. I've asked him to sit in with me during this interview if there are no objections. This interview is being videotaped and recorded for the protection of all those here today. We are about to interview Kelly Hart, who is a private investigator legally licensed in the State of Maryland. Ms. Hart is also legally licensed to carry a concealed firearm. With Ms. Hart is her attorney, Marie Barnett. Ms. Hart has been advised of her Miranda rights in the presence of her attorney and has agreed to be interviewed. Do either of you have any questions or concerns before we begin the interview?"

Marie voiced a concern. "Is it your intention to charge my client with any crime at this time?"

"No, this is just a fact-finding interview," Harbour responded. "Your client may stop answering questions or walk out at any time. You may also voice your objection to any question we may ask or advise your client not to answer any specific question. With that in mind, may we proceed?"

"Yes, go ahead," Marie said.

"Kelly, may I call you Kelly?" Harbour asked.

"Yes, Kelly is fine."

"Why don't you just start at the beginning as you know it? Tell us what happened that led up to the shootings we are investigating."

Kelly started, "Tom Shelby came walking through the door of my office and hired me to check on his wife and to identify if she was having an affair. Shelby provided me with an address where, he suspected, the person she was having an affair with lived. He found this address in the trash can at their home."

"I took the case and asked Shelby when would he be out of town next since this was when he thought was his wife's opportunity to cheat. Shelby told me Monday and Tuesday night. I told him to stop investigating and not to go back to that address anymore. Shelby agreed and left my office.

I was staked out when I saw a figure enter the house from the rear. I left my position and traveled toward the house, but before I got there I heard glass shatter and then saw three flashes of light along with the sounds of gunfire. I breached the house and saw two bodies lying on top of one another with blood on the back of the top body. The shooter was still in the house. I created a distraction to draw him out. Instead he fired his gun striking the door frame above my head. I spun low into the room with my gun pointing out. Our eyes met and I thought he recognized me, but he shifted the aim of his gun directly at me. I feared he was about to shoot me, which is why I shot first striking him twice in the chest. At that point, he dropped his gun and I moved forward to see if I could administer first aid."

Kelly was clear in her explanations and had her notes from her initial contact with Shelby right up to and through her surveillance of the boyfriend's house. Her notes stopped when she saw a person kick in the back door.

Kelly said, "I dialed 911 and there was no time for notes. I dialed 911 a second time after I shot Shelby and determined I could not help anyone in the house."

Harbour had a series of questions to ask her, but found most of them had been answered in her narration of what happened. He asked her what she was thinking when Shelby pointed his gun at her. Barnett objects, but Kelly waves her off.

"I was thinking, 'He's going to shoot me, he's going to kill me.'"

"Did you recognize him as Tom Shelby?" Harbour asked.

"Yes, in the split seconds before he pointed his gun at me, I recognized him and I believe he recognized me, but he aimed the gun at me anyway. He was going to shoot me."

Harbour looked at Brogan and said, "Brogan, do you have any questions?"

"Just one," Brogan said, "Kelly, do you believe in your circumstance, you had any other choice than to shoot?"

"No sir, I don't."

Harbour looked to Marie and said, "Marie and Kelly, this is an ongoing investigation. The forensic team has gathered evidence and will submit reports on their findings. With these reports and your statement, I will meet with the state's attorney for his input, questions, and/or suggestions on any potential charges. The state's attorney may wish to take this to a grand jury to see if they wish to seek an indictment. Finally, you will get this in discovery, but I want you to know we found Mr. Shelby's car parked right behind his wife's car, about two blocks from the scene. Mr. Shelby left a note on the passenger seat. It said, 'Forgive me for what I'm about to do.' Do you have any questions before I end this interview?"

Both women said they had none and Harbour noted the date and time the interview was concluded. He told Kelly she was free to go.

Kelly felt very awkward leaving the interview room with Marie. She wanted to say something to Brogan, but the right words didn't come to her. *I wonder what you're thinking. I did what I needed to do to survive. As a cop, you should understand that. I want to talk to you, spend time with you, get to know you. I realize this has fucked everything up, but maybe we still have a chance. Please, Brogan, don't think badly of me.*

24
WHAT DO YOU THINK?

After Kelly Hart and her attorney had left the police station, Brogan sat down with Jerry Harbour. "What do think Brogan? Her story is exactly what she told the responding officers. It appears she was hired to do surveillance on Shelby's wife, and she even had a retainer check from Shelby. I was able to call his boss this morning, and he told me Shelby called in Monday morning saying he was ill and might be out for a couple of days. The boss stated he had plenty of leave days, so it wasn't a problem. He continued that Shelby worked in the field and seldom had face-to-face contact with people in the office. Tom Shelby had always been reliable and did a good job. He knew he got married later in life, but had never met Shelby's wife. The man was completely shocked when I told him Shelby was dead."

Brogan responded, "I don't know Kelly Hart, but I've seen her around town and as recently as Saturday at the gallery event. I can check with Mrs. Abbott and see if she knows Kelly Hart and why she was invited to that event. I know it was by invitation only. I also saw her several weeks ago in a local restaurant. She was dining alone. We were sitting next to each other, but never spoke. I had no idea she had been a police officer or about her being in a shoot-out. I have a few contacts in Baltimore County and can get some additional history on her if you want."

"Yes, that would be great if you would. I'll see if Marie will share more information about her client since she shares office space with her. Marie and I have mutual respect, so I think she'll talk to me. I'll call you later this afternoon and compare notes," Harbour said.

Brogan left the station. His head was spinning. What a strange series of events. He had listened closely as she described what had occurred and the actions she had taken. She was calm and professional in her delivery. There was no hesitation while she prepared an answer that would serve her best interest or might be something you wanted to hear. She grasped the fact she had taken a life, but was able to compartmentalize her feelings while talking about the situation. Brogan kept thinking about what he would have done differently, but being in Kelly's position, he couldn't think of a thing he would have done another way. He hoped she would see a counselor to help her deal with her feelings and not keep them bottled up. *Unless the crime scene evidence points in a different direction or contradicts her statement, there is little doubt this will be ruled a good shoot.*

Brogan felt sorry for Kelly. Taking a life is hard no matter how justified you may have been. Taking two in just over a year was incredibly rare and might destroy her self-confidence. The worst thing that could happen was for her to doubt herself and hesitate in some future situation. Hesitation would get you or some innocent person killed as quickly as anything. It had killed one of his fellow officers last year. Brogan decided right then that as soon as a ruling was made on this shooting, and if it was made in her favor, he would reach out to Kelly and ask her to meet with him. He would reassure her that her decisions and actions were sound and based on training and circumstances. Yep, he would do the right thing.

What's going on in my head? Is my interest professional or personal? I'm spending a lot of time thinking about this woman. Hell, I'd normally just shake it off as being horny, but I think this is more than that. I used to think about Lynn Murphy like this, but I went into that relationship knowing it could never last. This is different. She isn't a cop, but she understands the job and what it entails. She's still in the business, so we have a lot in common and share a mutual unspoken bond. We both carry a gun. What could possibly go wrong?

Brogan chuckled to himself and privately hoped the forensic team and the state's attorney's office would expedite their investigations. Time was wasting! Brogan was on the hunt.

25
AT ALL COSTS

The *Daily Times* lay on his desk. The local newspaper's headlines normally proclaimed the high school's victory or loss from the night before. But now, on the front page and above the fold was the name Kelly Hart. The story proclaimed her to be a local heroine because of her actions during a double murder in Tall Pines. It said she dashed into a home without regard for her own life, where shots had just been fired, to save those inside. She met the killer head-on and dispatched him in a blaze of bullets. While written like a cheap crime novel, it made the point: Kelly Hart was not someone to be taken lightly.

Thomas Gordon felt a small shiver go up his spine. He always thought that he was fearless, but since this woman crossed his path he perceived the first crack in his armor. Thinking like this was just stupid and unproductive. Far more dangerous people had been in his life and when threatened, he had removed them. *Is it time to remove her?*

The buzzing of his burner phone interrupted his thoughts. *Shit*, he thought, *what other problem has raised its ugly head?*

"What?" he asked. Carlos began speaking without further introduction.

"We have a small problem, boss. One of the little girls is sick. Rosa thinks if we don't get her some treatment, she is going to die. She's given her medicine from the drugstore, but it is not working. Rosa thinks she needs an antibiotic to make her well. I know we can't go to the hospital or a regular doctor. The risk would be too high, and we have no papers for the children."

Gordon thought for a second and said, "I have a contact. She's a physician's assistant in a doctor's office and she's also strung out on pills. I'll have her steal a script for a child's dosage of an antibiotic to give to the kid. Carlos, if this kid dies, you know what to do. Bury her in a hole just like the others. We make our money when we sell them. They are merchandise we get for free from the border, so we will take only a very small risk to save one of them. There are many coming across the border every day. We have an endless supply. We need to protect ourselves at all costs. If we're caught, we will all rot in jail. I'll get back to you after I talk to the PA."

Gordon's mind returned to Kelly Hart. *She is a problem. She stumbled onto the farm. Or had she? What does she know? What was she working on? She's a loose end that needs to be clipped. Do I dare wait? If I take her, I'll have to interrogate her, so there would be no doubt about what she knows.* Gordon had all the skills and tools it would take to make her talk.

There was an outbuilding on the farm, far from the house, that provided the perfect setting for him to get to the truth. She was damn good-looking, so his methods of persuasion might begin with an intimate moment or two before it turned harsh. Gordon's face broke into an insidious smile.

26

IS THIS A DATE?

Brogan was elated. It took only ten days for the State's Attorney, Rudy Carol, to determine Kelly was exonerated from any wrongdoing in the shooting of Thomas Shelby. Her statement was completely corroborated by all the physical evidence gathered, including the autopsy report that showed gunshot residue on the hands of Shelby. The note in the car sort of sealed the deal when it was shown to be in his handwriting and the pen that he used to write the note lay in the center console. The gun and ammunition were also shown to belong to him. The preponderance of evidence made the SA's job pretty easy. The case would not be heard by a grand jury. Kelly's PI license, which had been temporarily suspended, was immediately reinstated. Kelly had been notified by the state's attorney's office of their findings and decision.

Detective Sergeant Harbour had shared this information with Brogan just minutes before Brogan picked up the phone and called Kelly at the phone number he had gleaned from one of Tall Pine's police reports. Kelly answered with a little smile in her voice.

"Hi, this is Kelly."

"Hi, this is Brogan. I got a call from Jerry Harbour and he told me the good news about the investigation into the shooting. I'm sure you're relieved."

Kelly's heart jumped in her throat, blocking her response. She sputtered an acknowledgment. "Yes, I'm very pleased. This is a huge weight off my shoulders. I expected this result, but you never know how these things will wash out with all these agencies involved."

"I'm very happy for you. You followed your training and did all the right things," Brogan said.

"Thanks for saying that. It means a lot coming from a guy with your experience."

"That's only part of the reason I'm calling. I was wondering if we could meet and just talk. I find you very interesting and would like to get to know you better. If you say no, it's okay, I won't be offended."

Kelly didn't say no. "Actually, I would like that very much."

"When's your next day off?" Brogan asked. "Are you a breakfast person? I'm an early riser and think breakfast is the best and most important meal of the day."

"I'm free all day tomorrow and I'm an early riser, too. I'd love breakfast and coffee."

As Brogan's voice went up an octave, he responded, "Great," How about I pick you up at your place at 7:30. I know it's a little presumptuous, but I got your address from one of the police reports."

Kelly came right back. "See you in the morning. I'll come down and meet you at the curb. What do you drive?"

"2021, dark gray Lexus RX350. Tomorrow is my day off, too."

They hung up. Kelly couldn't believe it. *That was close. I don't know how I stopped myself from saying it's a date! Can you consider breakfast a date? Yes, of course, you can and I am. Not sure about Brogan.*

Brogan immediately dialed the police station and asked for the chief. "Chief Richards," he answered in his baritone voice.

"Hi Chief, it's Brogan. I need off tomorrow. I have nothing on my calendar—any problems with that?"

"No, of course not. I'm happy to hear you're taking a day off. Must be something important and sudden, knowing you," said the chief.

"It's both," Brogan responded. "I'll have my cell phone if anything happens, although I may be out of the county. Both my detectives are working tomorrow, so you'll have coverage."

"Good enough. Enjoy your day," the chief said before breaking the connection.

Brogan then called and left a voice mail message for his senior detective, telling him he would be off, but with his cell, if something major happened and also that the chief was already dialed in.

27
TRACKER

At 7:20 a.m., Brogan was leaning against the passenger side of his recently cleaned Lexus. He was ten minutes early at Kelly's place. This fall day was sunny, but cool. Brogan was looking sporty with his creased dark brown five-pocket jeans, a white, collared shirt open at the neck, and Lucchese brown round-toe, highly polished cowboy boots tucked neatly under his jeans. To thwart the chill, he was wearing a moss-green Eddie Bauer jacket. Not visible was a soft, brown leather shoulder holster tucked under his left arm, holding a stainless-steel Sig Sauer 9mm semi-automatic pistol with customized wooden grips, fully loaded and ready to fire. His hair was neatly combed and his eyes shielded by a pair of Ray-Ban sunglasses. His posture was relaxed and his attire was that of a sharply dressed man. He glanced at his Tag Heuer watch, but in such a way that if Kelly was watching she wouldn't know he was early and anxious for this morning to start.

At precisely 7:30, Brogan saw movement at the front door of Kelly's building as she burst through the front door with a big smile on her face. She had just brightened his day. Kelly was also dressed casually in a soft pink, lightweight sweater, dark gray jeans, and a pair of short Freebird black boots that matched Brogan's in their luster. She was carrying a dark gray suede short jacket with an asymmetrical zipper draped over her left arm which matched her jeans. Brogan noticed the black shoulder bag on her right side and wondered if it contained her gun. He suspected it did and he was glad to see she had already climbed back on the horse and was prepared for whatever came her way.

One thing that attracted Brogan to Kelly was the fact she carried herself with confidence and had a little perkiness in her step. As she drew near, he saw she was clutching a pair of sunglasses in her left hand. Somewhat an aficionado of sunglasses, he recognized they were Louis Vuitton by their signature emblem on the exposed stem. *Damn, this lady is going to match me step-for-step or maybe even be a step ahead.*

Despite what he knew about her background and actions, he saw a beautiful woman whose skin was soft, lightly tanned, and unblemished. Her teeth were straight and white, but not artificially so. Her tight body and womanly shape aroused his male hormones. Her hair today was loose and hung just below her shoulders. She was definitely the full package.

Brogan turned to his front passenger door and held it open to allow her to enter. He smiled and bowed very slightly at the waist as if awaiting royalty to enter. She ignored the open door and came to him. She gave him a gentle hug in greeting and said, "Good morning Brogan. Where are we off to?"

He grinned and said, "To the best breakfast in Sandpiper."

"How's the coffee?" Kelly asked.

"Far better than police coffee and it's plentiful."

"Sounds good. Take me to this magical place." She then

climbed into his front seat and waited while he closed the door and circled the rear of the car to join her. Brogan loved her voice and her early morning banter. *She really is a morning person. I'm a lucky man.*

He pulled from the curb and drove the short distance to Coastal Highway and turned left. His destination was 17th Street and a breakfast fit for a king, or in this case a princess. A pastry counter emitted smells that would take your appetite to new heights while you waited to be seated. This was a local place and somewhere that Brogan was known well. He'd never brought a woman into this place, so heads would turn and tongues would wag when they saw this beauty in his company. He grinned at the idea of showing her off. It was a short drive and her conversation focused on the mystery place he was taking her. His attention was fully on her.

Four vehicles behind Brogan was a medium blue Toyota Corolla. Two cars behind the Corolla was a tan Chevrolet Silverado truck. Dark hair, dark-skinned Hispanic men drove each of these vehicles. Their attention was solely on Brogan's Lexus.

Brogan found a parking place behind Jack's. He turned to Kelly and said, "Doesn't look like all that much, but if you're going to be a local this is the place to come. The food will never disappoint and if you like pastries, we'll grab some on the way out. Jack Griffin is the owner and he likes the pastries more than the customers. He's a good guy and he'll find us a seat regardless of the crowd. He and I are friends and if you're with me you'll probably be his new best friend. Let's go."

They exited Brogan's car and entered the side door, which served as the entrance. The pastry counter was the first thing they saw and the smell of sugary delights battled with the smells of bacon and sausage. This was an old-time breakfast diner. Jack stood at the far end of the pastry counter surveying his employees. His hair was silver, but it looked like he had all the hair he was born with. His gray mustache was full, but neatly trimmed. His pale blue eyes were adorned with rimless glasses. He was greeting each customer. Most of them he knew by name. Jack saw Brogan and Kelly standing by the "wait to be seated" sign. He beamed at their presence and made his way to them. He was a little overweight, but that was due to his love of apple turnovers—his absolute favorite.

When Jack reached them, and before Brogan could say anything, Jack put out his hand and was met by Kelly's extended hand.

"Hi Kelly, it's so good to see you again," said Jack. "What are doing with this guy?"

Kelly laughed and said, "He told me he was bringing me for the best breakfast in Sandpiper and here we are."

Jack chuckled and replied, "Well, he's right, but you already knew that as often as you've been in here. Will you be having your regular?"

"Yes, Jack, that would be great," Kelly replied, barely able to contain herself.

Jack looked at Brogan, "You want your regular?"

"Yeah, Jack, I'll take the same. Where do you want us to sit?"

"I think Kelly's favorite table is available. You can sit there. Take him over there, Kelly, while I hustle up some coffee for both of you."

Brogan was totally deflated. *This woman is one step ahead of me! I seriously underestimated her abilities. I already like her way too much.*

Kelly saw his disappointment; his surprise had been crushed. She took his hand and led him to a small table for two, near a window facing Coastal Highway. Brogan realized he had never been seated by the windows. He didn't even have a favorite table.

After they sat themselves, Jack dropped off two coffees, assured them that their breakfast would be up soon, and moved away. Kelly said, "I'm sorry Brogan. This was just too funny not to take advantage of you. I've been coming to Sandpiper for years with my parents and we used to get breakfast here all the time. One summer, I even waited tables for Jack when he was short-staffed. When I moved down here full-time, I knew there was no place I would rather go for breakfast than here. Forgive me?"

Brogan grinned. "Only if you tell me all about yourself so I don't get blindsided anymore and make an ass of myself." The food arrived, and the dialogue between the two of them flowed easily.

Kelly said "I am an only child; my parents are still alive and the condo where I live belongs to them. I grew up in Baltimore County and studied Martial Arts as a kid and I still do.

I have a college degree in Criminal Justice and joined the Baltimore County PD when I was twenty-one. I have never married and have no children. At the age of twenty-four, I was fortunate to be assigned to the Dignitary Protection Unit with Baltimore County. I was there until last year when I was shot during a detail which forced me out on sixty-six and two-thirds disability. Marie Barnett and I went through the police academy together and she thought I would make a great PI. So here I am. Tell me about you Brogan."

Brogan began to squirm in his seat. "There is not much to tell really. I grew up in Baltimore City and joined the PD when I was twenty-one years old. I was married once, but we were both too young and it didn't work out. I live alone in a condo here in Sandpiper. I know I'm probably not at your level, but I have also studied martial arts and I still do. I've been here for ten years. Then about two weeks ago, I went to dinner and saw a beautiful woman who I knew I would like to meet. So here I am"

Kelly snickered and said, "I can see you are not used to sharing information about yourself."

Brogan chuckled, "I guess you're right, but I warm up the longer you know me."

Kelly thought it would take some time to peel this onion.

Outside the restaurant, Felix, in the Corolla, placed a cell call. Carlos answered on the first ring. "What's going on?"

"We were waiting outside her building this morning to take her, but some guy was there waiting for her. She's gone with him now. They're at some place on 17th Street. What do you want us to do?"

Carlos responded, "Did you bring the equipment I bought you?"

"Si, we got, we try it out a bunch of times. It works well."

"Okay, put it on and stay with them. I don't care where they go or what they do, you stay close. When you can, I want you to take her. If that fucking guy with her gets in the way, put him down. No witnesses, but I need her alive."

Felix answered, "We'll do what you want if nobody is around. She's good-looking. Can we play with her a little bit when we take her?"

"No! The boss wants her to himself. Don't touch her or I'll be sending someone to put you down. Call me when you get her and don't fuck this up. This is important and needs to be done quickly. Understood?"

"Si, Si, I got it Carlos. You pay us good for this job, right?"

"Yes. If the guy is a problem, you fix the problem. I'll pay you more. Just do it today."

"I'll tell Miguel," Felix ended the call.

Felix slipped from his vehicle and walked towards the restaurant on a path that took him by the rear of Brogan's Lexus. When he was at the trunk, he let his car keys fall from his hand. He glanced around and saw no one paying attention to him, so he bent over to pick up the keys. While down and hidden, he removed a tracking device from his jacket pocket and placed it on the rear frame of Brogan's car. The magnet on the tracker held it in place. It was out of sight of both foot traffic and vehicles on the road. It was turned on and transmitted a signal to a receiver unit on the front seat of the Corolla. It had a range of a mile or more in this flat terrain. Wherever this Lexus car went, a blinking red light would appear on the GPS-type map on the unit. There was no escaping from this device. The red blinking light would guide them to this car. The driver would never know it was there. Once they got the girl, they would pull the transmitter from the car. Only a trained eye would see the slight scratches it would leave on the vehicle's frame.

Felix told Miguel what Carlos had said. "Miguel, you follow me, and I follow the Lexus. If we get separated, you call me." They both had been given burner phones by Carlos. The phones would be tossed after this job.

"This guy is big, so we may take him out," Felix said. "If we do, it's more money for us. Bring your tire iron up on the front seat and make sure your gun is ready. No touch la chica no matter what. I don't know who the boss is, but Carlos says he's a bad motherfucker. He no put up with any shit. We'll wear masks when we take her. Only talk in Spanish. Okay?"

Miguel nodded his head and went to the storage area of his truck to retrieve his tire iron. Flex cuffs for her wrists and ankles, duct tape to cover her mouth, and a pillowcase to cover her head laid on the back seat of the Corolla under a blanket.

Felix and Miguel moved about a block away, out of sight of Brogan's vehicle. Both were in the country illegally. They had no ties to Maryland. Neither had ever been arrested in the US. Carlos had found them in the border town of Laredo, where they were accustomed to these kinds of jobs. He knew they had recently been pulling robberies in northern Virginia and Washington, D.C.

He reached out to Felix using a burner phone and asked him if they wanted to do a job for him. He offered them five thousand dollars each to kidnap a woman and deliver her to him alive. Easy money. If they had to kill her friend— business was business!

The blinking red light began to move, and so did they.

28
IN SYNC

They left Jack's restaurant stuffed with their breakfast selections. Kelly was carrying a small bag of pastries to take home. She allowed Brogan to pay for everything so he could redeem some of his manhood. Jack saw them to the door while gushing all over his close friend, Kelly. As the door closed, Brogan heard Jack say, "See ya', Brogan." The friendship pecking order had been defined. Jack liked her best. Brogan couldn't blame him. He liked her best too.

They were both laughing as they reentered Brogan's car. He started the car, but made no move to put it in gear. Brogan asked, "Are you having a good time?"

Kelly responded, "Yes, I really am. You're easy to talk to and you can handle a little self-deprecation. When we pulled up to Jack's, I had a hard time keeping a straight face and I knew Jack would be all over me. He's a nice guy and always has been."

"Would you consider this morning a date?" Brogan asked.

"Yes, I think I would," Kelly answered with a slight giggle.

Brogan asked again, "Then would you consider a second date with me? Perhaps lunch somewhere fun?"

"Sure, but my treat the next time. Give me a call, I'll let you pick the place again. We can figure out a time when we're both free. I'd like that."

Brogan smiled broadly, "Okay then. Are you free for lunch today? I don't want to take you home just yet."

Kelly felt her heart pick up its pace, and her face flushed slightly at Brogan's approach. She didn't have to think about it and said, "Funny, I don't feel like going home yet. What are we going to do while we digest the meal we just had?"

"How well do you know the Eastern Shore?"

"Not all that well, actually. I've served some papers outside the Sandpiper area, but I have relied on my GPS to get me there and to find my way home."

"Good, I have a full tank of gas and I'm about to give you a tour and I will narrate as we go. This is a very interesting place and I've spent a lot of time exploring and learning the area."

"Show me the way, big guy," Kelly responded, flirting just a little.

Brogan was an excellent tour guide as they traveled first to Salisbury and then south on Route 13. As the names of small towns and places appeared on road signs, Brogan told a story or a bit of history about each one. He even pointed out a few crime scenes from days gone by and explained how they were either solved or why they remained a mystery. He pointed to a house in one small town and said, "A school teacher once lived there. Her body was found in a field nearby. Turns out she was killed by her husband. It was big news while it was going on. The case was handled by the sheriff's department. Later a book was written about the murder; which I read. I still have it, if you would like to read it."

Kelly was excited to learn so much regarding the area where she now lived. She was also excited about being with

Brogan. *Slow down, this is the first time you're with this guy. It just feels like we're in sync or am I imagining this?*

They moved slowly south visiting towns that were not much more than a crossroads of a village. Old, well-maintained homes spoke of days gone by. There was always a church and sometimes two. They passed by graveyards, some big, some small, which held the previous residents of this usually quiet area of Maryland. With the leaves off the trees, Kelly could see homes and sights that were hidden in the summer and was reminded of the old woman and the big Hispanic man whose farms were both hidden by a band of trees. *I wonder if I could see those houses now.* She knew they were on the wrong road for those places and the memory slipped away. Brogan navigated the roads without consulting his GPS. He always brought them back to Route 13 as they headed further south. His stories of the areas she was seeing totally captivated Kelly. Though just a car ride, this was proving to be the best date she'd ever had.

"I love this," Kelly said. "Thanks for sharing your previous explorations with me. If you ever need a second career, you could be a tour guide."

Exploring had eaten away at the clock. They were both surprised when they realized it was almost 12:30. "You getting hungry?" Brogan asked.

"I thought the breakfast would hold me all day, but I am hungry," Kelly replied.

"You ready to stop?"

Brogan pulled to the side of the road and turned to Kelly. "I know a place that serves great seafood. It's another one of those local secrets that is nothing to look at and serves your food on cardboard trays with plastic utensils. The food is nothing less than spectacular. Any interest?"

Kelly brightened. "I love seafood. Take me there."

"One little problem," Brogan said, grinning at her. "It's about twenty-five miles south of here and it's in Virginia; if you don't mind me taking you across state lines."

Kelly rolled her eyes. "Let's go. It's not like I'm being kidnapped, and if I am, I'll take the risk for good seafood."

Brogan smiled and pulled safely back on the road still heading south.

One mile back, two other vehicles returned to the road as well. The drivers were frustrated and somewhat confused by the routes they'd been taking. Miguel called Felix on his burner phone.

"What's going on? Why are we driving all over the place?" Miguel asked.

Felix responded, "I'm just following the blinking light on the thing. You just look for me, you stay good." *Is this guy trying to shake me? Does he think something is wrong? He can't be thinking of anything. He doesn't even see my car behind him.* At one point, Felix closed the distance for just a few minutes to put eyes on the Lexus then backed off. *This gringo is crazy. I'm just wasting gas and he doesn't know where he going.* Felix had never taken a girl just for a ride. This was an unknown concept to him.

29
FACT OR FICTION

As the tour entered Virginia, Kelly was pleasantly surprised that Brogan continued his running commentary, spewing out facts about the places they were passing and occasionally taking a side road to show her something she might find interesting. She began to ask questions.

"Tell me more about yourself, Brogan. You know about me, but you have revealed very little about yourself."

He felt comfortable with his new friend. "During my youthful years in Baltimore, I played baseball, and basketball and hung out with my buddies at the city park. None of us had cars, so we got around using the transit buses. We kept our noses clean and never got caught for the things we knew we shouldn't be doing; like stealing beer off of a couple of old men's back porches. A couple of times we got lucky and snagged a pie or two left on the back windowsill cooling after coming fresh out of the oven. My parents were caught off guard and were worried for me when I told them I was applying for a position with the Baltimore City Police Department."

"Did you always want to be a cop?"

"I think so. I felt like it was a calling. It's a rush for me to investigate things and unravel clues and to follow leads taking me to a solution. Can't really explain it, but somehow, it's in my blood. I get up every morning wanting to go to work. When that stops or my body fails me, I'll retire."

Kelly responded, "I hope that's not anytime soon."

"I love every aspect of the job after I was selected and completed the academy. I was surrounded by plenty of negative personalities that bitched and complained about everything and everyone. I just put on my badge and did the job. I guess my approach worked because I was chosen for the detective bureau. After two years in the arson squad, I asked for and was given an assignment in the homicide unit. I knew these men and women were the cream of the crop and their daily banter contained very little bitching. They had made it to the top and work hard every day to stay there. I wanted to be a part of that unit. We all had a deep and dark sense of humor as we walked the beat of the dead. If I didn't, I'd probably go crazy. Every call started with at least one dead body. Gruesome as that may sound, each case was a great mystery waiting to be solved."

Brogan glanced over at Kelly before continuing, "I thrived in this atmosphere until one murder was my undoing. I touched the third rail of policing, when I arrested the son of a local politician for murder. He went to jail and my career in Baltimore came to a screeching halt. I needed to move on and that brought me to Sandpiper. I've been happy here." As Brogan spoke, he was non-braggadocios about his involvement in his many cases.

"You know, Kelly, I feel every case was always a team effort."

"I can relate. I felt the same way when I entered policing. I still miss the job to this day. We have a lot in common. Thanks for opening up to me."

Brogan became less revealing about his work at Sandpiper PD, especially in the most recent years. Kelly had heard about a serial killer who stalked Sandpiper last year and the death of a police officer. Brogan clammed up about that case and Kelly didn't push. It was fresh and surely brought with it emotional baggage that was better left alone for the time being. Like her, he would tell more when he was ready.

It took almost an hour to cover the twenty-five miles, but Kelly was delighted at the destination. A one-story white building advertised The Great Clam Shack. A parking space right next to the entrance had just opened up, and Brogan jumped on it. Inside it was exactly as Brogan had described it. The place was busy despite the fact it was 1:30 p.m., somewhat past the normal lunch hour. A friendly server guided them toward a table and provided them with menus. The menu offered many seafood delights and it was hard to choose, but choose they did. Kelly ordered the cream of crab soup and shrimp salad sandwich. Brogan's choice was steamed clams in butter and cream of crab as well. The place almost had a picnic feel to it. Their food was delivered pretty quickly and was delicious. Both of them would have to work hard to take off the calories they were absorbing today, but that was okay. Sometimes you just need to let go and enjoy yourself. This was one of those days. Kelly remarked to Brogan, "This place is everything you said it would be and more. You do know a lot of local secrets. Thanks for sharing."

Felix and Miguel had joined up and sat in the parking lot of a business that was closed. They saw the restaurant and the Lexus sitting close to the entrance. Felix evaluated their chances of pulling off the kidnapping. "Miguel, this is not a good spot. It's daytime, there are too many people, and they may have cameras. Do you think I'm right?"

Miguel nodded his head and said, "Si, we'll go to jail if we try something here. We'll wait?" Felix nodded slowly and replied. "We'll wait."

Felix and Miguel were patient people. Felix told Miguel, "Our time will come soon." So, they sat and waited with little talking, just watching the place where their prey had temporarily gone to ground. "Being in Virginia is a good thing," Felix said. "I don't see any police cars in two hours. This town probably doesn't have police. Police will not get here quickly. It will take a long time." *Perfect for us.* One at a time, Felix and Miguel went to a nearby gas station and filled their vehicles. They had no idea where they were going, but running out of gas would not be acceptable.

Kelly and Brogan shared their food with each other, tasting and commenting on the perfection of their lunch. You'd hardly guess they had a full breakfast only hours earlier. They ate like they were ravished.

As they finished their meal, Kelly declared, "I'm paying this time, and it's not up for debate." Brogan knew when to stand down, although it hurt him to do so. He nodded his head. "Okay." He got it. *An independent woman is making her mark in the sand.* "You can pay this time."

As they stood near the counter waiting for other folks to pay their bills, Kelly browsed a shelf containing paperback books. Most of them were authored by local writers and the majority of them were about watermen, ships, and everything nautical in the area. Brogan scanned the books without picking any of them up. His eyes settled on a book at the far end of the shelf. The cover depicted a beach with sandpipers, with a lifeguard stand and a knife sticking out of the sand below. Only two copies remained. He walked behind Kelly, retrieved a book, and then went to the register to pay for it. The lady behind the counter took the book and cash from Brogan. "Will that be all she asks?" Brogan nodded. She placed the book in a small bag and handed him the bag and his change from a twenty-dollar bill.

Kelly shouldered up to him with the bill for the food in her hand. She gave him the stink eye, thinking he had reneged and had paid for the food. Brogan put his hands up in surrender and took two steps back from the counter. After seeing the bag, she realized he had not paid, so she stepped up with her credit card. After signing the receipt, they turned to leave.

Kelly said, "Did you buy a book?"

Brogan answered, "Yes, I did and it's for you."

Kelly was surprised, "You bought me a book? What's it about? How do you know I read, or what I like?"

Brogan clutched his bag and said, "It's a fiction crime novel and I just know you'll like it since I saw you browsing all the local authors on that shelf in the restaurant."

"I do read a lot, but only a few authors who write crime fiction. Is it by Patterson or Connelly or someone I'll know?"

Brogan's lips turned up into a small smile, "No, this is a local guy, I had never heard of him. It's called *Vengeance*, and it's about some murders."

Kelly came back, "Who's the author?"

"His name is Jake Jacobs."

"Okay, I've never heard of him either."

Brogan handed her the bag containing the paperback book and said, "You can take a look at it tomorrow or whenever, we've still got a lot to see."

Kelly shoved the bag into her purse. "Let's get going."

Getting into his car, he thought, *this lady is such a presence. She's a good person and I want to protect her and stand between her and everything bad in this world.* He knew instinctively she would never stand behind anybody. They would stand side by side no matter what the world delivered their way. Brogan was looking at her differently than other women he had met. She seemed to know him far better than their brief time together should allow.

Kelly sensed Brogan was becoming interested. She caught him checking her out when he thought she wasn't looking and combined with the flirty banter told her that he may have wanted her. Kelly planned to give in to his desire if the opportunity arose.

"If you're still liking me, I have a question," Kelly said.

"Ask," Brogan responded.

"Has a woman ever asked to take you on a date?"

He thought for a moment and replied, "Not that I can remember."

Kelly looked deep into his eyes for a reaction when she said, "I'm asking you to go out with me on our third date. I want that to be today. Do you still have some eateries left on your list?"

His eyes said yes, even before he spoke. Brogan laughed. "It is a definite yes to your request for a third date and for having it today. I have many more restaurants in my inventory, but one jumps to mind, a little bit further down the road. We should try to get there around 6 p.m. for dinner. That will make us get home around 11 or 12 if that's not too late?"

"I'm game if you are," Kelly said. Brogan pulled from the parking lot and turned south.

30

THIRD DATE IS A KILLER

"Have you ever been to Williamsburg?" Brogan asked. "Yes, I went on a field trip with my class when I was nine."

Brogan laughed inwardly. "Sounds like it's time for a refresher course. We can walk off some of this food and then go to a restaurant I know near there."

"Oh, that would be so wonderful. I thought it was a grand place when I was nine. I can't wait to see if my memory serves me well."

Brogan and Kelly took in the historical splendor of Williamsburg, stopping at the homes, admiring the décor of days gone by and shops with all the replicated tools. They walked its uneven brick sidewalks and wondered what it would have been like to live in those times. Kelly remembered many of the sights, but stopped to read more of the informational signs to gain a far deeper understanding of what she was seeing. To her, it was still a grand place and one you could visit time and time again. The place was incredibly busy with tourists. The actors, dressed as inhabitants, played their roles well while answering questions that clearly showed they were well-versed in the period they were portraying. The two continued to enjoy each other's company. At one point, Brogan grabbed Kelly's hand to hold it while they walked and time flew by.

They eventually returned to their parking spot where dozens of other travelers were either parking or riding around looking for a place to park. A car, with several kids in the back seat, waited for Brogan to pull from his slot so they could immediately make it their own.

A short distance away, Felix and Miguel watched and again decided nothing could happen in this location without being seen by a lot of witnesses. Escape would be almost impossible. Patience is a virtue, but this was pushing their resolve. "We must wait a little longer," Felix told Miguel.

The next stop for Brogan and Kelly was an intimate steak house on the outskirts of Williamsburg. They arrived at 6:30 and found the parking lot dimly lit and only half full. The restaurant inside was also in soft lighting to enhance the atmosphere of a romantic hideaway. The dark wood throughout and cushioned chairs made the entire place inviting.

A couple at a nearby table were just finishing up. They seemed a strange match, a handsome Black man in his forties coupled with a young, attractive White woman, probably a teenager or in her early twenties. The twenty or more years difference in age raised both Brogan's and Kelly's curiosity. Both pondered what they were seeing. Was she a working girl on a date? Was he a sugar daddy with his young mistress? The few minutes it took them to gather their coats and her purse were punctuated with quiet laughter and exchanges of hushed dialogue. Whatever they were, they seemed to be enjoying each other's company. They left without further ado, leaving Kelly and Brogan to their recently received menus.

Walking through Williamsburg had again left them hungry, and they both ordered the petite-sized filet mignon with a blue cheese topping. Their two sides were baked potato and a salad with the house dressing. Both drank iced tea with their meals. The steaks were done to perfection, and everything was nice and hot when it was placed before them. They ate slowly, enjoying every bite. The aromas of the prepared foods heightened the ambiance. They never endured those awkward silences that sometimes occur when on a date with someone new. It was like they were long-time friends or lovers sharing a quiet meal.

Outside, Felix and Miguel were preparing to strike. They had found their perfect hunting ground and the opportunity they had waited so long for. They cautiously approached the restaurant parking lot and then backed into a slot side by side in a darkened corner, approximately twenty yards from the rear of the Lexus. Miguel joined Felix in his car.

"We have the perfect place," Felix said. "The plan is for you to open your door a little bit so it does not make noise when we get out. When we see the woman and the man getting ready to come out, we get out of the car. Then I'll tell you when to go. We need to stay low so nobody sees us. We'll hide behind the blue car next to the Lexus. You go to the driver's side with the tire iron. I go to the other side with my gun. When the guy opens his door to get in, you run up and hit him back of the head. Be sure you hit hard so he does not fight. I'll take the woman with my gun. I'll put straps on her hands and tape her mouth so no one hears her. Got to be quick. We take the woman back to my car and put her in the back seat and cover her with a blanket. If she fights, we'll knock her out. We'll not kill her. Miguel, you got the plan?"

Miguel nodded and replies, "Si." He opened his car door a few inches. Felix did the same. He had flex cuffs tucked in his pocket and a six-inch piece of duct tape stuck to his pants leg to place over Kelly's mouth.

Kelly and Brogan finished their meal and settled up on the check. Brogan prevailed and paid for the meal. Kelly thanked him for a wonderful meal and a spectacular first, second, and third date. As Brogan rose from the table, she followed. *Most good guys don't make any moves on a lady on the first date, and sometimes even on the second date, but by the third date, things usually begin to escalate. Hell, I just had all three dates on the same day. Is Brogan going to make a move on me? What am I going to do if he does? I've gotta think about this on the way back to Sandpiper. It's been a long time since I've been with a man. My emotions are all over the place between apprehension and growing desire.*

They made their way to the front of the restaurant. They stopped near the front door and Brogan helped Kelly put on her jacket. They pushed through the door and went to Brogan's car. Brogan, being a gentleman, opened the passenger door and Kelly slid into her seat. Brogan closed the door and proceeded around the rear of his car. He grinned. *What a flawless day.* He opened the door preparing to enter.

As soon as the woman appeared near the front door of the restaurant, Felix said, "We go now." Quickly exiting their car, they ran toward the Lexus, crouched down, and took up their pre-planned positions. They caught a break when the guy helped the woman put on her jacket. It gave them the few seconds they needed. They caught a second break when the guy allowed the woman to sit in the car first. She was in a position where she couldn't see what was about to happen to her friend.

When Brogan opened his car door, Miguel moved in silently behind him and raised the tire iron over his head to make his strike. The sound of a shot rang out and Miguel's head jerked violently to his right. Blood, brain tissue, and skull fragments flew from a large exit wound on the other side of his head. Much of the debris showered down the back of Brogan's head and upper back. The rest rained down on the back of his car. Miguel melted to the ground. The arm holding the tire iron collapsed and the tire iron fell straight to the ground, joining his now-deceased body. Without conscious thought, Brogan ducked to the ground. He saw the man lying behind him with his brains blown out and the tire iron beside him. An uncontrollable shiver passed down Brogan's spine as he realized he had almost died.

On the other side of the car, Felix had made it to the passenger window. He raised and aimed his gun at the unsuspecting woman. Kelly heard the first shot, feared for Brogan, turned to the door to get out, and found herself looking down the barrel of a gun pointed directly at her head. She moved back and began to raise her hands as if that would stop a bullet. A second shot rang a split second later before Kelly could go for the gun in her purse. She was still looking past the barrel of the gun into the face of the man who held it when a black hole appeared over his left eyebrow and he fell away with his unfired gun still in his hand.

Brogan's first and foremost thought was of Kelly. He said through his open car door, "Kelly, are you hurt? Are you okay?"

Softly she replied, "Yes, I'm okay. What just happened?"

Before he could answer, a male voice yelled out. "Virginia State Police, stand up and let me see your hands. Tell your girlfriend to exit the car with her hands up where they can be seen. Both of you place your hands on the roof of your car."

Brogan rose slowly, with his hands raised and empty. He was surprised to see two shooters. A tall, handsome Black man and a young White female. Both were locked in a two-handed firing position. *The couple from the restaurant.*

Brogan followed the officer's instructions, telling Kelly how to safely exit the vehicle and place her hands on the roof of the car. He whispered to Kelly, "Move slowly and stay quiet and calm. Don't make any moves that may be misinterpreted."

Brogan hollered, "I'm a police officer," but he stayed with his hands firmly on the roof. He knew he had two guns pointing at his back and two very pumped-up cops unwilling to take chances. *I would have done the same thing.*

When Kelly exited the car, her hands were high and empty. She turned slowly, placed both hands on the roof, and faced Brogan. She whispered, "My gun is unloaded and in your glovebox."

31
WTF

B rogan knew her permit to carry did not extend into Virginia. He didn't even have a permit for Virginia. They might be facing technical difficulties, but they were both still alive, thanks to the cops who now covered them with their guns. The adrenaline was wearing off and reality was setting in. Both of them had just faced grave danger and only the presence of two troopers saved them.

The next few minutes were intense. The cops faced two unknown suspects who might be involved in some type of criminal activity. Two men had just tried to kill them and had been killed themselves. Anything could happen now. Fingers were on the trigger, guns were pointed. These types of situations were gut-wrenching moments for all police officers.

The male trooper passed his handcuffs to the female trooper and signaled for her to cuff the suspects. She took the cuffs and moved forward approaching Brogan with caution.

"Are you armed?" she asked.

Brogan responded, "Yes, shoulder holster under my left arm. ID is in my inside jacket pocket."

She told him to spread his legs more, then removed his weapon from his holster and his ID from his jacket. She shoved the gun into her rear waistband and the ID into her pocket. She patted Brogan down for any possible additional weapons and found none.

"Put your hands one at a time behind your back," as she cuffed him snuggly, but not tight. Brogan remained silent and compliant during this process. He remained facing Kelly. His adrenaline was still elevated and he could only imagine what was going on with this very young cop. *I don't need to incite an accident.*

The trooper checked the body on the ground and determined he was clearly deceased and no threat, then repeated the entire procedure with Kelly who, truthfully, denied being armed and allowed the search of her body as proof.

"My gun is in the glove box, unloaded," Kelly said as she was being handcuffed to the rear. The trooper looked through the open passenger door and saw a purse on the seat and a closed glovebox.

She told Kelly, "Move away from the door."

The trooper then pushed the door closed with her foot, preventing Kelly access to anything inside the car. Kelly looked across the roof of the car at Brogan. She followed Brogan's lead and remained silent and as calm as she could be under the circumstances. He winked at her. She locked onto his eyes. She was rattled by what had just happened. She had been a cop for a long time, but this was the first time she looked down the barrel of a gun without her own gun in hand. It was a terrifying and helpless feeling. Her heart felt like it was beating out of her chest. She took a couple of deep breaths trying to calm herself. More comforting were the distant sirens she heard growing ever closer.

Taking the unknown man and woman at the Lexus into custody was a powerful few minutes, especially with the rookie trooper probably traumatized over what she had just done. Again, the female trooper followed directions and completed her tasks without error and without shooting any more people.

The first two vehicles to arrive at the scene were state police cars. They had to be prearranged backup. An ambulance with EMTs arrived next. They quickly confirmed both assailants were deceased. They looked at the two people in handcuffs and one asked, "Are you hurt?" Brogan and Kelly both respond negatively and remained still. The ambulance crew backed away awaiting further developments. It seemed half the Virginia State Police were arriving on the scene. Troopers were calling the Black guy, Sergeant, and the female, Trooper Baker. Neither was wearing a uniform, so it was impossible to tell the rank of the female.

The Sergeant and Baker surrendered their weapons to other detectives for future forensic examination. The detectives began interviewing them separately to find out what had happened. Brogan and Kelly were escorted, still handcuffed, to separate marked state police cars and placed in the back seats. As a precaution, and because they were technically in custody, they were read their Miranda rights.

Virginia troopers made calls to Sandpiper PD and Maryland State Police and determined that Brogan and Hart were who they said they were. Both were removed from the patrol cars, un-handcuffed, assumed a victim status and were treated accordingly.

An EMT came immediately to Brogan and offered him water, towels, and cleansers to clean off his hair and his clothes. Because he had rubber gloves on, the ambulance guy assisted.

Brogan asked for a pair of gloves before removing the debris from his hair. He removed his jacket, folded it inside out, and placed it on the trunk of the police car. Brogan thanked him, and the guy said, "No problem." Brogan saw the name Larry Ayers on his jacket and Brogan then said, "Thanks Larry, I appreciate your help." Larry nodded in recognition of Brogan's comment, gathered his supplies back into a plastic bag and returned to the ambulance.

Brogan heard one of the troopers call the sergeant, Sergeant Zigmeister. Sergeant Zigmeister was with Trooper Baker. Brogan could hear him telling her, "You acted properly and the man you shot left you no choice. You shot to protect the life of another." Baker had tears in her eyes and snot ran out of her nose. She wiped both away with her hand and stood straight.

In a strong voice, she responded, "Thanks, Sarge. What happens now?"

"Just follow my lead Trooper. Everything will turn out all right. You did good and should be proud of yourself. I'll vouch for your actions today and we'll get through this together."

As in any police-involved shooting, it was turning into a shit show of great magnitude. A lieutenant was in charge until a captain arrived and took control. Then a lieutenant colonel living nearby arrived and began giving orders. Finally, a plain-clothes first sergeant from the internal affairs unit arrived. The entire investigation defaulted to him under their departmental rules and regulations.

Order at the crime scene was restored. The brass disappeared when they realized they wouldn't be standing in the bright lights of the media. Superintendent Carl Wilson of the Virginia State Police, having been alerted to the officer-involved shooting, spoke briefly by phone with First Sergeant Gary Silk. The superintendent hung up satisfied that Silk had the situation in control. His people appeared to have performed courageously and he would be briefed in the morning. Wilson's mind drifted. *This is good public relations for my agency.* He shot a text to the PR guy and told him to go to the SP Office and hook up with Silk and prepare a news release for both print, TV, and social media and be prepared to do a stand-up press conference in the morning. He wanted Silk to be standing by his side. Richmond was not that far away from the scene. Before going to bed, Wilson dialed the duty officer at the Governor's Mansion.

First Sergeant Silk approached Zigmeister and Baker and handed each one of them a service weapon. He said, "No trooper should be unarmed. You two just relax. We'll all be going to Area 37 State Police Office soon and getting our heads together so we can tell the superintendent what's happened here. You keep these guns until forensics returns yours to you. Then, I want my guns back." The troopers holstered their newly acquired weapons. This sign of trust went a long way. A cop feels naked without their gun.

Because neither Brogan nor Kelly had displayed or used their guns, the fact that they were in Virginia was ignored. The two assailants were dead. At first look, it appeared to be a robbery gone bad, until the tracking monitor was found in the Corolla. A check of Brogan's car had revealed the tracking device on the frame of his car. This turned the investigation in a whole new direction. A techie-trooper showed the investigators how to operate the reverse tracking mode of the video device. Both Brogan and Kelly were asked to join Silk as he viewed the device. It showed a meandering path leading from the restaurant where they now stood, north all the way to the restaurant on 17th Street. This had been a targeted attack, but on whom was the question? Neither Kelly nor Brogan recognized either of the dead men.

Brogan and Kelly approached Zigmeister and Baker. Brogan spoke first. "You saved my life and probably Kelly's too. I don't know how to thank you. I had my guard down and it almost cost me my life."

Kelly jumped in and spoke directly to Baker. "I know how you feel right now. I've had to take a life in the line of duty. But take my word for it, what you did today was courageous and speaks volumes about you and the training the Virginia State Police gave you. I am forever in your debt. Thank you is not enough. I was scared to death and your actions saved my life. I am sure of that."

Baker, in the true tradition of a cop, said, "Thank you, ma'am, I was just doing my job."

Brogan turned to Baker and said, "You did your job very well today. I also thank you for saving our lives." The four exchanged handshakes. The brotherhood of law enforcement knows no state lines.

When the crime scene investigators arrived at the location, they took pictures from every possible angle. When they determined Brogan's vehicle would produce no evidence relevant to the shootings, they released the car back to him. First Sergeant Silk asked them to drive to the State Police Office for some additional questions and their insights on why these men may have been after one or both of them. Circumstantially, the flex cuffs and duct tape made it appear they were intending to take Kelly with them. Brogan probably would not have survived the blow to the head with a tire iron. Kelly would have probably faced a worse fate had she been taken. The drive to the State Police office took them an additional fifteen miles further west on Virginia Route 64. They drove in silence. Both were deep in worried thought.

When Brogan and Kelly arrived at the State Police office, they were taken to a conference room and given coffee and donuts. Soon they were joined at the conference room table by Sergeant Zigmeister, Trooper Baker, First Sergeant Silk, and plainclothes investigators, Detective Lewis and Detective Verzi.

It was then that Brogan and Kelly learned what they didn't know about Sergeant Zigmeister, Trooper Baker, and the shootings.

Sergeant John Zigmeister introduced himself as a detective with twenty-two years on the job. "This is Trooper Probationer, Cynthia Baker, fresh out of the police academy with two weeks in the field and under the close supervision of a Field Training Officer (FTO). Her normal patrol FTO called in sick today, so we reassigned her to work the three to eleven shift with me as her acting FTO. Luckily for Ms. Hart, Baker was the top shooter in her class. We stopped at that restaurant because of their great steaks and the twenty percent police discount.

"After finishing our meal, we were returning to our unmarked cruiser when we saw the two Hispanic men pull into the parking lot and back in side by side in a darkened corner. One man got out of his truck and entered the car. I thought I saw a training opportunity and asked Baker what she saw.

Baker expressed, 'It looks like a drug deal about to go down, but since the men are staying together for too long, maybe it's a sexual thing.'

"When both men propped their car doors open and the interior light did not come on, Baker admitted she didn't know what was going on and I agreed. Baker asked me, 'Should we approach the car and find out what they are doing?'

"I told her let's wait for a while and see what happens. Anytime you're surveilling someone, give them a chance to reveal themselves and their intentions.

"I radioed for two back-up units due to the suspicious circumstances, but told backup units to stay out. I also told them to be prepared to block the road at either end at the first intersecting road. We sat low in our car, concealing our silhouettes.

"When you both left the restaurant and the two assailants immediately left their vehicle and hid behind a car, I quietly radioed backup units to move in. I started giving orders to the rookie. I told her, "I'm going out my door and move to the trunk area. You follow me out the driver's door and move to a position behind the left front wheel. I'll take the guy on the driver's side. You take the one on the passenger side with gun out and up. I'll give the verbal commands, but be prepared to shoot if you see your guy is armed. You'll have to make the call to shoot or don't shoot. Just don't hesitate after you make your decision.

"The guy approaching the driver's side kept both hands down until he was right behind you. He lifted the tire iron high over his head. It was obvious he was going to split your skull. I didn't hesitate. I shot the guy. Yelling stop or freeze never entered my mind as it would come too late to prevent irreversible damage. Then I heard Baker's shot. When my guy fell out of sight, I moved my focus to the other man. He had a gun in his hand, but he was already reacting to being shot. He also fell out of sight. Everything happened in a couple of split seconds. The rookie did good."

Baker blushed from the compliment. She had clearly regained some of her composure. Sgt. Silk asked, "Baker do you have anything to add or does anyone else here have a question?" Everyone shook their head no.

The crime lab people reported that the vehicles provided no substantial evidence, as both were reported stolen months ago from the Washington, D.C. Metropolitan area. They had found no identification on the bodies nor in the vehicles. Both guns found in the possession of the perps had their serial numbers ground off. The computer crimes unit of the state police would be delving into the tracking equipment and two burner phones found on the men. The dead men would be fingerprinted and their prints would be compared against computer records. Investigations wouldn't start before early the next day. It was a wide-open investigation and the shooting of the two men seemed to be a lesser part of a much larger crime investigation. These guys were unquestionably hitters, but who hired them and why?

Sitting at the State Police office conference table and going over Brogan and Kelly's movements during the day brought investigators no closer to a solution or a suspect. At midnight, they decided to call it quits for the night.

As the internal shooting investigation continued in the coming days, both Zigmeister and Baker would be ordered to submit written reports, and to visit with a counselor, and sit with investigators who would go over their actions. Both would be ordered to take paid administrative leave for a period of time and then return temporarily to administrative duties. Once it was determined to be a clean shoot, both would be returned to full duty with the incident fully documented in their personnel files. Neither officer would forget this night for the rest of their lives. Brogan and Kelly both said they would return for any internal hearings or trial boards concerning the shootings, if necessary.

The attempted attack on Brogan and Kelly would be turned over to their major crime investigators. Someone would reach out to them sometime the next day. Hopefully, they would have information from the tracking unit, the burner phones, and fingerprints that might help Brogan and Kelly put this puzzle together. Unfortunately for Brogan and Kelly, all agreed this was a Maryland-born crime and the answers lay in the Sandpiper area.

When Brogan and Kelly left the State Police office, they retraced their route back to Sandpiper, realizing they were driving toward the danger. That's what cops and PIs do. They run to the danger. In this case, they didn't even know who was bringing danger into their lives.

Somebody was there waiting for them. Brogan and Kelly acknowledged this obvious fact and made a pact to turn this situation around and take the hunt to whoever was hunting them.

A few miles north of the State Police office Kelly asked Brogan, "Can you pull to the shoulder of the road?"

When he stopped, she opened her door and threw up. Brogan wasn't sure what to do, but leaned across the seat and gently laid his hand on her back. After a couple of minutes, she straightened up and wiped her mouth with a napkin that had been stuffed in his door panel. Brogan handed her a bottle of water and she drank some while she leaned out the door and cleared her mouth. She sat up again. With red eyes, she said, "I'm so sorry. I thought I was going to die and I can't get it out of my mind. I was so scared."

Brogan knew there was nothing he could say that would erase what she saw or how she felt at that particular moment. He had seen people far stronger than her lose it when the adrenaline wore off and they were left with nothing but their emotions and thoughts of what might have been. He gently rubbed her shoulder.

She turned and said, "You still liking me?"

Brogan took her hand and said, "Yes, Kelly, I'm still liking you very much. You ready to go home?"

She nodded and meekly said, "Please." She pulled the door shut, and Brogan put the car in gear and returned to the road.

32
A LONG RIDE HOME

Kelly and Brogan faced a three-and-a-half-hour drive home. Not quite the ending of the third date they had hoped for. Both were quiet for the first hour, mulling over what had happened and who might be behind it. Coming up with nothing individually, they began to beat it back and forth among themselves, but they had received no recent threats or locked up anybody who showed enough rage to seek revenge. It had been so long that he couldn't remember the last Hispanic guy he had arrested. There was nobody getting out of jail that might have wanted to do him bodily harm. He had just gone through that last year. Odds were this was something entirely different.

Kelly had even fewer people she may have pissed off. She thought of that little worm from Dundalk, but couldn't fathom him having the balls or the money to pay hit men to come after her. How could he have even found them? She was pretty confident he wasn't involved in this. She didn't think this was coming from Baltimore County or her law enforcement career. Her years with executive protection had been completely devoid of any violence or felony arrests until the day of the shooting. That guy was dead and no family had been located. He wasn't Hispanic. No Hispanic connections had come up during the internal investigation.

Only one Hispanic guy came to mind. *I remember that big Hispanic guy at that farm. But he wasn't one of the shooters that had been killed. My contact with him had been brief and had nothing really to do with him personally. I remember the Hispanic children and the woman there, but I didn't have contact with her. But there was something! Why were cameras in the driveway? Who did they think was going to come down that driveway? What were they hiding or protecting? There had been no daycare sign! Something was just off. But I chastised myself for being overly paranoid. That situation happened several weeks ago. Shit, am I being overly paranoid again?*

"Brogan, you know what? I attempted service of a summons that turned out to be an error in the address by one of the attorney's staff. The error had caused me to visit two farms looking for this guy named Bowker. Mr. Bowker was later served at his correct address.

"In my search for Bowker, I visited the farm where I was met by a big Hispanic guy and I saw a Hispanic woman and a bunch of Spanish-speaking children ranging in ages from three to five. There were security cameras and no sign for a daycare. I had a gut feeling at the time, but considered it a cop's paranoia and forgot about it."

Brogan listened intently to her story. In his years of policing, he knew many cases had been turned, or lives saved, on nothing more than a gut feeling. He said to Kelly, "I know it's thin, but we've got nothing else. We're going to need to rest up for tomorrow, but I think it's worth checking out. We need to find out more about these people and what's going on at that farm. We're both too tired to come up with a game plan tonight. When I get up tomorrow, I've got to brief the chief on what happened today and tell him we have one slim lead outside of Sandpiper that needs to be followed. He gives me free rein, so it won't be a problem. Do you have anything you're obligated to do over the next couple of days? A surveillance might be needed."

Kelly responded, "No, I don't. Normally, I'd be calling around to attorneys' offices looking for papers to serve, but this is far more important to me. I will call Marie and tell her about today. I'll tell her I'll be out of the office for a couple of days, but available by phone. I'll let her know to be on the lookout for any strange activity around the office or anyone inquiring about me. Marie used to be a cop, so she'll know what to do. She carries a gun and I suspect the secretary in the office has one in her desk. The Eastern Shore is full of people carrying guns and you know what? It makes me feel safer."

Brogan brought up the fact that they really didn't know when the men began following them. The tracking monitor took them back to 17th Street, but that was only the location where the device was attached and turned on.

Brogan pushed his mind to recall how he had left his place and gone directly to Kelly's. *This movement didn't show up on the monitor, so how would they know we'd be at the restaurant unless they followed us from Kelly's place?* Kelly was the most likely target. The restaurant was probably their first opportunity to attach the tracker. It pissed Brogan off that these two slime balls had spent the entire day following them on what Brogan had considered a private, romantic drive. He was grateful the Virginia State Police had saved Kelly and him, but he wished he had been the one to have killed them. He needed to find who hired them and settle the score with that person. Only bad guys had died so far, but the chances were that the person responsible would not stop because of this one failure. Someone was either filled with hate or was hiding a secret they couldn't allow to see the light of day.

Brogan had one other lead and he explained it to Kelly. "Whoever is behind this has money. Hiring two hitmen and equipping them with tracking equipment and burner phones is not cheap. One of us, most likely you, has worried someone who has the resources to keep coming at us. We need to stay vigilant. Unfortunately, the evidence is pointing to you as being their main target. The tracker was to follow my car because you were in it. The flex cuffs and duct tape were on the guy who was at your car door. They definitely wanted you alive for some particular reason. Two sexual predators working together are rare. Ransom is a possibility, based on you living in a high-dollar condo, or maybe they needed to talk to you about something. Think hard about that possibility. Something you think is nothing might be very important to someone else."

They stopped in Parksley, Virginia, at the Royal Farms store and got coffee to keep them awake for the last leg of their journey. Kelly found the bag of pastries in the back seat, and they shared them. They rolled into Sandpiper around 3:30 a.m. and Brogan took Kelly home and insisted on coming in to clear the condo to be sure nobody was waiting for her. Normally, Kelly would have thought this was a little over the top, but she found in Brogan what she had lost when she left Baltimore County. Brogan was her backup.

He searched the entire condo, including closets and any

area large enough to hide a human being. He found nothing. Then he checked the locks on the door and found them to be adequate.

He suggested she lean a dining room chair under the door handle and set some other noise makers against the door to act as an early warning system. Satisfied that she would be safe with her gun on the nightstand next to her bed, he said, "Kelly, I know this day started out perfect and I'm sorry it ended as it did. Can we try again sometime soon?"

Kelly moved to him, leaned up and gently kissed him on his lips. He responded in kind. She held the kiss long enough for him to know it was special. When her feet returned to the floor, she looked into his eyes and said, "It was perfect, every second of it. I enjoyed all our dates and when things turned to shit, I knew I would be okay because you were there. Brogan, I'd love to do it again and again if you'd like."

Under normal circumstances, this would have turned into a lust-filled next couple of hours, but both knew fatigue would render it less than memorable. Memorable is what they both wanted, but for now it could wait.

She followed him to the door and said, "Goodnight, I'll be safe. Please keep your head on a swivel and be safe. Call me tomorrow when you get up and we'll meet to decide our next steps. Thanks for a wonderful day."

She knew he would stand outside in the hall until he heard all the locks engaged and the bumping of the chair against the door before he would retreat to his car.

The door was secured, and she had a moment just to think. *He's not only my backup, he now wants me to be his partner in figuring out what's going on.* As bad as things were, she couldn't help but have a warm feeling of companionship come over her. It felt good. She called and left a message on Marie's office phone, telling her briefly to be wary and that she would call her as soon as she woke up and fill her in. She undressed, slipped into an oversized tee shirt, brushed her teeth and then did a face plant on her bed. She didn't move for the next seven hours.

Brogan left Kelly's and drove straight to a do-it-yourself car wash. There was no way he was going to let blood and brain tissue sit on his car overnight. Once he got home, he washed himself even more thoroughly than his car. His clothes went in a plastic bag and then into the trash can. All could be replaced and the thought of what had been on them ruled them disposable. He then joined the rest of the sane world and fell asleep.

33

SOMETHING IS WRONG

Carlos paced in his kitchen; he had been doing so for what seemed like hours. It was 2 a.m. and his men had failed to report. Surely, they'd had an opportunity by now to take the girl. If they were doing shit to that girl, he would kill them both. *Where the fuck are you guys? Something is wrong! Very wrong!*

Felix had called him when they entered Virginia just to let him know they were still on the woman, and they were in Virginia. Carlos had said, "It doesn't matter where they go. Just stay on them and get the woman."

His burner phone sat silently on the kitchen table. *Should I call them? What if they had gotten themselves locked up?* He didn't want the police to answer the phone. If they were arrested, he was already fucked, because Felix had called him earlier and they would have his burner's number in the phone. The phones couldn't be directly traced to him. He had paid cash for them in a small market. He had made sure there were no cameras in the store before making the purchase. He had traveled all the way to Easton to add another layer of concealment.

He had to call Gordon in a few hours and he had to be

able to tell the man something. Right then he knew nothing, but knowing nothing did not fly with Gordon, he would go ballistic. Carlos had assured him that these guys could get the job done and deliver the woman to him. Carlos had been convinced they could do the job and that's why he knew something had gone wrong, but what? At 2:30 a.m. he couldn't stand it any longer and called Felix. The phone rang and rang, but no one answered. What did that mean? He still didn't know shit.

If he had known, he would have gone crazy. The phone sat in an envelope, locked up in a police evidence room, in a state police office. The last cop to have the phone had put it in the envelope and failed to turn it off. The battery was dying slowly. The embedded eSIMs recorded any numbers calling the phone and saved them to a missed calls file. The police would find it tomorrow when the computer crimes guys began their work on the recovered burners.

Carlos planned this operation and he now recognized a flaw. *These guys do not know where I live and the only contact information I gave them was the cell phone number of the burner.* That phone laid quietly on his table. *Christ, there was also the tracking system I provided to them to worry about.* Carlos purchased the system from a fence that dealt primarily with electronics. The guy's name was Sweet Johnny, so named because of the sweet deals you could get from him. Carlos had met him in Pocomoke City after being referred by another Hispanic friend. Carlos had been careful and never revealed his last name, where he lived, or anything personal about himself. He even parked his truck several blocks away and carried his purchase away in a plain cardboard box. Cash had been the method of payment. The tracking unit was expensive and purchased specifically for this job. *If they have the girl, it's worth it, but if these dickheads have lost it or just aborted the mission and kept it, Gordon will be hiring guys to look for them. He is just not a guy to be messed with.*

Carlos was afraid of Gordon. Carlos could easily take him in a fair fight, but there was nothing fair about Gordon. He was like a wolverine; not very big, but extremely nasty and violent. God forbid if he felt cornered or threatened. He would tell Carlos to throw all those kids in a hole and bury them, or he would just disappear leaving Carlos and Rosa holding the bag. *How can I find out what's going on?*

Carlos went to his truck and brought in another burner phone. He got the phone numbers for all the hospitals and police stations near Route 13, south of the Maryland border to Williamsburg. He began calling each one using the ruse that two of his Hispanic workers were supposed to pick up supplies in Virginia and bring them to Maryland, and are now overdue. He said, "I am worried that they may have been in an accident." He knew this method carried some danger, but he knew no other way.

The next forty minutes passed with nothing learned. Carlos came to a phone number for a fire department in York County, Virginia. The phone rang and a young voice answered wide awake, alert despite the hour of the morning. "Cadet Meadows," the voice reported, "How can I help you?"

Carlos went through his routine and prepared to hear the usual response, sorry, I don't know anything about something like that happening. Instead, Meadows said, "No accidents in the area, but two Hispanic guys got killed earlier in a shootout at a local restaurant."

"They're both dead?" Carlos asked. "What happened?"

"Yep, both dead, not sure of the details. Our ambulance was on the scene with the state police. I'll give you their phone number."

Carlos heard a voice in the background. "Meadows, who are you talking to? Give me that phone."

Meadows's supervisor snatched the phone from the cadet's hand and asked, "Who is this?" The supervisor was talking to dead air. He instantly began dialing the state police while glaring down at Meadows.

Meadows looked up innocently and said, "What?"

Carlos heard enough. He took the burner from his ear, opened the back, removed the card and crushed it under his heel. The phone laying on the table met the same fate. He would take both phones, along with the crushed cards, and bury them. He left the house with the phones and broken plastic in a baggie and walked fifty yards to the barn. He started up the excavator, which emitted an eerie sound at this time of the morning. He drove down near the wood line and scooped one large divot into the ground. He tossed the baggie and pushed the removed soil back into the hole. He patted it down with the bucket and returned to the barn. He was shaking from the dread building in him. He thought hard. *How can I spin this with Gordon?*

Back at the house, Carlos jumped on the internet looking for local York County, Virginia news. Sure enough, the incident was wall-to-wall with local postings:

TWO DEAD IN WHAT APPEARS TO BE A ROBBERY GONE TERRIBLY WRONG.

TWO UNIDENTIFIED HISPANIC MEN WERE KILLED TONIGHT IN THE PARKING LOT OF A YORK COUNTY RESTAURANT.

TWO VICTIMS, OUT-OF-STATE TOURISTS, WERE REPORTEDLY UNHARMED. VIRGINIA STATE POLICE ARE INVESTIGATING.

NO FURTHER DETAILS ARE AVAILABLE AT THIS TIME, AS THE INVESTIGATION CONTINUES, A PRESS CONFERENCE HAS BEEN SCHEDULED FOR 10:00 A.M. AT THE STATE POLICE OFFICE IN RICHMOND.

Carlos knew little about what happened, but he knew in his heart that these were his guys. Both were dead. The boss had a right to be afraid of this woman. If she wasn't after him before, she was now.

The sun began to peek through the kitchen window. Carlos thought to himself, *I need to wake Rosa up. We need a plan of our own that doesn't include Gordon. I'm not panicking, but I'm not just going to sit by and hope for the best.*

34

DO IT RIGHT. DO IT YOURSELF.

When his special cell phone rang at 7 a.m., Gordon was already at his desk in Sandpiper. A call from Carlos this early could go either way. He would be told the woman had been taken and he would give Carlos instructions on where to take her, or he would be told excuses. Thomas Gordon did not suffer fools or failures.

Gordon answered, "Tell me."

Carlos was nervous when he spoke and for good reason. The news was not good. Quite the contrary, it was just short of catastrophic.

"The two men I recruited to do the job are dead. They were killed in some sort of shootout, in York County, Virginia. The woman has not been taken and apparently was not injured in the incident. She has a boyfriend who may have done something to interfere with my men completing their tasks." Carlos paused, but Gordon said nothing.

Carlos continued. "Boss, I planned this with safeguards. We have lost two men who are of no concern to us. There is no link from them to me except for the equipment I gave them. I made sure the equipment is also not linked to me. My cell phone was destroyed immediately and, of course, so was the burner. All the burner phones were purchased in another town, in a small market, with no cameras. I paid cash. Likewise, the tracking equipment was purchased from a fence in another town, and he has no knowledge of who I am or where I live. He didn't care why I wanted it or where I was going to use it. This was also a cash deal, so all links to me are nonexistent. The cars they were driving were stolen in Washington, D.C. and the guns they had were untraceable, with ground-off serial numbers. Again, I had no part in that, so there is no link to me." Carlos almost ran out of breath trying to get all his excuses and information out before Gordon could remark.

Gordon took a deep breath, before speaking. "Carlos, this is still a mess, but I can see you've done a good job of protecting us throughout this job. I will do some research to see what happened in Virginia, then we'll make our next move. We cannot waste time. The tracking device will tell them they were targeted. We still don't know why she was at the farm or if she is investigating what she saw. It is more important than ever that she is interrogated then dealt with quickly. The woman has no way of knowing who is really after her and her boyfriend. Do we know who the boyfriend is?"

"No, boss, we don't," Carlos said. "He picked her up yesterday morning. My men were positioned to take her at her car on her way to work, but she walked directly to this guy who was waiting for her at the curb. They went for breakfast and that is where we put the tracker on his car. When they left the restaurant, they began driving all over the place. They went to Salisbury and then turned south on Route 13 and just kept driving, crossing into Virginia, which was the last update I got. I kept waiting for them to call, but then I heard about the shooting near Williamsburg, that two Hispanic guys had been shot and killed and just put it together, that it had to be our people. You can look it up on the internet and there is supposed to be a press release this morning at 10 in Richmond. That's all I know."

After another deep breath, Gordon said, "Carlos, I just want you and Rosa to stay on the farm and keep a low profile. Stay on high alert and call me immediately if anything happens. Do you understand?"

"Yes, boss, but what about the sick little girl?"

Gordon's voice hardened. "What about her? Let her die and stick her in a hole. Understood?"

"Yes, boss." The connection died in Carlos's hand. He had his marching orders. Rosa would not be happy.

Gordon rolled back from his desk and took a moment to think. *Want something done? Do it yourself. I'll deal with that little investigator bitch and her boyfriend if I catch them together. Maybe it's time to pull the stakes and move on. I'll have to take care of Carlos, Rosa and the kids. Messy, but not undoable. I got to think about this. Damn, things here were so sweet and the money just kept rolling in. If that woman and her boyfriend were gone, things could go back to normal. I'll fire up my computer and find out what's going on in Virginia! Everything's on the internet if you know where to look. And I do!*

35

BROGAN, IS THIS TRUE?

Dazzling rays of sun lit up Kelly's face. She awoke unsure of her whereabouts. Moving her head only slightly on the bed she saw she was home, at her parent's condo. Kelly was overwhelmed by images that came rushing back. *Williamsburg, the shootings, the police, Brogan, throwing up on the side of the road, and being dropped off at home; I don't remember anything else.* She saw that she had at least made it into night clothes. The small clock on the nightstand said 10:00. *Wow, I slept seven hours without moving.* She turned her head and checked the other side of the king-size bed. *No Brogan. Guess he did drop me off and didn't stay. Now I remember him insisting on me locking down.* She wandered into the living room area and found all the lock-down mechanisms still in place.

Her first duty was to call Marie and bring her up-to-date. Marie picked up before the first ring died in Kelly's ear. Marie spoke rapidly. "What the hell are you into now? There was a shooting? Are you hurt? You said Brogan was there. Is he hurt?" Kelly was immediately sorry she had slept so long, leaving her friend worrying about her well-being. Kelly took ten minutes to run the whole story by Marie. Then she had to answer an additional dozen questions from Marie. After Kelly answered Marie's questions, Marie's voice returned to an almost normal level. She had one final question for Kelly. "Who is behind all this?" For that, Kelly had no answer but assured Marie that Brogan and she intended to find out.

"You and Brogan?" Marie inquired. "He's a cop and you're a PI. How's that going to work?"

"I don't know, but this is personal, and he wants me to work with him, and that's what I'm going to do."

Marie chuckled for the first time. "Yes, it sounds personal. I'm more concerned for you now that Brogan's in the picture."

"What do you mean," asked Kelly.

"Brogan is the best cop this area has ever seen. He will stop at nothing to find out who's done this, but sometimes he leaves a lot of damage in his path. Just be careful around him. He seems to draw danger to himself, not to mention what he might do to your heart."

Kelly smiled and replied, "Not to worry, Marie. I'm a big girl and danger is nothing new to me. He makes me feel safe when I'm around him. As to my heart, it's been safe for way too long. He'll have my back and I'll have his. I'll call you if we get into any legal trouble, so don't turn off your cell for the next few days. I'll check in to let you know I'm okay."

"Oh, Kelly I almost forgot. Stacy may have found a place for you to live in Sandpiper. She has a friend who is moving in with her boyfriend. She's been living in a really cute cottage on 18th Street, bayside. The lease runs out in four weeks and the owner doesn't know Stacy's friend is moving out. It's fully furnished and has a small but nice yard and porch. I think there's even a small patio in the back. Are you interested?"

"Absolutely, I'm all over it. Is Stacy there? I want to thank her," Kelly responded.

"No sorry, I sent her up to the courthouse to retrieve some court filings. But I'll tell her you said thanks and you will call her tomorrow, if that's okay?"

"Yes, yes, that's perfect. I'm so excited at the opportunity. I'll definitely call her tomorrow morning to thank her and get the details. You just made it a perfect day, especially after the uncertain day I spent yesterday."

After ending her call, Kelly started toward the shower. *I've got to get my shit together, get dressed, and get in touch with Brogan. Hope he hasn't gone off without me because I've been in bed all morning.* Twenty minutes later, she was clean and presentable, no worse for wear and tear.

She returned to the living room and put her gun back in her purse. She saw the bag and remembers the book Brogan bought her. *Why would he want me to read this book?* She took it out of the bag and perused the cover. She flipped it over and saw a picture of the author. Still nobody she knew or recognized. She began to read the blurb on the back. She got no further than the first paragraph before putting it down and dialing Brogan's number. He answered with his single identifier, "Brogan."

Without introduction, Kelly started, "Brogan. Is this true?"

"Is what true?"

"Is this book about you?"

Brogan smiled to himself. "I told you that you needed to read it, that you'd like it."

"No, tell me. What's it about? Just tell me," Kelly begged.

"We don't have time for that book. We've got the here

and now to worry about. Are you ready to go to work? We've got to make a little road trip this morning and then a surveillance tonight. Do you have any dark or camouflage clothing to wear?" Brogan asked.

"I've got blue jeans, sweaters, and a jacket that's dark gray, and black tactical boots I can wear," Kelly responded.

"If it will keep you warm, that should work. I have an old camouflage jacket that is too small for me that I'll bring if you need another layer. Bring your binoculars and gun with some extra ammunition. Gloves too, if you have them. We've got some bad guys to go after if you're ready. Can I pick you up in about thirty minutes?"

"I'm ready," Kelly said as she went to her bedroom and began to fill a small duffel bag with all the things she would need. Her pulse began to race.

36

I THINK WE'RE GETTING CLOSER

Thirty minutes later, Brogan showed up driving a strange car and Kelly threw her duffle in the back. He told her, "This is an undercover car that is used only during surveillance situations. We also have a van, but it would be too obvious if spotted near the farm."

He said, "I received a call from the Virginia State Police. They had tracked the cell phone purchases to a market in Easton and asked if I could check it out. I told them I would."

Kelly pressed Brogan, "Tell me about the book."

Brogan said, "We need to focus on what we are doing. The book can wait." With that, Kelly decided to forget about the book for the time being.

It was almost one in the afternoon when they pulled up to a small, nondescript market in Easton. The windows were covered with beer signs and advertisements for the Maryland Lottery. Located in a shabby part of town it was probably not really safe for strangers. The sun was shining and the presence of a White male and female screamed cops, so the locals just watched to see what was going to happen next. They parked right in front of the store, so they could keep an eye on their car. They climbed the two concrete steps and pushed the entrance door inward. The place was old with narrow aisles stuffed with various products. It was the corner store for the neighborhood and serviced the people who would pay a few cents more rather than drive to the larger grocery stores in nearby shopping centers.

An older Black gentleman in his 80s stood behind the counter wearing an apron that at one time might have been white. It was probably as old as the wearer, but was still serviceable. He smiled, showing a mouthful of teeth tinged dark by years of smoking. His hair was gray and receding in the front. A cross hung from a chain around his neck. He looked at the pair of strangers and said, "Can I help you?"

Kelly and Brogan had decided that Brogan would do all the talking, and he spoke up and said, "My name is Brogan. I'm a detective from Sandpiper and I'm looking for some help with a shooting investigation."

"Been no shootings around here," the old gentleman said.

"You're correct, but someone tried to kill my partner and me and we need your help to figure out who that is."

"Okay," the store owner said. "I'm Timothy Moore. That sounds serious. How can I help?"

"You sold six cell phones to somebody about three weeks back. I'm sure they paid in cash, but perhaps you have surveillance cameras?" Brogan said.

"No, we got no cameras, and the guy did pay in cash, so I don't have a credit card record, but I remember him. That was my biggest sale of the day. Actually, it was my biggest sale of the week. I should have known he was up to no good."

"Do you remember what he looked like?" Brogan asked.

"Yep, I sure do. First time I'd ever seen him. He came in and walked up and down the aisles for a while. I got a little scared he was casing the place and was going to rob me, so I made sure my gun was within reach. But finally, he came to the counter and said he wanted to buy burner phones like it was a normal request. I guess in this store it is, but not in the quantity he was asking for. I only had eight and he took six and paid cash on the barrelhead."

The man paused for a moment before continuing. "Haven't seen him since, but you were asking if I can describe him. He's a Hispanic, big Hispanic fellow, not all that fat, just tall and big. Big as you, but probably heavier than you. Had a full head of hair and brown eyes. Didn't see any tattoos or anything. He was wearing jeans and a plain gray sweatshirt. To me, they all look the same, but this guy was bigger, so I remember him. I didn't see a car, which I thought was unusual, so when he left, I went to the window and watched him walk out of sight. A couple of minutes later, here he comes cruising by the store in a pickup truck. It was dark colored, but I didn't pay attention to what kind it was or the tag. That's all I know."

Brogan looked at the man and said, "You've been extremely helpful and I thank you, Mr. Moore."

Brogan and Kelly both bought a soda from the ice chest at the front of the store and got the telephone number of the store, and left. Kelly waited until they got in the car and said, "Are you thinking what I'm thinking?"

"Yeah, I think we're getting closer," and started back towards Sandpiper.

37

IT HURTS MY HEART

The sun was up at the farm and the kids had been fed. They were burning off pent-up energy in the backyard, running, laughing and playing like normal kids their age. All were happy, but one.

A little girl was inside and unable to join the other kids. She was so sick she could no longer eat normal food and was having trouble even sitting up to drink. Her fever came and went. A small stand sat next to her bed. The top was half-covered with over-the-counter medicines. Nothing was working. Rosa had sat up all night with the child and watched in horror as her condition worsened. She attempted to get soup into the little girl to nourish her. She begged Carlos to let her take the child to a clinic to be seen. Carlos said, "It's too dangerous. They will ask too many questions that we can't answer. It will bring unwanted attention to us. If anyone finds out what is going on at this farm, we will go to jail until we die. Do you understand Rosa?"

"Yes, yes, I know, but it hurts my heart to see this baby lie here and suffer so."

"Listen, she may be the lucky one," said Carlos. "We don't know where these kids are being sent. There are far worse things than being sick or even dead. We have joined hands with the devil and we must remain hidden. I've been saving all our money and have almost enough so we can leave and start a new life far away from this place. It will take time, but someday we will forget all this and have our own place and maybe even a child of our own. Rosa, you must remain strong for a little while longer. I promise we will leave here soon."

Rosa understood that they had been involved in unbelievable and unforgivable things since coming to the farm. She could no longer remember the number of children who had come and gone. She hoped that most of them had found good homes and were happy. She was not a stupid woman. She had trouble trying to reconcile herself with the knowledge that most had probably gone to predators who were evil like their own boss. *Mr. Gordon is a very bad man.*

Gordon frightened Rosa when he came around. She knew that Carlos was afraid of him too. She prayed every night that God would forgive her for her role in all of this, especially for the children who had died while in their hands and had been buried on the farm. No priest, no service, not even a coffin. Just an unmarked hole in the ground, comforted only by their favorite toy or dress. She visited these now-covered holes, frequently praying for their souls and her own. She knew this little girl now in her care would soon join those other little ones in a dark, damp hole. Tears rolled down her face as she cried for forgiveness.

38
TIME TO LAY LOW

While Brogan and Kelly were returning to Sandpiper, they were making plans for that night's surveillance. They discussed and decided to set up at dusk. Both hoped to gather more intelligence into what was going on at the farm. They discussed whether they should contact the sheriff's office and advise that they were conducting a surveillance. A review of their gear was conducted. The only question left was what could they do during the hours before darkness?

They were not the only ones making plans. Thomas Gordon was making his own plans. The previous night's online auction of the children had gone far better than expected. He sold all eight healthy kids at the farm to new homes. The clock on the three-day delayed delivery was now ticking down the hours. All the monies had been transferred into off-shore accounts. That single night of sales had grossed them 1.2 million dollars. He would be free of the kids in just over two days.

The shootings in Virginia had changed everything. Gordon realized an investigation was out there, churning around like a tornado. The bitch PI was behind it and another move on her was too dangerous. Out of caution, Gordon decided to shut the farm down, at least temporarily. He called Mexico and they mutually agreed to stop everything for the short term.

Gordon called Carlos and said, "I'm sending you on vacation. I want you to gather everything relating to the children and dig a hole large enough and bury it. It's all replaceable, and it connects us to human trafficking, so it has to go. I'll give you plenty of money to keep you and Rosa away for at least a month or more. Then, I'll re-evaluate and give you a call. The farm can just sit idle, so no one will be the wiser. Tomorrow night, drug the children and transport them to our secret location and turn them over to our man for delivery." He then whispered to Carlos, "Bury the sick girl. If necessary, put a pillow over her face. Do you understand?"

Carlos knew the right answer. "Yes sir, it will be done."

Gordon contemplated his next moves. *I will begin dismantling the operation tomorrow. I need a vacation too. A few weeks in the Islands will do me good and I can get some sun. If I get lonely, I can buy companionship. I'll be well out of the jurisdiction of these small-town cops and private investigators. I'll be making a good thing out of a bad thing. The real estate business can survive for a few weeks without me.*

The dark web would remain dark until Thomas Gordon decided to light it up with new selections. He would tell Carlos and Rosa to enjoy themselves and would promise to call them when it was safe to return to Maryland. The next night, Carlos would transport all eight children to the middleman, who would then pass them on to their unknown futures. Four days from then, Gordon would be booking a flight to the warm and sunny islands of the Caribbean.

39
THEY'RE IN THE WOODS

Carlos and Rosa were happy beyond belief. They were getting out of there. Carlos said, "Rosa, we need to move quickly and bag up all this kid stuff. I will bury it in the back field in the morning. The dresses, soccer balls, bicycles, and plastic playground equipment must also be buried. Leave each kid with one toy to keep them occupied for the day and make sure the six girls have their favorite dress to wear for the trip to their new home. The two boys will have their soccer balls and we don't have to dress them up for the trip."

"Carlos, do we have to come back?" Rosa asked. "Can we just go somewhere and then slip away for our own life? Do we have enough money?"

"Yes, I think it's time to go and stay gone. Mr. Gordon scares me, and I fucked up that kidnapping in Virginia and I don't think he's going to forget it. We must be careful and do everything he says and pretend everything is normal, but once we're gone, we're gone!"

"Where will we go, Carlos?" Rosa asked.

"West, far away from this place. Just keep packing this shit up, so Gordon doesn't have anything to be mad about," Carlos said as he continued to throw stuff in boxes.

I'll dig a big hole in the field and throw all the cameras and monitors in it with all the kid's things. Gordon has no idea how much stuff I bought when he told me to guard the farm. He thinks I just have a couple of cameras on the driveway, but I've got this whole farm being surveilled by motion detection night-vision cameras and video monitors to see what's out there. It's Rosa and me who will go to jail if the cops show up. Gordon thinks I'm stupid, but I'm not going to jail while he gets off scot-free.

Brogan and Kelly spent two hours in the courthouse looking at land records, property transfers, settlement papers and deeds. It was like chasing a ghost. Things had been misfiled or lost when it came to the property they knew only as "the farm." The property was owned by Gerald and Barbara Zappa until about three years ago. They put the property up for sale for eight hundred thousand dollars through the Thomas Gordon Real Estate Company in Sandpiper. Then the property disappeared into a rabbit hole. There was no record of the sale or of the property being taken off the market. There were some documents on another piece of property in the Snow Hill area and other papers concerning a property just outside of Snow Hill, but it was not the farm they were inquiring about in the file. The clerk tried to help them, but also became confused and lost in the maze of documents. The clerk pledged to search the files until she straightened everything out. Both Brogan and Kelly had searched land records in the past, but neither was an expert, especially when the wrong documents were all they could find. Online searches, such as Zillow and Google, didn't give them the answers they sought. There were no records of showings or offers to buy.

While searching the land records, they did discover one interesting fact. There was a large tract of undeveloped land on the south side of the farm. It was a ten-acre plot deeded to Marvin and Deanna Teacher, purchased in 1994. This is the old lady Kelly previously visited. *Good to know. This might be to our advantage. Approach the farm from this direction. Better to ask for forgiveness than for permission.* Deanna Teacher would not be brought into the loop about their intentions.

Kelly suggested they call the real estate office to see if they could help. Brogan made the call, hoping the full force of the law would expedite obtaining the information they sought. Unknown to him, he was falling over another tripwire. The receptionist answered and listened while Brogan explained their dilemma, then asked to speak to Mr. Gordon. Following normal protocol, the receptionist rang Mr. Gordon. "There's a Detective Brogan on the line."

"Did he say what he wants?"

"Only that it was about a farm property this office handled about three years ago. He didn't share the location or the names of the buyer or seller," she replied.

"Please tell him I'm not in the office and get a phone number for him, so I can call him back. I'm tied up on another matter right now," Gordon said.

"Yes, sir, will do."

A moment later, Brogan hung up and turned to Kelly. "He's out of the office and will call me as soon as he can be reached."

Kelly had been thinking about Thomas Gordon. "I met that guy at the Gallery Gala. Do you know him?"

Brogan shook his head. "No."

"He's a weird little guy. Gave me the creeps when I met him. Thought he was going to start hitting on me."

Brogan laughed, "Sort of like me and our series of dates?"

"No, nothing like you. You were sweet and clever; big difference. Plus, you're not a weird little guy. You're big!"

"Oh, I'm a weird, big guy, huh?"

Kelly snickered, "I'm still investigating your weird aspects."

"Miss, you haven't even seen weird yet. Stick with me and I'll show you weird," Brogan said, flirting back with Kelly. "We may have to find out who owns it later. We're still going to be watching it tonight to see if we can figure out what's going on out there. Let's double-check our gear and go get something to eat. It will be dark around 5:30, so we need to get rolling," Brogan said while heading for a nearby sub-shop, so they could grab a quick sandwich.

Fueled with sandwiches and coffee, Kelly and Brogan arrived in the area of the farm. They slowly cruised along the road past the driveway twice. Still, no signs announcing the presence of a daycare center.

Kelly told Brogan, "The first camera was positioned around the first curve in the driveway so it would not be seen from the main road."

"Let's go to the little dead-end drive that you explored before," Brogan suggested.

Kelly said, "Good idea. I think it was long enough to pull the car off the road and hide it in the tall weeds near the gate."

They had created tire tracks in the driveway, but they would disappear in the dwindling daylight. They had seen no other traffic during their exploration. This rural road was quiet and had no street lighting. Dark and private. Perfect place to hide criminal activity.

They grabbed their gear and began walking the road toward the farm. They were prepared to enter the weeds and woods, at the side of the road, at the first sign of headlights, but no one came.

Half a mile later, they came to the beginning of the heavily wooded Teacher property. "Should we go into the woods?" Kelly asked.

"Normally I would say yes, but with no traffic, let's stay on the road until we're almost to the driveway. That way, we can move faster and easier," Brogan replied.

Finally, they were near the driveway and entered the woods on their right. Brogan was correct. Moving through the woods in near darkness was slow and noisy. The farm was not visible, but Brogan had a good sense of direction, and it helped he had studied the Google Earth satellite pictures during their downtime after lunch. This kept them in a straight line paralleling the farm property. He knew the farmhouse sat approximately two-tenths of a mile off the road. His experiences hunting on the Shore helped him in calculating the distance they had traveled. He stopped and Kelly, with her head down, bumped into his back.

"What?" she whispered.

"I think we're here," Brogan responded. "Now we turn to our left and approach slowly to the edge of the woods where we can find a good place to observe our target."

Kelly nodded her head and followed Brogan. Kelly's mind had drifted to the night in Tall Pines when she was on what was supposed to have been a simple surveillance, but it had turned into a night of extreme violence and death. *Was this just a surveillance? Was there such a thing? When you intentionally go looking for bad deeds, you're bound to find them more often than not.*

The woods slowly started to lighten as they approached its edge. Moonlight illuminated the farmhouse approximately one hundred yards away. This was a side of the farm Kelly had not seen and she was surprised when she saw there was a pond between them and the house. The pond was surrounded by natural growth, but it did not block the view of the house that sat slightly elevated in the distance. An occasional frog croaked his dissatisfaction at having visitors near his home.

The pond was a two-edged sword. Anyone wanting to reach them from the farm would have to circle the pond, conversely, to reach the farmhouse they would have to do the same thing. They both stood in the shadows of the pine trees lining the edge of the woods. Lights showed from different windows of the farmhouse. This was not the best place to observe from, but for tonight it would suffice. They may have to try a different surveillance location on another night. A fallen tree near the edge of the woods provided the perfect place to set up. They settled in and brought their binoculars to bear on the house. The windows were large, so they could see figures moving in front of them from time to time. They waited and watched.

Inside the farmhouse, a beeping sound alerted Carlos that one of the night vision cameras had sensed movement on the south side of the farm. Probably another deer wandering onto the property, but with what Gordon had said, Carlos immediately went into a small room set up as a security chamber and checked the appropriate monitor. His eyes grew large as he saw something that chilled him to the bone. Two figures standing in the woods behind the pond. Too distant to distinguish who they were, but definitely people and not wildlife. He watched as they moved a few yards to their left and lowered themselves to the ground, disappearing from sight. He watched and saw their heads peek over what must be a fallen tree. From the position they were in, he could tell they were holding binoculars and were looking straight at the house.

Carlos had planned for such an occasion, but now that it was here, he was in near panic. He reached for another burner phone he kept in this room for emergencies only. This was clearly an emergency. As he reached for the phone, his hand brushed against a gun he also kept in this little hideaway. Carlos called Gordon.

Gordon didn't recognize the phone number, but with all that was going on, he answered it immediately. "Gordon," he said.

Carlos spoke in quick clipped words. "There are people in the woods watching the house. What should I do?"

"Can you see how many people are there?" Gordon asked.

"I think only two. I watched for a couple of minutes and saw no others," Carlos reported.

Gordon went into an immediate rage. "It's that fucking PI and her cop friend, I bet. Well, they're fucked this time. Carlos don't do anything. Tell Rosa, but neither one of you look out the windows or do anything to scare them away or let them know that we know they're there. Are they in the woods on the south side of the property?"

"Yes, sir," Carlos responded.

"Carlos, I'm coming to the farm and I'll come in from the north side. Unlock the door on the north side of the house. I'll be there in about forty minutes. Do you still have the AR-15 in the house?"

"Yes, sir, it's locked in a closet, but it is ready to go and I'll get it out before you get here."

"Excellent. Have all the children been fed?"

"Yes, they are fed and Rosa is reading to them," Carlos replied.

Gordon was thinking on the move. "Give the kids ice cream laced with their sleeping medication. They must be asleep before we can do anything."

"It will be done," Carlos assured him.

"Do nothing else until I get there. We will end this interference tonight. You've done good, Carlos."

Gordon ended the call as Carlos went to tell Rosa what they must do.

Gordon never asked how Carlos saw the intruders, and Carlos would keep the surveillance closet his little secret. It would tell him when Gordon was arriving and he would then turn off the beeping alert so it would not sound while Gordon was in the house. It sounded like he may be digging holes again tonight.

40
I'LL KILL THEM BOTH

Gordon was on fire. All his synapses were firing. He was focused and his mind felt electric as he quickly changed into dark clothing, armed himself with a silenced handgun, and raced to his car. Two people had been interfering with his operation and that could not stand. He would kill both of them. He had thought about it and remembered a cop named Brogan being at the Gallery event at the same time Kelly Hart was there. *They're in this together and tonight I'll kill them both.* He and Carlos, with his AR-15, could easily overwhelm the two of them and then stick them in a hole on the farm. His rage was heightened by the risk he faced from the Mexican cartel. They were an unforgiving bunch of cutthroats who would not accept excuses and the consequences for failure were nearly always fatal. His thoughts ricocheted as he sped along the back roads to the farm.

Gordon arrived just after 7 p.m. He drove in from the north side of the property and turned his headlights off long before anyone might see them near the farm. No traffic was present tonight. Located only about fifty yards from the farmhouse, was a patch of woods running parallel to the property. It was a trail made by the farm tractor. Gordon drove slowly, bumping along until he was beside the house.

He disabled the overhead light and left the vehicle quietly, pushing his door closed slowly. He carried the silenced gun, loaded with a seven-round clip, in his hand. Before he left home, he made sure there was a round in the chamber. *Calm down so you don't miss anything or make a mistake.* He moved toward the house with his gun in both hands, low and ready should he encounter opposition. He looked up and noticed the upstairs windows were dark, telling him the children had been put to sleep for the night.

He reached the side door and found it unlocked as directed. He was in the mudroom which connected to the kitchen. He found Carlos and Rosa sitting at the kitchen table, curtains drawn. He whispered to them, "Is it safe to come in."

"Yes, Boss. All is good," Carlos said.

Gordon observed the AR-15 propped against the wall behind Carlos. He saw Carlos had a handgun shoved in his waistband. Gordon entered the kitchen and moved to the other side of the round kitchen table.

Lying in the woods was new to Kelly. She had conducted surveillance operations from cars, houses, apartments, and even from an airplane once, but this was her first trip into the woods, at night, to watch. It was pitch dark in the woods. One would think it would be dead silent, but at night, things change in the woods. Critters that have slept or stayed hidden all day long were now on the move. She couldn't see them, but they were there. She could hear them. Leaves rattled, branches snapped and stuff went bump in the night. She reminded herself this was Worcester County, Maryland. *No lions, tigers, scorpions, or snakes here. Oh, shit, there are snakes here! I wonder what kind? Deer are in here, too. Will they step on me? Probably not. They can see in the dark, I think. Spiders are probably crawling all over me by now, looking for some bare skin, or an opening in my clothing to get in.* Brogan lay a few inches from her, perfectly still. *Why isn't he afraid of all these possibilities? City girl meets country. Quit being such a girl!*

Brogan whispered, "Someone is coming to the windows. It's the Hispanic female and she's closing the curtains." One by one all the curtains closed. They had caught a break. The curtains were not lined and they could still could see shadows and make out shapes through them. The lights had been blazing in the upstairs windows and then they were extinguished minutes before she closed the curtains.

"This is probably her nightly routine," Kelly said. "I think she put the kids to bed and now she's closing the curtains for privacy. I know I close my curtains every night."

Gordon slid into the seat across from Rosa and Carlos. "Has anything happened yet?"

"No sir, I think they are still there," Carlos responded. Then he thought to himself, *I'm smart using the words 'I think.' How would I know without looking out the window? I know because I just checked the monitor before turning off the beeper, and I knew you were on your way. I warned Rosa to stay calm and follow orders. I got to stay next to her.*

"Are you guys okay?" Gordon asked.

"Yes, we are fine," Carlos assured him.

In rapid-fire talk, Gordon told them that, after tonight, everything would be closed down. The children would be taken away tomorrow and then all of them would be taking a long-deserved vacation. He reminded Carlos that all the toys and things associated with the kids must be buried. Carlos continued to nod his head in agreement through this dialogue. Rosa did her best to keep eye contact and act normal. Her nerves were on edge, but even she was glad to hear this would be over soon.

Gordon said, "Give me a few minutes to think about a plan of attack so we can remove this threat. I assure you this must be done and the bodies buried deep, before the sun comes up.

"Those people in the woods are the only witnesses who can arrest us and send us to jail. They will be missed, but before anyone goes looking for them, the three of us will be long gone. Free to do what we want and then get together again, possibly at a new location to begin making money again." Carlos and Rosa smiled at this proposition.

Gordon was now pondering his next moves. *I have killed before, but never a cop, and never two people with guns who are probably far better shots than I am, with my periodic visits to the range. I've killed, but I've never been in a gunfight. Will the AR-15 be enough to give me the edge?*

Just like that, he decided what to do about the two witnesses. He stood, lifted his gun and shot Carlos through his right eye. Rosa's mouth opened as she began to scream. She was immediately silenced when Gordon's second shot chipped her front teeth as it entered her mouth and exited the back of her neck. Carlos's head snapped back, but then fell forward to rest on his chest. Blood streamed from his right eye. Rosa's head had fallen slightly to her left as if she was seeking Carlos's shoulder to lean on. *They're probably dead.* Gordon quickly circled behind them and shot each in the back of the head. *No doubt now.* He had realized the two witnesses who could hurt him were sitting across from him the entire time. *Those assholes in the woods know nothing.*

Gordon reached over and grabbed the AR-15 to take with him. He reached into Carlos's jacket pocket, fished out his cell phone and pocketed it. Rosa had never called or been called on her cell, so Gordon spent no time looking for it. The silencer and the sleeping medicine had done their job. The kids slept on as Gordon glanced around, realizing he had never spent enough time here to know the layout. He saw a closed door off the kitchen, but guessed it to be a pantry and ignored it. The time between making his decision and exiting the northside door was less than two minutes. *That's how you get business done.*

41

RUN FOR YOUR LIFE

The sounds of the shots never reached Brogan and Kelly, but the flashes of the gunfire showed clearly through the fabric curtains when a shadowy figure rose and pointed something at the couple across the table. The figure then circled the table, pointing at the heads of the unmoving couple. Two more flashes of light signaled two more shots. It was abundantly clear. They had just witnessed two people being executed.

Brogan and Kelly were on their feet with guns out. They rushed around the pond toward the house. Without verbal communication, they stayed together approaching the front of the house to make entry. Brogan's mind tried to grasp what had just occurred. *Where did the third person come from? No one came up the driveway. Had they been in the house the entire time or did the person come into the house from the north side we couldn't see? I'll figure it out later. Get inside. Are kids inside? Were they being eliminated too?*

Together they mounted the steps to the front porch. Brogan gave a vicious kick to the front door. They were in the house and immediately began clearing rooms on the first floor. The house was silent and an overwhelming smell of gunpowder filled the air. The odor was the distinct smell from a recently fired gun. When they reached the brightly lit kitchen, they found two people seated at the kitchen table. Kelly checked each for a pulse while Brogan continued to provide cover. Kelly found the victims warm to the touch, but neither had a pulse.

"These are the two people that were here the day I came by," Kelly said. She walked to a door standing ajar, "A mudroom. Empties out to the north side of the house." Cautiously, Brogan opened a closed door in the kitchen. They were surprised to see a security room containing monitors that covered all sides of the house. One monitor showed the exact area where they had been lying under surveillance. A handgun was visible on a shelf in the room. Kelly grabbed it and stuck it in her waistband. It was clear the people inside had known they were in the woods. Somebody was cleaning up loose ends.

Brogan pointed a finger toward the ceiling. Kelly nodded her head. She knew they must now clear the upstairs, unsure of what they would find. They heard no noises coming from upstairs, but was someone lying in wait? Knowing kids were up there and knowing their location was too far away for backup to arrive soon, they couldn't wait. This was still an active shooter scene and the rule was you kept moving toward the danger. It did not mean you had to be reckless or stupid.

Brogan took out his cell from his pocket, dialed 911, relayed the address, and indicated the location was an active shooter scene with at least two dead already. He requested police, ambulances, and an alert to social services for an assist with multiple children in need of help. He quickly gave the operator Kelly's and his description and told her they were about to clear the second floor. Hopefully, this would keep the first responders from shooting them by mistake. The call took just a few seconds. They moved to the foot of the steps leading to the second floor. The level of danger increased since someone else might hold the high ground. Guns up, they began their climb.

Gordon knew he was running for his life. He hoped his execution of his two associates had gone unnoticed by those surveilling the house, but he couldn't rely on hope. He ran quickly out to his vehicle, flung open the driver's door, tossed the AR-15 onto the passenger seat and climbed behind the wheel. He cranked the key and the engine sprang to life. A very bumpy, but quick U-turn pointed him back toward the main road. Within seconds, he was at the intersection and thumped up onto the blacktop surface. He headed north. Not the quickest way back to his home, but he would avoid going by those lying in the woods. Inside his chest, his heart was beating fast and hard and a bead of sweat formed along his hairline. In a scary sort of way, he was enjoying the adrenaline rush he was feeling. A smile formed on his lips.

I'm clear and I'm going to get away. I have planned for this moment and now all I have to do is execute my plan. It will take hours for the cops to search the farmhouse, deal with the children, and remove Carlos and Rosa. Those hours are my getaway time. I've got a big head start and I intend to use it. Sooner or later they will be chasing Thomas Gordon, but by then I will be someone else. I'm a ghost slipping into the night. Tomorrow morning, I'll be driving towards a new life in a new location.

Training took over and they moved in perfect harmony up the staircase. They met no resistance and stood silently on the wood floor in the hallway. A single night light plugged into a receptacle provided their only lighting. The hallway presented them with four closed doors. Rather than violently breaching the doors, they each hugged a wall and Brogan called out, "Police! Open the door and show your hands. Come out now and you won't be hurt."

Nothing happened. He repeated his message, but silence was the only answer. Brogan and Kelly moved in unison to the first door, which was on the left. The door was unlocked and the knob turned with ease. Brogan gave it a push and it swung inward revealing a bathroom. Kelly went in. The door was against a wall, so no one could be hiding behind it. The shower curtain was closed. She turned the bathroom light on while simultaneously ripping the shower curtain back. No one was there. No place else to hide. She pointed to a camera mounted in a corner near the ceiling. It was pointed at the tub. Brogan's steely blue eyes turned to flint as they registered the possible horrors these kids had been forced to endure.

Further down the hallway, they tested a door on the right side and found it unlocked. Again, it swung inward exposing a darkened room. Brogan took a calculated risk, reached around the door jamb, and found a light switch on the wall. He flicked it and swiftly pulled his hand back to the safety of the hall. Nothing happened. Brogan and Kelly exchanged hand signals and then breached the door. She went in low, covering the left side of the room. Brogan went in high, covering the right side of the room. Nothing happened. A double bed was pushed against a wall. A small lump in the center of the bed gave them pause. Something was wrapped in a sheet. It was not moving. Kelly approached carefully, while Brogan covered the rest of the hallway.

She nudged the sheet while pointing her gun directly at it. It moved slightly, but rolled back to its original position. *Obviously, not pillows.* Kelly gently tugged at a corner of the sheet and dark hair fell from a child's head. Kelly violently pulled the sheet off, thinking whomever it covered may be suffocating. Kelly stared at the body of a small female child. *Too late for this baby.*

Brogan's heart clenched when he saw the child was dead. His attention turned to the final two doors. There was no time to waste. Kelly joined him and they moved down the hallway. The rooms were revealed without encountering any opposition. In one room, two small boys were sleeping. In the other room, six little girls were also asleep. Kelly unsuccessfully tried to awaken one of the boys, but he would not be roused. His pulse was strong, but his sleep was abnormally deep. Kelly turned to Brogan and said, "I think these kids have been drugged. We need medical help here now!"

Brogan was standing on the lighted front porch holding his badge in his hand raised high with his other hand in a position of surrender when the first sheriff's deputy roared up the driveway, turned his car sideways, and then sought cover behind the hood of his car. Gun in hand, he evaluated Brogan as a possible threat. Second and third police cars arrived. An ambulance followed closely behind.

Brogan was able to diffuse the tension and soon the ambulance crew entered the home and joined Kelly on the second floor. A second ambulance arrived and additional medical attention was directed upstairs. Kelly found herself in the way and returned downstairs to be with Brogan.

They went directly to the security room and examined the equipment. Kelly was far more astute with surveillance equipment and quickly found out how to rewind the video on any of the cameras. Their focus was on the north side. Their effort was rewarded when they observed a vehicle traversing along the woods and then stopping parallel to the house. A figure emerged and walked at a hurried pace toward the farmhouse. About halfway to his destination, the figure looked upward as if examining the windows or roof line. Kelly reacted. "I know that guy. I met him at the Gallery event. He came up to me and introduced himself. His name is Thomas Gordon."

Brogan responded, "I think I do too. That's the guy we called about the property today. I've seen him at numerous events in the county where the politicians and high-dollar folks get together. What the hell is he doing here? Let me call my office. PCO Scott is working tonight and if anybody can track this fuck, she can."

42
CHASING THE GHOST

Maggie Scott had been monitoring the police activity at the southern end of the county and was only moderately surprised that Brogan was in the middle of it. She raised an eyebrow when Brogan called.

"Scott, Kelly Hart and I were on a surveillance detail that ended up in a double homicide. I need your help. The only solid lead I have is an individual named Thomas Gordon who owns a real estate business in Sandpiper. I need everything you can find on him. Business and home address, full description including date of birth, any vehicles registered to him or his real estate business. Scott, this is important. I think we've stumbled onto a human trafficking operation that has been preying on kids under the age of six. I believe he just murdered two of his associates to keep them from talking. He's on the loose and we need to bring him in. Call me the second you have anything you believe will be helpful. I've seen you in action. Just do your thing and then call me. Thanks in advance."

Kelly and Brogan reviewed the tape again and paid more attention to the car Gordon arrived in. Although the video was in black and white, the vehicle appeared to be light gray in color. It could have been a Lexus or a Cadillac. It was a four-door car. Not an SUV. They asked one of the deputies to put out an immediate BOLO on a car fitting their vague description and added a warning to be cautious and to obtain backup before stopping, as the operator was probably armed and should be considered extremely dangerous. Brogan knew this was a long shot as most of the cops working in this area were parked in the front yard.

Crime scene techs and the medical examiner had arrived on the scene. In spite of the remote location, things were running rather smoothly. An hour had passed since the shootings. Detectives for the sheriff's office had claimed jurisdiction and had already done a preliminary interview of Brogan and Kelly to find out what happened. Additional law enforcement was called in to assist with a thorough search of the residence once a search warrant had been obtained. A member of the state's attorney's office and a deputy were with a judge trying to secure the warrant.

The Department of Social Services sent four workers to the scene. Two of them spoke fluent Spanish. Slowly, the children were waking up. Bewildered and afraid, many of them were crying and asking for Rosa. But she could not hear their cries. They would be the only ones who cried for Rosa after the details of this investigation leaked out.

43

HE'S GETTING AWAY

Twenty-three minutes after Brogan spoke with PCO Scott, she called back with some of the information needed. Despite the pressure, Scott spoke in a professional and level tone. "His name is Thomas Gordon, and he owns the Thomas Gordon Real Estate Company headquartered in Sandpiper and with an office in Easton. He has been in business for approximately three years and here is where it gets interesting. I can't find any record of him before three years ago. He owns a home in Snow Hill worth over two million dollars, purchased three years ago. He lives at 13254 River View Drive, Snow Hill, MD. The house sits on a three-acre property facing the Pocomoke River. His business and personal banking are done through the Virginia Maryland Trust Company with branches in Sandpiper and Snow Hill, Maryland, and Norfolk, Virginia. Don't ask me how I know this. The branch office here in Sandpiper is only two streets away from his office. He has a 2022 Lexus Sedan registered to him at the Snow Hill address. I will text you a copy of his current driver's license. His driving record begins three years ago and he has no tickets or fines.

I'm still digging and have a couple of friends who are checking databases that are unavailable to me. Don't ask about that either. He has no criminal record and a perfect credit history. I'll get back to you as soon as I have more."

"Great job, Scott. I can always count on you to get the intelligence."

Brogan contemplated their next move. He looked at Kelly and said, "There's nothing else for us here. If the sheriff's office finds anything, they can call me. The deputies will be a while gathering the children and arranging transport to Social Services. They have their hands full. Gordon has a home approximately fifteen minutes from here on the Pocomoke River. We need to go there and see if that's where he's hiding. I'll call in my other detectives, Patty Ryan and Bob Carr, and have them begin search warrants for his business in Sandpiper, his car, and his home in Snow Hill. Tomorrow, if we need to, we'll go after bank records with a warrant."

Brogan cornered the deputy in charge, Detective Sergeant VanHorn, and told him that he and Kelly were going to get out of their way and that if they needed anything from them, just call. He promised they would go to the sheriff's office the next day to give formal statements. With dead bodies, kids, and searches all pulling him in different directions, the detective told Brogan he appreciated their help and that he, or one of the other detectives, would take their statement in the morning. Kelly and Brogan quietly cleared the scene and walked to the shoulder of the road to their vehicle still concealed near the fence. No one had asked how they got to the scene or where their vehicle was. No one had even asked how the house had come under surveillance. The farmhouse looked like a war zone and a lot can be missed in the fog of war.

When they got to Brogan's car, he called his detectives and briefed them on what had occurred and the need for search warrants. He suggested they call the state's attorney's office for support. He promised to keep them abreast of any new information as it developed.

Brogan said, "I want you to let PCO Scott know what you're doing so that she can provide you with information that would enhance the probable cause in the search warrants. All right guys, call me if you need anything."

Brogan sat silently for a minute and then began searching his phone for a particular phone number. He found it and pushed send. A few seconds later it was answered. "This is Detective Zigmeister. Can I help you?"

"Yes, Sergeant, I think you can. This is Brogan. I believe we have found the reason for the shooting in Williamsburg and may have identified the guy who ordered the hit."

"You have my attention, Brogan. Regardless of what I was doing, I'm all ears now."

After almost ten minutes of talking, Brogan had revealed everything he currently knew.

"Sergeant, Thomas Gordon is on the run and might flee to the south to get out of Maryland."

Zigmeister responded, "I'll immediately alert all Virginia troopers and local police patrolling along the route into Virginia to search aggressively for the suspect and his known vehicle. I'll start by posting troopers at the Maryland-Virginia line. Keep me informed."

Brogan knew Zigmeister would not sleep tonight. He felt a common brotherhood with Zigmeister and knew he was as wound up as tight as Brogan was.

Brogan recognized he had possibly wasted valuable time,

but he appreciated the wheels of justice had been set in motion, and Gordon couldn't escape now that traps had been set. Brogan needed more information to tighten the noose on Gordon. He knew where to find it and began driving toward River View Drive.

Kelly turned to Brogan. "Is he getting away?"

Brogan flashed a quick smile and said, "No, not on our watch. We'll get him."

Kelly grew quiet while considering what Brogan had said. *Not on our watch. We're a team. We have a common goal and we have each other's back.* Kelly believed with all her heart that they would get this loathsome individual. She was not sure how, but she was certain that she and Brogan would find a way.

44

SOMETHING IS KEEPING HIM CLOSE

They cruised by Gordon's house. By all standards, it was truly a mansion. His home was picturesque, surrounded by up lighting that enhanced the stone workmanship on the exterior of the home. The house had a black gated driveway, but the gate was open. Several windows showed lighting from lamps within, a warm and welcoming sight.

To Brogan, an open gate was an invitation to come in and visit. He hoped that Gordon had not realized they were on to him and would try to bluff away any accusations he and Kelly made. Brogan decided this guy would be arrested on sight and any resistance would be met with overwhelming force. He could not shake the sight of the small, brown children at the farm. They were there to be sold into slavery, more depraved than most people could even imagine. Someone must be held accountable and the unexplained wealth of Gordon was now explainable.

Kelly and Brogan parked in front of the house in the circular driveway. No one came outside to greet them. They walked between the Greek-inspired massive columns on the porch. The porch was adorned with rich, dark brown wicker furniture. Light, tan cushions beckoned a visitor to sit and wait for a server to appear with drinks. Kelly thought the porch furniture was unusual at this time of the year, but reconsidered the possibility that it was all for show. Rich people do that kind of thing. The guy who lived here sickened her even more. He made his money off the backs of small children.

The front door was a massive wood creation with wildlife carvings. Ducks, dogs, fields, and armed hunters were all present. The cost must have been astronomical. A lighted doorbell glowed on the door frame. The porch was fully lit, making Kelly and Brogan feel entirely exposed. Brogan and Kelly exchanged a look. Brogan signaled her to step away from the door as he pushed the doorbell. They could hear it ringing inside the house. Nothing happened. No dogs barked and no one opened the door. Brogan tried it again. It sounded loud even from outside where they stood at the ready. Still no response. Brogan turned a decorative door knob and the door opened. It was nearly 9 p.m. so the door should probably be locked, but it was the Eastern Shore and locking doors was still optional.

They entered a grand foyer. Brogan called out, "Mr. Gordon, this is Detective Brogan. Please show yourself." Nothing. He tried again and got no answer.

"Brogan, there could be kids sleeping in this house," Kelly said. "We've got to take a look for their safety."

Brogan chuckled to himself. *Sounds like a line that will be used in court when we get accused of making an illegal search.* He wished he had thought of it. They decided to clear the house, looking for the children, concerned about their safety. It took almost an hour to check all the rooms. Brogan cautioned Kelly not to search in places where a child could not be concealed. He didn't want to lose this bastard on a technicality. They were about to give it up and regroup outside to give the situation more thought.

Brogan suggested they take one final look in Gordon's home office. He might have left a note or other communication about where he had gone or how to reach him. Brogan told Kelly, "This never happened," as his search for the note extended into opening drawers and flipping through personal papers. One drawer had nothing but brochures of cruises, vacation locations, guided tours, horseback riding, and hiking locations. They searched all the drawers and reviewed the personal papers, but they did not find any incriminating documents or clues that showed where Gordon might be.

At 10:15, Brogan's phone rang. PCO Scott said, "A Snow Hill police officer has found Gordon's car parked near the edge of town in a Dollar Store parking lot. It has been cleaned out and there is no sign of Gordon." Brogan wondered, *does he have another accomplice who's helping him escape? Maybe he has a safe house near where he abandoned his vehicle? I bet he has a second vehicle that he's switched into.*

Scott continued, "The Snow Hill guy says the car can't have been there more than an hour or so because he had patrolled that lot and it wasn't there before."

"Why is Gordon still in the area?" Brogan thought out loud. "He should be long gone by now. If he had just fled, he could be deep in Virginia by now. Why is he staying around?"

"Fuck if I know, keep looking," said Scott.

Brogan turned to Kelly and said, "A man might hang around for a woman, but no one has said he has a wife or even a girlfriend. What else would hold him close?" *Money!* "Maybe he has money concealed somewhere that he needs to begin his flight from justice. Where would Gordon hide money? Maybe in plain sight. Maybe he needs to make a withdrawal from his bank. An ATM will only give him about three hundred dollars on any single day, but a large business account might finance a trip abroad or at least across the country."

"You may be right. How are we going to find out?" asked Kelly.

Brogan called Scott back, "One other thing, can you get the name and phone number of the president of the Maryland Virginia Trust in Sandpiper? If you can, I'm going to wake him up."

Brogan remembered that among the brochures in the office, there was a county map. He retrieved it and spread it out on the large kitchen island. He found a black marker and put a mark at the house where they were, and then another mark at the Dollar General Store. He estimated they were about five miles apart. *What am I missing?*

Kelly studied the map and suggested he might be on foot because he was afraid of being arrested while driving his car. *Where would he go and why would he abandon his vehicle at the Dollar Store?*

Kelly asked Brogan for the marker and drew what she estimated to be a one-mile circle around the Dollar Store. A wanted man, walking more than a mile or two, would be taking a huge risk. She didn't think Gordon was foolish enough to try it and he was not prone to take risks. She studied the map for a safe harbor for Gordon. If she found nothing, she would expand the circle by a mile and search again.

Brogan looked over Kelly's shoulder and tried to figure out where Gordon might have gone. A couple of warehouses were within the circle, but Brogan knew these places and knew they were locked and guarded by lights and cameras. Neither was a place a fugitive would run to. He saw a storage facility just outside the circle and something clicked. Brogan ran back into Gordon's office and jerked open the brochure drawer and spread them across the desk. He rummaged through them and there it was. A brochure for the storage facility. He scanned the verbiage, and it touted the size of their storage units, including ones big enough to house a car. "That fucker has another car," Brogan barked.

Brogan grabbed Kelly's hand and said, "We gotta go. Bring the map." Brogan was waving the brochure from the storage facility. It was called "Easy Access Storage" and it was about eight miles away.

Kelly wasn't sure what was going on, but if Brogan thought they had a lead, she trusted him. He explained his excitement as the car charged down the driveway and made a left. Brogan floored the accelerator, throwing Kelly against her seat as they sped into the night. Kelly was not used to being pinned to her seat for what seemed to be an eternity. She was then thrown into her seat belt as Brogan came to an abrupt stop in front of a storage facility. Six long buildings separated by wide driveways laid behind a high, wrought-iron fence. The gate was closed. The sign told renters to use their passcode to enter and the gate would close behind them. There was also a button to alert the caretaker and speak to them through an in-house intercom system. The car had barely stopped before Brogan was out and leaning into the button as if pushing hard would make it work better.

Kelly heard a female voice come through the intercom system, but was unable to hear what she was saying. Brogan's voice boomed. "Detective Brogan here on an urgent police matter. Please open the gate or come to the gate, so I can explain what's going on." The female voice said something, and Brogan walked back to the car and leaned on the door. He bent down and said to Kelly, "The owner is on her way to the gate to let us in." The ten minutes, which seemed like ten hours, passed before a tall woman appeared heading for the gate. As she moved across areas of the storage unit property, the motion-sensor lights came alive turning dark into day. Brogan met her at the gate. Kelly remained in the passenger seat watching, but did not hear the exchange. Brogan was very animated, holding his identification card so the woman could examine it. The woman seemed troubled that a cop from Sandpiper would try to get onto a property in Snow Hill. Kelly thought the woman was lucky to have the fence between herself and Brogan. She was wasting his time and there was no time to waste. The woman raised her cell phone to her ear, and after a brief conversation, pushed a button on her side of the fence and the gate swung inward slowly.

Brogan returned to the car and said, "She called the sheriff's office and they told her to let me in." He pulled his car up to the sign that said Office.

The woman was already inside, lighting up the place. "I'm sorry. I just don't know you and there are so many people trying to scam me. I wanted to be sure."

Now that Brogan was getting his way, his demeanor cooled quickly. "You did the right thing. Don't ever open that gate at night to someone you don't know." Kelly smiled. *Of course, that rule doesn't apply to you!*

The woman identified herself as Tammy Johnson, and Brogan told her they were looking for a suspected murderer and, during their investigation, the name Thomas Gordon had come up and a brochure at his home had led them to her door.

Tammy shook her head and said, "Do you think I'm in danger?"

Brogan tried to reassure her and said, "There is no reason to believe you are. The information you provide will just help further the investigation. Tammy, do you have a client named Thomas Gordon?"

Without checking any records, she said, "Yes, I do. He's had a large storage unit here for at least three years. Pays a year's rent, all at one time, at the beginning of each year. He comes here every few months and goes into the unit for about an hour and then leaves. I'm not nosey, but I can be curious. One day when he came, I went down the aisle where his unit is and opened a vacant unit across from him. I pretended to be attending to that unit, but I was really checking him out. He has a car in there. I saw it. He has it up on jacks or something because the tires are off the ground. He had the car running and was revving the engine. I don't know cars, but the engine was loud, and I was afraid it was going to jump off the jacks and crash into the units across from him. It didn't jump off, of course, and he shut it off after a few minutes. There is electricity in there and I think he has something plugged into the engine compartment. A friend of mine, whom I told about it, suggested it might be a trickle charger to keep the battery charged. The guy's a little weird, but friendly. Is he a witness or a potential victim?" Tammy asked.

Kelly responded, "Why do you ask that question?"

"Well, maybe I should have told you right away, but he was here tonight. Came in here on foot and opened the gate and walked down to his unit. He's never been here at night before and being on foot was unusual too. I figured he had broken down in his other car and was looking for transportation. Sure enough, after about fifteen minutes, he drives out of his unit in the car and leaves. I checked, and he's closed his unit and locked it up, but I'm pretty sure there's nothing in there except maybe those jacks. Oh yeah, almost forgot. The one time I did see him in there, he had a red plastic gas can and was putting gas in his car."

Brogan was dumbfounded that Tammy had held the best for last. *I should slap this woman silly, but I am the one that didn't tell her he was our suspect.*

Brogan took a breath. "How long has he been gone?"

"Maybe fifteen minutes. Have I done something wrong?"

"No Tammy, you haven't. Did you get a good look at the car when he left?"

"No, I'm sorry, I glanced at it as he went out the gate, but all I saw was a dark car with a loud motor. It was a two-door if that helps. I didn't see any tags or stickers on the car. Wait 'til I tell my friends a murderer was hiding his car here."

Kelly gave her a warning look, "We didn't say he killed anyone. This is an open investigation, so we're not at liberty to talk about it. Soon the press will get hold of this story and it will all come out. We appreciate your help tonight. If Gordon comes back or contacts you, call 911 immediately and don't let him in your house no matter what he says."

"Don't worry," Tammy replied, "I have a gun and I know how to use it. I'll be extra careful until I hear he's been caught."

Brogan made another call. Zigmeister answered after one ring. "Did you get him?"

"No not yet, but we found out he's got another car and we know it's a dark color and it has a loud motor like a race car and it's a two-door. No make or model yet, but he could be anywhere by now. I thought I'd be waking you up."

"No, you didn't. You knew I'd be awake and out on the street. I'm near the Maryland-Virginia line, but if he has a different car, he may have slipped by us."

"I don't think so," said Brogan. "He hasn't had time to make the Virginia line yet, but if that's where he's headed, he should be there soon. I'm texting you a copy of his driver's license with his picture. Then you'll have his face and a loud motor to look for. How can you miss?"

"Anything else we can work on?" Zigmeister asked.

"Maybe. It's a slim possibility that he needs money to jump-start his trip. Maryland Virginia Trust Company is his bank and there's a branch near his office in Sandpiper and Snow Hill. However, there's a branch in Norfolk, Virginia. Any chance you can get someone to cover that branch in case he slides in there to use the ATM? Before you say anything, I don't believe ATM money will be what he's after. He may be there when they open to get what he needs. How about someone covering it right through opening, until about noon tomorrow?"

Zigmeister came back sarcastically. "Sure, I'll roll out the whole fucking Virginia State Police to look for the guy who ordered your head caved in. We better catch this guy, or I'll have a lot of explaining to do for assigning so much manpower to help out Sandpiper fucking PD."

"Yeah, I know it's a heavy lift," Brogan said, "but you have broad shoulders, so I know you can handle it. If that probationer female sharpshooter is working, get her somewhere close if we need her."

Zigmeister laughed and hung up, not giving the suggestion the importance of an answer. The last thing that a new trooper needed is a second shooting.

Brogan's cell phone rang and he didn't recognize the number. He answered, "Brogan."

"Hi, this is Melvin Weaver. I'm the president of the Maryland Virginia Trust branch in Sandpiper. Your PCO tells me you may need some help with a guy named Thomas Gordon. What can I do to help?"

Brogan explained the situation to Weaver. "Gordon is a suspect in a felony case I'm working, and I'd like to get a look at his bank records. I would like to have one of my detectives come by in the morning, so we can start to get legal access. He will be able to share with you the name of a state's attorney who is helping with this investigation."

Weaver said, "Look, I get in the bank around 8 a.m. to get stuff done before we open. Can your detective meet me there at 8? We should be able to work out what needs to be done before the phones start ringing at 9."

"He'll be there," Brogan assures him before hanging up. He then texted Detective Bob Carr and directed him to meet Weaver at 8 at the Sandpiper branch of the bank. Carr acknowledged the text. Brogan slid his phone back into his pocket.

There were a lot of moving parts at this point. He and Kelly had identified the right guy and now only needed something in this investigation to break it wide open. He had to tell Kelly they would camp out within view of the drive-thru at the Snow Hill bank branch. It was almost midnight. They would take turns sleeping. It was going to be another long night.

Brogan fired off a long voice email to the chief, explaining all that had happened. He left it up to the chief on how much to tell the mayor about one of the town's upstanding citizens. This would set the town buzzing again. Things were just about back to normal after last year's debacle. The sunrise would be in about six and a half hours. Maybe a new day would give them a new perspective. He was kind of wishing he would get the opportunity to sleep with Kelly, but not in the front seat of a car and especially not while one slept and the other stayed awake. When this was over, he was looking forward to a few days off from work. *Maybe I can talk Kelly into going someplace together. Too soon for that kind of thinking, better stay focused on this case before thinking about what's to follow.*

45
Gone To Ground

"Pocomoke City Welcomes You," read the sign. The light said, "Vacancy," even though two of the letters in the word vacancy were dark. The parking lot was gravel and the motel was circa 1960s. Gordon was not sure he would be able to sleep in this place. He could only imagine what kind of action the beds in this place had seen. Still, it was 11:15 p.m. and most of the other motels in the area had turned their signs off or read, "No Vacancy."

He had his car and he had gotten something to eat. Now he needed a few hours of rest before he completed his plan to disappear. One more little hoop to jump through and Thomas Gordon would be no more.

A tiny bell rang when he opened the door to the office. The lighting was dim, not to set a mood unless that mood is dirty. *What a dump.* A man of undetermined age came through a curtain that protected a doorway off the office. Somewhat surprisingly, he appeared to be wide awake and had a coffee cup in his hand. He looked past Gordon to the car parked in front of the office. He appeared to be surprised there was no bimbo sitting shotgun. He turned to Gordon and smiled, revealing a few missing teeth. "How can I help you, partner?" he asked.

"Need a room for the night."

"Just you?"

"Yep, flying solo tonight. I keep falling asleep, so I figured I'd catch a couple of hours before hitting the road again," Gordon told him.

"Okay, we got some vacancies," the guy said while looking down at a map covered in plastic that showed the layout of the motel. "Any rooms without an X through them are available."

Gordon looked at the layout. This was a one-story building with eight rooms facing the road and eight rooms facing the parking lot and woods in the rear. Gordon put his finger on room number sixteen. It was in the back and was the furthest from the office and the highway. No one was in rooms 14 or 15.

The guy said, "Okay, that'll be fifty dollars and I'll need to see some ID to register you."

Gordon produced a hundred-dollar bill and said, "My name is Benjamin. Mr. Benjamin and I left my ID at home if that's okay."

The hundred-dollar bill disappeared from the counter and was replaced with a green oblong plastic disc bearing the number 16 and a single key attached. Gordon hadn't known these kinds of places still existed, but he was glad they did.

"Enjoy your stay, Mr. Benjamin. There are clean towels in your room and the sheets were put on fresh today. Dial 8 if you need the office. We don't have no cable, so the TV only gets three local channels."

Gordon scooped up the key. "Thanks," he said and headed

out the door and into his car. He pulled into a parking slot in front of room 15 as a precaution. His room was a tad better than expected, but it was not the kind of place you'd want to visit more than once. Everything in the room was thread-bare from years of repeated use, with the typical burgundy and hunter-green motif. The bathroom showed a little rust around the fixtures, but was clean with a paper-wrapped bar of soap on the sink. No body wash, shampoo, lotion, or other niceties were being offered.

Gordon was bone tired, and after checking the bed and finding no running roaches, he laid down on top of the spread without removing his clothes. He might have to leave in a hurry, so he was prepared. He placed his handgun on the side table next to his backpack. The AR-15 was locked in the trunk of the car and the car alarm was set.

He knew he needed to be out of there by 7 a.m. to be in Snow Hill by a little after 8. He was going backward, but he felt safer than trying to hide in the town. Gordon wanted to be the first through the door when the bank opened. A quick trip into the safe deposit room, clean out his box, and head south, leaving Maryland in his rearview mirror. Having a good plan was everything. Going to ground in this shabby ass motel was not in the plan, but you had to be flexible to survive. He set the alarm on his watch so he wouldn't oversleep. He closed his eyes and he was gone.

46

SNEAKING AROUND SNOW HILL

The sun was rising in the sleepy little town of Snow Hill. The county's seat of government was coming awake. Unknown to the residents, armed combatants were merging for a possible confrontation.

Kelly snored softly while slumped in the front passenger seat. It was her turn to take the watch an hour ago, but Brogan didn't have the heart to wake the sleeping beauty. *She'll be pissed when she finds out what I've done, but she'll come to understand I've begun to elevate her to a pedestal over which she has no control. She's in this investigation for the long haul. Not complaining, not wanting to go home. She is a fearless companion.*

The distance to the bank was considerable, but it was an unobstructed view from their parking spot. The spot was next to the end of a strip mall that sat slightly elevated behind the bank. The last vehicle through the drive-thru took place around 1 a.m. Brogan watched a white pickup truck advertising a local construction company through his binoculars. The older driver spent only a few minutes completing his transaction. A Snow Hill police officer had passed by only once during the night. Chief Leonard had been notified of the surveillance and potential danger that would arise if Gordon were to show up. Brogan knew Chief Leonard well and could count on his cooperation without question.

Chief Leonard had spoken by phone to his lone night shift officer and told him to avoid the area near the bank, but to be ready to respond to a dangerous situation if called upon. Officer Franks was a seven-year veteran and was hyped at the chance his normally quiet shift might turn into something far more exciting. He was parked about two miles away with a radar gun hanging on his window. It was turned off and was used as a prop for his presence on a road that would take him directly to the bank.

A low, but persistent beeping awakened Gordon. He pushed a button on his watch and silence washed over him. It took him a few seconds to realize where he was, but when he did, he became fully awake and moving. It was 7:00 a.m., time to get going. If he was careful and kept to his plan, he would escape today. Gordon was still dressed, so he spent just a few minutes in the bathroom cleaning up. He pulled a shaving kit from his backpack. He shaved and brushed his teeth. His hair was wild from sleeping on it, but a handful of water rubbed all over his head, followed by the assistance of his small brush, made him look almost human. He put some drops in his eyes to clear the red out. He pulled a dark blue Ralph Lauren Polo baseball cap low on his head and put on a pair of Maui Jim Baby Beach aviator sunglasses. A perfect disguise for a man on the run.

Good to go, he peeked out the curtained window and saw

his car sitting as he'd left it. Nobody was stirring but him. Out the door in minutes, he retrieved the AR-15 from the trunk, put it on the back seat within easy reach, and covered it with a blanket. Gordon was behind the wheel heading north. He detoured into a McDonald's drive-thru for a coffee and a sausage biscuit. Fully focused on the road leading to Snow Hill, he paid strict attention to the speed limits. He was well aware of the engine noise produced by the three-year-old metallic-blue Camaro muscle car he was driving. It was a gorgeous car and was faster than most of the police cars in the area.

Gordon rolled cautiously into Snow Hill. It was 8:15 in the morning and the town had come alive with people going to work and populating breakfast venues. School buses were moving about after their morning drop off of children to school. Gordon knew the town well, having spent a great deal of time driving its streets and weighing possible escape routes. The bank would open in forty-five minutes, so he was killing time while performing counter-surveillance moves. He had already decided he would park away from the bank, so his car would not be captured by their ever-present cameras. He thought his hat and sunglasses would give him sufficient cover as a pedestrian walking the sunny streets near the bank. In the back seat was a well-used briefcase he would carry as a prop when going into the bank.

There was a small delivery road that led to the back of a strip shopping center behind the bank. As long as he didn't block a loading door, this might be a good place to park. He pulled into an area he felt would be safe and left his vehicle locked and pointed out for a quick getaway. Gordon rounded the corner of the building and immediately stopped and stepped back quickly behind the building. *Holy shit, that was close.* Parked on the side, near the front of the building, was an unmarked police car. In a second, he was around the corner thinking he saw the outline of two people sitting in the car. *It's the fucking cop and his PI partner.* His mind shifted to survival mode. *I'll use the AR-15 and take out these two assholes. Bad idea, disregard that idea and come up with a better plan. I'll move my car and come to the bank at an angle that will be invisible to the police car. I need to check possible surveillance cameras on the other side of the bank before going in.* Gordon returned to his car and drove slowly and quietly away.

Gordon found a parking space at a busy restaurant on the main road leading by the bank. Parking in plain sight was the plan. He would walk the two blocks to the bank and use the natural cover of the businesses along the way. It was now 9:00 am. *Time to shit or get off the pot.* Gordon jammed his handgun into his waistband, hiding it with his jacket. He strolled slowly toward his destiny, never turned his head searching for trouble, but used his peripheral vision and sunglasses to scan his surroundings. *So far, so good.* If his timing was right, he would reach the bank about ten minutes after it had opened. He wanted the employees to be attending to other customers so his entrance wouldn't bring any special attention to him.

Just before entering the door to the bank, he removed his hat and sunglasses. The hat stayed in his left hand with his briefcase and the sunglasses were hanging on the zipper of his jacket. *Don't want to go into the bank looking like a potential bank robber.* He resisted the urge to turn and run when he looked through the interior glass windows of the bank president's office. Two people faced the president with their backs to Gordon. He recognized them at once. *It's that Detective Brogan and PI Kelly Hart. I was right. They were the two in the car watching the bank.* Gordon's right gun hand hovered close to the bottom of his jacket. *This shit is about to get real.* Gordon saw one of the female clerks coming out of an employee restroom hidden in a small alcove. He quickly approached the clerks and said, "Hi, can you help me? I have an emergency."

Her eyes widened. "What's your emergency?"

Gordon had his back to Kelly and Brogan as he explained, "I got a call last night from New York where my mother lives. She's fallen and has been taken to the hospital. The hospital is saying she's not badly injured, but can no longer live alone. They say her balance problems will result in her falling again. They recommend I find a facility where she can receive care and monitoring. She just turned ninety, two months ago. I have important records concerning my mother in my safe-deposit box here at the bank. Can you help me retrieve all these documents and other items I'll need to take to New York? Of course, I'm a customer of the bank and I have my identification and my key to the box." *This clerk is buying my story. This was the perfect ruse.*

"Yes, sir, I can help you if you'll just step this way." She led Gordon from the lobby into a private area of the bank where the safe deposit room was located. After checking his identification and verifying he had a key to the box, she inserted her key into the box while Gordon inserted the key he had removed from around his neck. The box slid easily from its nook in the wall. The clerk excused herself from the room and said she would be nearby when he was ready to leave.

Once the door closed, Gordon hurriedly lifted the lid. Everything was as he had left it. All the items were neatly packed into a nylon gym-sized duffel bag. He placed the safe-deposit box on the waist-high table that occupied the center of the room. He unzipped the bag and saw its contents were undisturbed. He re-zipped it and pulled it from the box. Gordon decided to abandon the briefcase, sitting it next to the wall. He closed and returned the now-empty box to its slot. He took a deep breath. *It takes a big set of balls to do what I'm about to do.*

He pulled the room's door open and the clerk was standing just a few feet away looking at her cell phone. She looked up and her eyes widened as she saw the duffel bag now slung over Gordon's shoulder. "Wow," she said. "You had a lot of stuff in your box. Will you still be needing the box?"

Gordon smiled at her. "Oh yes. When I return from New York, most of this will go back in my box. I just don't have time to go through it all now. I'll have time when I get on the train. Thank you so much for helping me today." The clerk smiled, nodded, and stepped aside to let Gordon pass. This entire give-and-take, plus emptying the box of his money and new ID, took less than five minutes. He glanced toward the president's office and saw everyone was still in place talking. He strode out the door, hat and sunglasses back in place, strolling up the street with an air of confidence in his step. The bank clerk checked the safe deposit room and saw the briefcase leaning on the wall. She remembered Mr. Gordon brought it with him. She grabbed it and rushed to the bank lobby. She moved to the front door and stepped outside. *He's gone, but where?*

She stood there for about a minute, thinking he'll realize his oversight and return. She then observed a dark blue muscle car drive past the bank. The driver was wearing a baseball cap and sunglasses. *Could that be Mr. Gordon? I do believe he was wearing that jacket.* She yelled out and signaled to him with the briefcase waving in her hand. She was surprised when he continued to look straight ahead. She couldn't believe he hadn't seen her or acknowledged her. She went back into the bank and saw the bank president leaving the copy machine and passing out papers to other employees.

She approached him, and he handed her a blown-up picture of Mr. Gordon. The words **Use Caution Extremely Dangerous** in bold letters were under the photo. She looked the bank manager in the eye and said, "Mr. Gordon was here. He just left with the contents of his safe-deposit box."

Brogan and Kelly rushed to her side and Kelly asked, "What did you just say about Gordon?" The bank clerk repeated her statement. "He was just here. He took everything in his safe-deposit box."

The man growled, "Where did he go?" The clerk was confused and answered automatically to his demanding tone. "He just went by the bank in a dark blue car. He's wearing a baseball cap and sunglasses. He's headed toward Route 113. He left his briefcase."

She lifted the case so everyone could see it. She offered no resistance as Brogan removed it from her hand and snapped it open. It was empty! Brogan handed the case back to the clerk, turned to Kelly, and said, "Let's go."

Both sprinted towards the exit and entered Brogan's car parked near the rear of the bank. Brogan left tire prints on the road, as he roared from the parking lot onto main street, after seeing it was clear. Gordon only had a few minutes head start. Maybe they could catch him before he got too far. They scanned the road ahead looking for a blue car. They drove toward Route 113 knowing a T-intersection was ahead. A left turn would take them toward Sandpiper and a right turn to Pocomoke City. "We need more eyes looking for this car," he told Kelly.

The last mile to the 113 intersection was flat and clear. At the intersection, still half a mile away, there was a flash of brake lights and then another flash of blue going right without a turn signal. Just as quickly, it disappeared behind a corner house. Brogan saw his target. It was balls to the wall now. Brogan made the turn to go south on 113. After completing his turn, Brogan grabbed his mike.

"Car 3 to Headquarters, I'm in pursuit of a dark blue, two-door vehicle traveling south on 113 toward Pocomoke. The driver is the suspect in the double homicide that occurred last night."

Brogan was glad the undercover car he was driving had been seized by the department from a drug dealer. He had driven it before and knew it had a lot of horsepower and was faster than any unmarked car they had in their fleet. Maybe the wheels of justice had just taken a turn in the right direction.

47

PURSUIT

The roar of the engine and the rush of the wind was deaf-ening as they continued their pursuit south. Radio chat-ter increased, but it became clear there were no cars in the immediate area. Pocomoke City PD advised their cars were on the wrong side of Pocomoke handling a violent domestic call. If the chase turned north on Route 13, they would try to intercept. If it turned south on Route 13, they would get there too late.

Kelly had never been the passenger in a chase like this one. Lacking the heavy traffic, multiple traffic control signals, and devices of the Baltimore streets, this was wide-open driv-ing. The flatland and primarily straight roads of the Eastern Shore were conducive to high-speed driving. Brogan made the turn clocking thirty miles an hour without stopping. Kelly was not fully prepared and was thrown violently around in her seat. A Coke can worthy of an antique collector's notice rolled from under her seat, striking the back of her shoe. She bent, scooped it up, and stashed it in the door panel before it could do any real harm.

Kelly leaned to her left and saw the speedometer which read eighty miles an hour and rising. Pine forests bracketed this rural setting on both sides. An occasional dwelling, cut deep in the woods, flashed by. Without the mailbox markers, these homes would probably be missed completely. Knowing Brogan was focused on the road, she took up the responsibility of looking for potential hazards. Not an easy job in an area she was just vaguely familiar with. They blew by a car that was doing forty in the fifty-five zone. A gray-haired older woman was hunched over the steering wheel with no idea of what was going on. Kelly checked the side-view mirror and saw the old woman pulling onto the shoulder. *Good chance she's peed herself and would turn for home at the next crossover.*

Brogan said, "The car we're chasing is a Camaro, I recognize the trunk design." Kelly could tell the car was blue, but couldn't ascertain any further descriptors at this rate of speed. Even a slight mistake would be a death sentence. Regardless of Brogan's speed, the blue car was maintaining at least a quarter-mile separation.

The Pocomoke City intersection at Rt. 13 came up fast. The blue car caught a green light and turned left, at a harrowing speed, heading south toward Virginia. As impossible as it seemed, Brogan arrived at the intersection just as the light turned yellow. Kelly anticipated the wild left-hand turn and Brogan did not disappoint. Kelly got only a glimpse of the startled faces of other drivers at the intersection. The undercover car's tires were squealing like a stuck pig, but they maintained traction.

Brogan placed his blue bubble light on the dash and jammed it in the corner to keep it from flying from side to side. It was a very weak substitute for the modern bar lights on marked patrol vehicles. The light had magnets on the bottom so it could be affixed to the roof, but Brogan knew at these speeds it would blow right off and bang along the side of the car, until it was totally demolished. He had activated the siren, but it was worthless at such high speeds. They were outrunning the sound of the siren. Keeping the citizens safe was solely on Brogan, but he couldn't let this killer get away.

The blue car had the advantage of its low profile and design for high-speed driving. Brogan doubted the driver was used to these speeds and saw some near misses due to his lack of experience. Victims of these near misses slowed down and gazed unbelievingly out their car windows. When Brogan and Kelly went by with lights and siren blasting, they imagined the people cheering them on to get this motherfucker.

Police do a lot of high-speed driver training, and even more high-speed driving, because of the nature of their business. Brogan used everything he had learned to close slightly on the fleeing vehicle. Brogan yelled above the pursuit noises. "Kelly, do you have Zigmeister's cell number?"

She yelled back, "Yes, it's in my phone!"

Brogan continued the screaming match. "Call him and tell him we're headed his way, at a high rate of speed! Tell him the guy is driving a blue Camaro and we're closing on a hundred miles an hour on the straight-away!"

Kelly placed the call and Zigmeister answered.

She yelled into the phone, "This is Kelly Hart! Brogan and I are chasing the suspect and we're headed your way, at a hundred plus on the flat stretches! Suspect is driving a blue Camaro and he's probably armed! He's killed two people in Maryland! We can't catch him and are just barely keeping him in sight!"

Zigmeister replied in the voice of a seasoned trooper, "Be careful. My troopers and I will be at the state line with all our emergency lights on. We'll be ready with spike strips across the road if he tries to get through. I'll have a couple of cars further down the road to deal with him if he decides to run on his rims."

"Thanks, Sarge. See you in a few minutes at this rate." The line went dead as Kelly turned to Brogan and said, "He'll be ready. Spike strips across the road, so don't chase him between the Virginia guys."

The normally thirty-minute drive was eaten up in what seemed like seconds. Brogan was white-knuckled on the steering wheel as the Virginia line dwindled from twenty to ten to five miles away. Lights had been run, multiple collisions had been skillfully averted, heart attacks had been incited. Through it all, Brogan had handled his vehicle with an ability seldom witnessed over such a great distance, at such tormenting speeds. Gordon had still kept ahead. *Wonder if he's experienced or just lucky.*

The final two miles to the Virginia line loomed before them. It would take them just minutes.

Gordon was scared shitless. He had gone one hundred miles an hour only once before in his life. He had been sixteen when he and his buddies drove his dad's car down a Kansas highway. Scared him then and it scared him now. *I'm coming up on the Virginia line and I hope that running out of Maryland will mean running out of the jurisdiction of Brogan and his bitch companion. Deep down, I know Brogan won't stop unless he runs out of gas or wraps himself around a pole. Either would be fine with me.*

"Virginia State Line," the sign read, "One Mile." It was flat and straight to the finish line. Despite the blurred vision at those speeds, Gordon saw the heart-stopping red and blue lights of multiple police cars waiting in the distance. His foot slipped off the gas pedal for the first time in over thirty minutes. *Crash the roadblock or pull a U-turn? Running the roadblock will result in me, and my car, being shot to pieces by the police. I probably won't survive that. Need a new plan.*

Just as quickly as he thought it, he saw an opportunity. A stretch of pine trees was approaching on his right side. Gordon saw a clearing that appeared to go deep into the woods. It was his only chance, and he took it. Leaving the road at approximately sixty miles an hour, he was propelled over a low drainage ditch. He bellied out on the other side, but the soil was soft and he survived the jump, and regained control as he entered the cutout into the woods. What he didn't realize was that several trees had been harvested from this area, creating this divot in the woods. The vehicle was still doing about fifty miles an hour. The four-and-six-inch stumps reached up and ripped at the undercarriage of the Camaro. Gordon went from fifty to zero in record time. His seatbelt was the only thing that saved him a trip through the windshield. The airbag deployed, burning his face. He was shocked, but conscious. He undid the seatbelt and reached for the AR-15 on the floorboard. Once in his grasp, he exited the car and looked back toward Rt.13. Brogan had stopped on the shoulder and was being joined by Virginia State Police vehicles. Unbeknownst to Brogan and Kelly, a small army of Maryland troopers and sheriff's deputies had been following the chase and were now filling the shoulder of the road behind them.

Brogan and Kelly were the first ones on foot, forging

their way across the drainage ditch. They saw the Camaro had come to a violent stop, listing to the side with a tree stump raising the frame two feet in the air. The driver's door flung open and Gordon emerged armed with a rifle of some kind. As they reached for their weapons yelling, "Police," a volume of bullets spit at them. Kelly and Brogan hit the ground, as did all the supporting troops gathered behind them. Gordon obviously had no experience with the weapon, as all his rounds flew harmlessly high and into the woods on the other side of the highway. He fired with reckless abandonment, until it locked back empty.

Gordon had no replacement magazines, so he threw his AR-15 to the ground, pulled his handgun, and retreated into the wood line. Brogan and Kelly were still the closest to the suspect and rose in unison to continue the chase on foot. They were cautious because they saw Gordon carrying a handgun, but they also had their guns out and up. Not firing yet, because of the distance, but closing on this piece of shit who had caused so much pain and suffering. The troopers on the shoulder of the road came together to form a plan to surround the woods and bring in nearby canine assistance to help in rooting this guy out safely.

When Brogan and Kelly got to the edge of the woods, they could hear Gordon crashing through the woods ahead. In far better physical condition than Gordon, they were closing in on him. Gordon was spitting, cussing, and breathing heavily, as he plunged into thickets and vines in his efforts to elude. The noise reassured them that he was not waiting to ambush them. They continued to thunder through the woods chasing him.

Without aiming, Gordon spun and fired a shot at his

pursuers. The round struck a tree about two feet from Kelly, causing her to hit the ground again. Although, if it had been properly aimed, it would already be too late. She jumped back to her feet and moved forward. Brogan took note that this asshole had almost scored a lucky shot that could have ended Kelly's life. Brogan redoubled his efforts to close and end this chase. The shot at Kelly had given Brogan every right to shoot Gordon if he could get a bead on him.

The woods went quiet in front of them. They could still hear the troopers closing from behind, but Gordon had stopped making noise. He was catching his breath, or waiting to ambush them when they drew near. Brogan raised a closed fist to Kelly, the universal signal to stop, and then signaled her to move around to her right and flank Gordon. He pointed to himself and then to his left, indicating he was going to flank Gordon on the left. There was a certain amount of danger in this move, because they must be careful not to shoot each other in the crossfire.

Brogan wished the troopers coming from behind would stop, because their noise was blocking out any warning movement of Gordon's. Brogan used all his developed hunting skills to move slowly forward. What happened next took him completely off guard. Gordon, hiding behind a tree near where Brogan was standing, swung a broken branch downward knocking Brogan's gun from his hand. Luckily, no damage to his hand or arm. Brogan saw Gordon reach for the gun stashed in his belt.

Still on his feet, he rushed toward Gordon, tackling him. *Should have shot me, asshole.*

Gordon was wiry and spun away. Gordon's clever move caused his gun to go tumbling off into the underbrush. Separated from Brogan, Gordon frantically crawled toward where he last saw his gun just a few feet away.

Out of nowhere, a form appeared. Kelly came flying into the fight, tackling Gordon and knocking him to the ground. She was reaching to gouge out his eyes. Gordon felt her fingers beginning to sink into his eye sockets and rolled viciously to his left, bringing his right elbow up and back. The point of his elbow struck Kelly's right temple. Stunned by the blow, she fell away. Gordon was on her in a heartbeat, trying to strip her of the Sig Sauer in her holster. Kelly, still dizzy, held the gun in place using both hands. Gordon balled up his left hand to a fist, striking Kelly twice on the right side of her face. As he drew back for his third strike, Brogan breached the distance. He grabbed Gordon by both his chin and the back of his head and executed a violent rotation. A loud cracking sound announced Gordon's neck and spine had broken, ending his life. Brogan threw him aside, knowing he was no longer a threat.

Brogan sat on the ground, pulling the semi-conscious Kelly into his arms, cradling her head in his lap. He brushed the hair from her face. The right side of her face was red from being struck, and her right eye was beginning to swell. She looked up, saw Brogan, and said, "Did we get him?"

Brogan answered in a soft voice. "Yes, Kelly, we got him. He won't hurt anyone ever again." She nodded in understanding. "Just stay down and we'll get a stretcher in here and take you out of the woods."

"Fuck we will," Kelly exclaimed. "Help me up. I'm walking out of here on my own."

Brogan tried to be persuasive. "You may be hurt worse than you think. Let the EMTs do their job and get you out of here."

Kelly reiterated, "No, help me up." Brogan made no move to help her up.

A strong voice said, "You heard the lady. She's ready to get up!" An arm and hand reached past Brogan and grasped Kelly's hand. She was gently raised to her feet.

Zigmeister smiled and said, "You okay?"

Kelly returned the smile and said, "Yes, thank you."

Brogan was now sitting on the ground by himself, looking like half a goof. He got up fast, hoping the rest of the police, now flowing into the area, had not witnessed the exchange. *I keep underestimating this woman and that damn Zigmeister has seen in her what I haven't. She's tough and resilient. She's even going to be cute with a blackeye.*

Brogan's gun was returned to him and Gordon's gun was photographed and placed in an evidence bag. As Kelly, Brogan, and Zigmeister exited the woods, they met and passed by the local medical examiner, headed in the opposite direction. They acknowledged each other in passing. The broken man who lay in the woods was now the coroner's responsibility. Everyone had a job to do. Today, everyone had done it well.

Although there are now just victims and witnesses to what had occurred, Brogan, Kelly, and Zigmeister all had common thoughts. *The bad guy is dead, the children at the farmhouse are safe, and as a result, the paperwork generated will be massive.*

Stopping at the ambulance, Kelly received an icepack, which she immediately applied to her face.

48
LET ME TAKE YOU HOME

Zigmeister, Brogan, and Kelly reached the shoulder of the road. Two canine dogs waited anxiously to join in the chase. Brogan thought, *Too late, guys. The bad guy is down.* Handlers began to guide the dogs back to their patrol cars, after rewarding them with a small treat.

The three amigos turned and faced each other. The shootings in Virginia would be cleared. The shootings in Maryland would be cleared. Children had been saved, children had been lost. A crime ring so sinister it lacked description had been disrupted and hopefully shut down. Time to share the information with everyone, so they can climb on the credit-taking train.

Zigmeister raised his hand above his head and spun his index finger in a circle in the air, alerting his Virginia troopers that it was time to get back across the line. The action here was over for the day. He shook hands with Brogan and Kelly. "I'll see you somewhere down the line. Thanks for your help and I can be available if they need anything from me or my troopers." He started to leave, but turned back and said, "You two take care of each other." With that, he was gone, joining a gaggle of his fellow troopers.

Brogan and Kelly had been awake for over a day and a half and it was starting to take its toll on them. Kelly was trying to ease the pain in her face. Both looked like they had slept in their clothes because they had. They returned to Brogan's car and fell into their respective seats. Brogan said, "You ready to go home?"

Kelly gave him a crooked smile. "Yes, I'm ready."

Brogan dropped the car into gear and negotiated a U-turn. "Good, I'll take you home."

The ride home was subdued as they rehashed in their minds and in conversation all that had transpired since their first three dates. Each doubted they could keep up the pace. Just before arriving home, Kelly smiled as she read the welcoming sign for Sandpiper. Everyone who needed to know had been notified during the drive home. When they got out of the car, Brogan brought his go bag in with him.

Brogan was still worried about Kelly having a possible concussion or some lingering damage because of her fight with Gordon. "I know you need rest and I'm going to stay with you in case you need further medical attention."

"I'll be okay," she said, but easily relented to his wish to stay with her. Despite their growing need for something more, he tucked her into her bed after she showered and changed into cotton pajamas.

As she began to nod off, he whispered "I'm going to take a shower and change. I'll be back in to check on you. Try and get some rest."

Brogan grabbed a pillow and blanket and set up residency on her living room couch. Throughout the night, he awakened her every couple of hours, checking her eyes and cognitive reactions and her answers to routine questions. He was relieved when her response to his care turned from smiles to aggravation. He knew she was herself when she said to him, "You go to sleep and leave me alone." He took her advice and fell into a deep sleep. His last thought before drifting off was of Kelly. *The need is growing, but like before, the time's not right.*

49
TREASURE TROVE

Kelly and Brogan awakened early despite all that had happened. Brogan went home and changed into fresh clothing. Kelly was doing the same at her place. They agreed to meet an hour later at the PD. The swelling in Kelly's face had receded and makeup almost hid her black eye. She wore her injuries as a badge of honor. She arrived at the PD and the Duty Sergeant ushered her into the detectives' area where Brogan was talking with the chief. She stopped to give them privacy, but the chief waved her over and shook her hand. "Kelly, I want to thank you for being Brogan's backup on yesterday's events. You showed great courage under extremely stressful and dangerous conditions.

"The sheriff called and heaped praise on both of you. He told me that, in the duffel bag recovered from Gordon's car, they found a treasure trove of documents and information concerning the kidnapping, smuggling, and sale of children. Unfortunately, a search of the farm had revealed six small, unmarked graves in an adjoining field. Autopsies would tell more, but so far, the bodies were children who died of illnesses they possibly had contracted before they entered the country. Had they received medical care, they might have survived.

On a more positive note, the FBI and the Taskforce for Missing and Exploited Children had assigned investigators to the case. They were saying they had never had so much written and documented information on the workings of the dark web, and its involvement in the selling of children. They believed, over the long term, they might recover many of the children already sold, identify the pedophile buyers, and charge them for their actions.

This case and the death of Thomas Gordon attracted the national attention of multiple federal agencies. It was destined to go international, as many of the children had been sent to various locations around the world and, apparently, to anyone with the money to pay for them.

Sandpiper was back in the news for its participation in the investigation. Gordon had been fingerprinted, which resulted in a match for a man named Harold Johnson. Johnson had been wanted on felony charges, involving the solicitation of a young woman for the purpose of prostitution, in southern California. He was also a suspect in the murder of a real estate broker in California. Two investigators from California were now flying across the country hoping to gain evidence that would clear their cases.

The Maryland State Police were aiding the Maryland Real Estate Commission as they did a deep dive into who assisted Gordon in obtaining the Maryland documents he had needed to become a real estate broker. They were intent on rooting out the wrongdoers and placing appropriate criminal charges.

Federal agents interviewed Brogan and Kelly for hours at the PD, about everything that had happened. It was plain to the interviewers that only Brogan and Kelly Hart were responsible for the work that exposed the criminal syndicate. However, both parties requested the credit for the closure be distributed between all the agencies involved, and to direct questions in Virginia to Sergeant Zigmeister.

While questions arose involving tactics used, civilian involvement, and jurisdictional confusion, no one could criticize the final results. The only person who might complain was dead, killed in the most unusual manner of having his neck snapped while he was committing assault; and while he was trying to strip Private Investigator, Kelly Hart, of her legally carried firearm. Numerous state and local police officers witnessed the conclusion of the struggle and, to the person, they felt the actions were justified and necessary. Brogan had the right to shoot Gordon, but left without his gun, he had resorted to his martial arts training to take a life and to save and protect other lives. No state's attorney would dare consider bringing charges against these local heroes.

Everyone in Worcester County who had sought Thomas Gordon as a friend, because of his apparent wealth and status, was now distancing themselves and expressing they hadn't known him that well. They described him as a loner who made them uneasy when in his presence. It was the buzz of the entire community and people were reevaluating their own selection of friends. Being the closest neighbor to the farm, Deanna Teacher had been interviewed by local and national media. Her answers to questions were very short and pointed to a lack of civility across the country. Many reporters found themselves facing a closed door signaling the end of the interview.

50
THE MOUNTAIN STATE

Several weeks had passed swiftly for Kelly and Brogan. Kelly was working on some investigations for Marie, mostly interviews with witnesses that would help her in pending trials. Attorneys were still feeding Kelly papers to serve. The work was steady and had increased considerably since she and Brogan made the news together. A PI who helped take down a smuggling and child-selling organization was a story straight out of a television series. Curiosity churned around the case. Brogan and Kelly ducked reporters who were relentless in their efforts to uncover more details. Slowly, the calls dwindled and interest faded away as new news stole the headlines.

Kelly contacted and negotiated the rental terms, with the landlord, for the cottage she was about to rent. After visiting it with Brogan, she decided it was just right for her. It was small, about 1000 square feet, and would be easy to care for. It was actually larger than the space she left in Baltimore County, and it was a single home providing a higher level of privacy. The house on one side was occupied by a single woman. The house on the other side was empty until summer, when it would accommodate young employees during the tourist season. All the backyards were cordoned off with waist-high picket fences that added to the cottage effect. Kelly hoped the summer residents worked at night, so she could get some sleep. She remembered when she was their age and had endless energy. She and her friends would stay up all night long and think nothing of it. *I may have to pay them a visit and set some neighborhood rules - just a friendly warning.*

One day, Brogan stopped by to help her unpack boxes. He opened the front door and yelled out, "Anybody home?"

"I'm in the back," Kelly responded.

Brogan started down the hallway where he was met by a small gray dog. It was a terrier of some kind. The dog stared at Brogan as if he was an intruder. Brogan loved dogs and bent down, to extend his hand to be sniffed. A quick sniff and a tail wag meant Brogan had passed the dog test. Brogan walked into the back bedroom, now followed by his new friend. "Did you get a dog?"

"No, not really. He belongs to my neighbor, Journey-Rose. He found a small hole in the fence out back and comes to visit me, presumably, to make sure I'm doing things right."

"Journey-Rose sounds like a country music singer. I like it."

"Yeah, it does. She's very nice and has apologized for him coming here on his own, but I told her he was welcome anytime. I wish I had the work hours that would let me have a dog, but it would be unfair to have any pet with the hours I keep. Journey-Rose is a waitress working at multiple restaurants, so her hours are not much better than mine. He's decided to adopt me as an additional human to take care of him. I love him already."

Brogan cocked his head. "He's really cute and friendly. What's his name?"

"You're going to love this, since you're a cop. His name is Duncan, and he has an affinity for donuts, just like the rest of you boys in blue. Maybe that's why I love him so much."

Brogan had been busy too. He spent many of his days liaising with other police and federal agencies, seeking more details about what they were now calling, The Child Selling Case. There had been little time for each other. They had gone to lunch twice and dinner once. They shared a few intimate kisses, but nothing more. Both knew a volcano of desire was building and the right time would be soon—or the wrong time would work.

During a phone call late one night, they made a life-changing decision. Brogan suggested they take a long weekend together. He named a place called The Greenbrier in West Virginia. He told her, "I've never been there, but I've only heard great things about it. It's in the Allegheny Mountains and flanks the Eastern Seaboard. It dates back 240 years. It's a National Historic Landmark and an award-winning resort. It has served many purposes. It was once a secret hiding place for US government officials to conduct business, in case of war or a potential bombing of Washington, D.C. It was also a hospital for veterans injured during World War II. Now it's a beautiful hotel and year-round resort. What do think?"

Kelly didn't hesitate. "I've never heard of the place, but if we're together, I know I won't be disappointed. When can we go?"

He surprised her and said, "I've made reservations from Friday through Monday of this week. Are you feeling spontaneous?"

Kelly laughed. "Spontaneous is my middle name. I can't wait."

"Oh," he said, "It's decorated for Christmas and, if there's snow, we can take a sleigh ride. No snow, it will be a carriage ride. Bring some warm clothes for outside, so we can explore the area."

"I'm so excited. I wish we were leaving tomorrow!" she exclaimed.

"Tomorrow is Tuesday, but I can make it happen."

"No, no. I was just kidding. I need to get ready. I need to go shopping. Can we leave early Friday?"

"Does sunrise work for you?" he asked.

"Sunrise it is. I'll be ready. Will you pick me up?"

"You just be ready," he replied. "I'll be there and I'll come in to get your luggage."

Friday was a gift of beautiful weather, with local temperatures predicted to rise into the low sixties. Sunrise in Sandpiper was always a special time. The sun breaks over the ocean and bathes the beaches, hotels, condominiums, and private homes that sit on this little spit of land. Beach lovers find serenity every morning when they soak in the rays of the sun. Friday was one of those days.

Kelly was as nervous as a cat with a new puppy in the

house. *This is it. The time is right. The man is right.* But these thoughts didn't stop the anxiety from building inside her. *Will I be up to his standards?* The thought of making love with the new man in her life was crazy exciting, but scary. *Just calm down and everything will be fine. You know he's a nice and considerate guy. You know he has feelings for you. Just be yourself. Something about you has drawn him in. What happens, happens. Oh shit, am I ready for this? Hell, we've been ambushed together, shot at together, rolled around on the ground with a murderer together. Why would I think getting in bed with him would be any scarier than what we've already been through?*

The tapping on her front door broke her thoughts and announced Brogan had arrived. Her luggage was sitting next to the front door. A large suitcase, a small suitcase, and a leather bag made up her travel needs. Oh yes, a purse large enough to hold her computer and the stuff she just had to have on hand. Brogan smiled when he spied the 3 bags she needed for a short trip, but he didn't care. The fact she had agreed to go with him was all he could think about. *I'm looking forward to four days to ourselves. I'm surprised she didn't decline my invitation. I'd have had to cancel the reservation. I know she's out of my league. I'm even more ready for this trip.*

His one suitcase and a few things on hangers left plenty of room for all of Kelly's luggage. She was beaming when she came to the door and let him in. Her face showed no lingering signs of the injuries she had received. Brogan knew she had suffered some loss of confidence in her appearance over the last few weeks. All that had disappeared. Kelly radiated as a healthy, beautiful woman. She helped carry her luggage, after arming her recently acquired alarm system and double locking her front door. "Can't be too safe."

There were cameras on the front and rear of the house which allowed her to check those areas on her phone in live-time. Brogan had been the driving force behind all those upgrades to her cottage. She knew she had gotten a special deal when the installer told her that he and Brogan went hunting and fishing together. It was still pretty expensive, but it also made her parents extremely happy when they heard about it.

Kelly had told her mom about her trip to the Greenbriar, but they had kept her dad in the dark. He would not approve, having not officially met Brogan. *Once a daddy's girl, always a daddy's girl.* She liked it that way and would not intentionally bust his bubble. She knew, eventually, her dad would approve of this overly protective cop. *Time to go to Greenbriar.*

Kelly was surprised when Brogan turned left on Rt. 113 and headed south. She had been to West Virginia before and it always included a trip around the Washington Beltway.

"Hey, don't we take Rt. 50 towards Washington?" she asked.

"Nope, we're going through the Chesapeake Bay Bridge Tunnel and then across Rt. 64 to West Virginia. We'll go by where our new buddy, Zigmeister, works, hit the outskirts of Norfolk close to the restaurant where he saved us, and then close to Richmond Virginia. The rest of the trip is pretty much an open highway with great scenery all the way to the Greenbriar. Sit back and relax."

Brogan took his time and they stopped for breakfast and later for lunch. Kelly was in charge of picking the spots to stop. No chain establishments were the only rule. Even the meals were part of the adventure.

"How about that place on the left," she yelled out. "It looks interesting."

Brogan glanced at the place and agreed it looked interesting, but it also looked like it might fall down while they were eating there. *Why not?* The breakfast was wonderful. The owners were true Virginians who lived by the code: you should eat until you're full, then eat a little more. Just the right amount of grease helped the plentiful offerings go down. Kelly paid. Brogan kept his mouth shut.

Back on the road, they talked about the houses tucked in the mountains. Most would be invisible during the summer, but with the leaves off the trees, log cabins dotted the landscape.

"Would you like to live out in the woods like these people?" she asked Brogan.

"I've never given it much thought, but I think I might. I like to hunt and fish and sometimes it's nice to get away from the crowds and the crime."

Kelly agreed. "Yeah, it would be kind of cool to have a place at the shore and a place in the mountains, if you could afford it. I think you and I have chosen careers that will take a lot of penny-pinching to ever have two places in desirable locations."

"Yes, you're right. I feel extremely fortunate to have a job I like and being in a resort town is a huge plus."

"Growing up, I always loved coming to Sandpiper with my parents," Kelly said. "Working there is a dream come true."

Kelly picked another interesting place for lunch, and they lucked out and got great sandwiches and chips. A lot of laughing and joking made the time go by. They had turned a six-hour drive into an eight-hour adventure, but since they left early, they still arrived at the Greenbriar around 2:30, impressed when their GPS took them to the entrance. A stone gatehouse prohibited entry until a security guard greeted them, "Hello folks. Welcome to the Greenbrier! Will you be a guest of the hotel?"

"Yes, we are."

"Wonderful, may I see your ID." Brogan handed him his driver's license. After a quick review, the security guard handed Brogan back his ID and the gate slowly opened.

Once inside the gate, they followed a long driveway. Brogan and Kelly admired the luxurious surroundings of the resort. The lawns were impeccably manicured, the trees and shrubs perfectly trimmed, and a feeling of Christmas began to loom in the air. The property was adorned with Christmas lights and Christmas decorations and the most beautiful Christmas tree. In the center of the garden, the size of the tree was equal to what you would see in Times Square or the White House in Washington, D.C.

The drive brought them to the front of a huge, stark white Georgian-styled building with two sweeping staircases. Kelly and Brogan felt immediately like they had been swept back to grander times. They were met by a valet parking attendant. Their luggage was snatched up and placed on a gold-plated luggage cart, with red carpet, by a bellman dressed in tails. He accompanied them to the check-in counter. Several couples were lined up in front of them, so Brogan looked at Kelly and said, "Why don't you go visit the shops and meet me back here in the lobby? It looks like this might take a while." She grinned, spun on her heels, and was gone.

Brogan worked his way to the counter and gave the desk clerk his name. She found it immediately and welcomed him to the hotel. Brogan asked if flowers could be delivered to the room along with a bottle of champagne. The clerk said, "Complimentary champagne is already being chilled in the room and all rooms have fresh flowers." Brogan was pleased. *This place is expensive by Sandpiper standards, but the service is already exceeding anything I have ever experienced. I hope Kelly is impressed.*

The check-in went smoothly and the bellman stood ready to escort him to his room. Kelly was nowhere in sight. Brogan got an idea and texted her their room number as he entered the elevator. He told her to take her time and he would meet her in the room with the luggage.

She texted back and said she would be up in about fifteen minutes. When Brogan arrived in the room, the setting was captivating. It was a mix of a classic old-style Virginia mansion with some updated amenities. A large claw-foot tub and a frosted glass shower were major features in the bathroom that were concealed by two sliding pocket doors. Two luxurious white terry robes, with the Greenbrier logo, hung from hooks. He tipped the bellman and went directly to the tub and started the hot water running. There were mixed fresh flowers, and he extracted a white rose and laid it on the sink while the tub began to fill. He noticed a champagne bottle chilling when he walked in. He went to it, unsealed it, and carried it into the bathroom. A small table sat next to the head of the tub where two champagne glasses sat waiting to be used. He poured one glass half full. He saw some bubble-making soap and tossed a small quantity into the tub. It immediately covered the water with pink froth. He took the flower and pulled the petals off and tossed a few on the floor leading to the tub and then spread the rest over the bubbles covering the entire surface of the tub.

He checked the king-size bed and found it firm like he preferred. The view out the window overlooked the tennis courts surrounded by evergreen trees. A beautiful setting.

They were on the fifth floor, which gave them a view of the surrounding mountains. The room temperature was perfect after coming in from the cool weather of the mountains.

He heard the door mechanism release as Kelly came through the door. She was carrying two Greenbriar bags and was grinning all over herself. She took in the room and her grin turned to a full-out, blushing smile. "Oh my, this is so perfect. Thank you, Brogan."

"I'm glad you like it. I think it's nice too. Come look at the bathroom." Brogan waved her toward the closed pocket doors. He opened them with flare and they disappeared inside the walls. Brogan stepped aside allowing Kelly to go in first. Kelly stopped cold at the entrance. She was paralyzed by the romantic scene: bathtub, bubbles, petals, and champagne which made a setting fit for the front of a magazine.

Brogan turned and said, "Been a long day and I felt you might like a bath to relax after the drive. The champagne is optional, but I thought that might relax you as well. While you soak, I'd like to run down to the gym to loosen up, if it's okay with you. I'm tight from the drive.

Kelly smiled, impressed by Brogan's efforts. "It's more than okay. It's thoughtful and I appreciate what you've done. You go to the gym, and I'll take advantage of your offer. Take your time because I'm going to take mine."

Brogan grabbed a small gym bag he brought with him and, before he left, he apologized saying, "I'd turn on some music, but there's no radio and I doubt you want to turn the TV loud enough to hear it in the bathroom. Do you have something to read?"

Kelly rushed to one of her pieces of luggage, threw it on the bed, and dug around. Finding what she was looking for, she spun around, holding it in front of her. It was the book Brogan bought her when they were on their extended date.

"Yes, I do. I've been saving it."

Brogan shook his head. "Not sure. It's a little dark, especially after what we've just been through."

"No, I've been saving it. You go to the gym. See you in an hour or so." Before he left, Brogan leaned down and gave Kelly a passionate kiss.

51

ARE YOU SURE?

Brogan finished his workout, dripping with sweat. It felt good walking into the gym's shower. He wondered if Kelly had thought his efforts to make her feel special were over the top. *This woman is special. I wonder if she knows what she means to me.* The showerhead dumped chilly water on his head and shoulders. It cooled him down, but did nothing to reduce the fire growing within him. His nerve endings tingled in anticipation of returning to their room.

He dried, slipped back into his travel clothes, and then hurried back to the room. *He hoped he hadn't left Kelly for too long.* When he entered the room, he glanced anxiously around. She wasn't in the bedroom. He walked to the bathroom door. He was pleasantly surprised to see her still in the tub. She must have refreshed the bubbles and hot water. Her head was leaned back on a folded towel and her book was clasped between her hands in the reading position. Brogan leaned against the door frame and said, "What's up?"

"Nothing yet", she joked. "This book is scaring the hell out of me, but I can't put it down."

"I've heard that," Brogan said. "I want to take a shower and clean up."

Kelly stopped reading long enough to say, "Good idea. Go ahead." She made no sign or effort to remove herself from the bathroom.

Brogan smiled. *Okay, Miss Tease. I'll play your game.* He grabbed a towel, threw it over a hook by the shower, and undressed. When he was naked he looked over to the tub and caught her peeking. A smile crossed his face as he stepped behind the frosted glass. He took soap to his body and a razor to his face. While he lathered his body, he couldn't hold back a grin. *Is she still peeking? I hope so.*

Kelly stared at the shower stall. She had just caught a glimpse of his large cock. It's wasn't hard, but the sight was causing her to quiver with anticipation. *If he can get that up, he's checking all the right boxes. Should I get out of the tub and join him in the shower? No, I'm going to leave him in charge.*

His body was clean, his hair shampooed and his face smooth. Brogan rinsed and then reached out for his towel. After drying, he wrapped the towel around his waist. He stepped from the shower and saw the book folded on the table and the champagne glass sitting empty. Kelly asked, "Can you come here and help me?"

Always a gentleman, he closed the distance quickly and reached for her hand. She braced herself with her left hand and allowed him to slowly draw her nude body to a standing position.

He gazed slowly at her body, something just short of a full stare. Soap bubbles clung to her thighs and an occasional flower petal did its job to paint the perfect picture of the female form. She was wet and the sudden change in temperature from the tub to the room brought her nipples to attention. Her pink areolas surrounded her twin peaks. Brogan had completely lost eye contact. Kelly's body was flawless, except for a fading red scar running down her right forearm. Brogan considered it the mark of a warrior. She made no effort to conceal it from him. He had plenty of his own battle scars to share with her.

"Will you bring me a robe?" she asked in something just above a whisper. Brogan turned immediately and retrieved one of the two robes and another towel. He strategically placed the towel on the tile floor to provide her with a safe place to step. He steadied her hand with his hand as she stepped from the tub. Standing on the floor, she turned her back to him so that he could wrap her in the robe. Brogan looked at her back and perfectly formed ass. He encased her with the large soft robe.

Kelly shook her hair free from the loose bun she had used to keep it dry. Her pale blonde hair fell gently just past her shoulders. She slid her arms into each sleeve of the robe and cinched the belt closed. She turned to face Brogan. She took his hand and led him to the bed. Kelly pulled back the covers, faced him again, and undid the robe letting it fall to the floor. She pressed her ample bare breasts and hard nipples against his hair-covered chest. She moved into him and felt his stiff penis pushing against his towel.

Kelly sat on the edge of the bed, "Come climb in bed with me and keep me warm." Without comment, Brogan released his towel and it fell to the floor near the discarded robe. His cock was fully erect and only inches from her face, Kelly took her turn staring. She slipped into and across the bed allowing room for Brogan to join her.

He hesitated for a moment and said, "Are you sure?"

She again beckoned him into the bed and answered, "Yes, I'm sure."

Brogan joined her in bed and pulled her in close. She was cool from her recent exposure to the room's temperature, but he was like a furnace. He gently embraced her as their lips met and they enjoyed their first horizontal kiss. The next few minutes were full of gentle caresses, tender kisses, and touching as they explored each other's bodies. His fingers danced lightly across her back and sides and drifted across her stomach and breasts. His hand wandered between her legs, but stopped short of touching her most intimate area. Kelly was responding to his touch and used her tongue to explore his mouth. He matched her movements and they both felt his erection grow even harder and larger.

Kelly wrapped her right hand around his burning hot prick and slowly massaged it while moving her hand up and down. Her first impression was confirmed. This was the biggest cock she had ever held. It was as hard as steel. She licked her palm and slid it over the head in a circular motion ever so gently. It shivered at her touch.

Feeling his urgency grow, he rolled on top of her, pushing her into the mattress without bringing his full weight to bear. He used his right hand to brush back the hair that had fallen partially across her face and stroked her face softly. *I enjoy the feel of this woman. I want her. I need her.*

She spread her legs slightly and then surprised him by gently pushing him onto his back. She swung her right leg over his body straddling him. She gazed into his eyes and saw a shade of blue he must reserve for his most intimate moments. They were now the deep blue of a tropical island pool. She hovered just above him and held her position with her bent legs. Kelly smiled at Brogan and whispered, "What did you ask me before you got into bed?"

"I asked you if you were sure?"

She answered his question by grasping his penis. She moved it to the lips of her vagina. She was wet with anticipation. She slowly rubbed the head of his dick over her clit making it just as hard as he was. Then she slowly lowered herself onto his erection. The feeling of pleasure was overwhelming. She continued her descent until he was buried deep inside her. She clenched her knees into his sides holding their position. Kelly thought, "*This feels so good I don't want to move.*" She could feel the tension growing in his body. *I can't let this end quickly.* Kelly raised slowly and then lowered herself again. She began a gentle rocking motion while putting her hands on his chest, she arched her back, and her hair swayed with her movement.

Using his mind, Brogan recovered control of himself. Brogan began to meet her gentle rocking motion. Her breasts bounced to the rhythm of their bodies. Kelly's breasts were gorgeous globes from Brogan's current perspective. He laid his hands on her hips, not pushing or pulling, just enjoying the ride. Her rocking increased in speed and a low moaning sound emanated from her throat. Brogan was holding back as best he could, but felt himself slipping over the edge. Kelly produced a passionate sound Brogan had never heard before. It wasn't loud, but intense and matched the throbbing constrictions of her vagina as she reached her high. Brogan joined her and for a moment he tightened the grip on her hips for fear he might throw her off. Their simultaneous orgasms were powerful.

Her head fell forward to her chest. Her hair hung down concealing most of her face. Her entire upper body lowered until he could feel her nipples burying into his chest. Tremors continued to run through her entire body for a few seconds. It had finally been the right time and the right place.

To Kelly's surprise, Brogan didn't withdraw or fall out. Her eyes widened as she felt him growing within her. He was ready to go again and she did not disappoint him. This time it was a much more feral ride for both of them as they moved with a deep need to satisfy. After the second time, they parted to catch their breath.

They snuggled and began again exploring each other's bodies using their hands and mouths. Brogan used his lips to trace beads of sweat between Kelly's breasts. His kisses ended between her legs. His tongue probed Kelly's sweet spot and her body shuttered before she reached another full-throated orgasm.

Her response brought Brogan swiftly back to life. Taking charge, he put himself on top this time, and entered her smoothly and deeply. His arms lifted her legs until her knees were near the side of his head. His penetration was deep and she energetically met his thrusts. Just minutes later they again shared a mutual release. Lying on their backs naked, they stared at the ceiling and then at each other. Both laughed. The experience had left them pleasantly exhausted.

Hungry from their workout, they ordered from the room-service menu. When a server brought the food up to the room, Kelly ducked into the bathroom while Brogan answered in his robe. The server rolled the meal into the room.

When the server departed, Brogan tipped generously. Kelly joined Brogan as he pulled the silver dome covers off the steaming hot food. They ate in bed which was something neither of them ever did. They ate naked which was something neither of them had ever considered. All their defensive walls were down and they enjoyed each other's company completely and without reservation. A fondness and trust had formed between them.

The rest of the night was spent in exploration and sharing. When they were finally spent, they were bathed in sweat and the bedding was wet from their lovemaking. Brogan found a soft blanket in the closet and they wrapped themselves in it. They fell asleep in each other's grasp. In the morning, they showered together and had their first slippery vertical fuck.

The next three days were a repeated variation of the night before mingled with a smattering of day trips, tours, carriage rides, shopping, and even a visit to the on-property casino.

On the ride back, Brogan turned to Kelly "Where's your head?"

"I was just reliving how wonderful the past few days have been. You made this time so magically romantic. I have never experienced anything like this in my life."

"This is just a fraction of the way I would like to treat you, given the opportunity. I think you are a beautiful and special woman."

Kelly blushed at his compliment, but returned, "I'm looking at special." Brogan could not hold back a small grin.

"How about Jack's for breakfast tomorrow?"

"It's a date."

Tuesday morning Brogan walked into his office to the ringing of his desk phone. "Brogan," he said. The caller's voice came down the line, "Hi, this is Jake Jacobs. Would you allow me to interview you for a book I'm writing?"

"Sorry, it's still not my thing," Brogan responded and ended the call.

Jake looked at his phone after Brogan had hung up. *Guess I'll have to do it the hard way.* He turned to his long list of sources, informants, and witnesses he had culled from news coverage and court records. He punched in the first phone number that he hoped would help him tell a new story about this amazing detective and his new PI sidekick. A voice answers, "Kelly Hart."

AUTHOR'S MESSAGE

We all go through life with family, friends, and acquaintances. If we are lucky, we have a lifetime filled with friends and lovers. Sometimes they are the same person. People who carry guns in war or law enforcement have an additional category. They have backup. Backup is an individual you can trust with your life. Someone who will always be looking out for you. Someone who will stand in defense of you. Someone who will be your wingman and cover your six.

The story you have just read speaks to the beginning phases of Brogan and Kelly developing the role of each other's backup. Becoming backup for someone has no official start or end date. You recognize when you have it. Hopefully, everyone who reads this has someone in their life they can consider backup. If not, you have the Brogans and Kellys of the world to be your backup when you come face to face with evil.

Brogan and Kelly have now intertwined their lives, and together or apart, they will face new dangers and mysteries that will call upon all their mental and physical resources to overcome. The third book in this series is just around the corner. Stay vigilant. Head on a swivel. Be aware of your surroundings. And of course, keep reading.

Please follow Jake Jacobs at www.authorjakejacobs.com

ACKNOWLEDGEMENTS

Wow, this was a barn burner; from concept to finish in just months. I was not alone in this endeavor. The lion's share of thanks goes to my wife, Tobie. She has lived the life of a martial arts black belt, private investigator, and Executive Protection Specialist. Her contributions to the narrative have brought clarity and realism to the book. Blended with my years as a state police detective, fiction and fact merge into a fast-moving storyline. Tobie has again tapped into her artistic side to do the artwork for the cover of this book.

Tobie and I spent countless hours reviewing this work. Making the story flow and bringing the characters to life was paramount in the telling of this story.

A special thanks to my friends, Ricky Haynes, Anne Weiss, Robin Laird, and Renae Dryer for reviewing the draft of this novel. Their opinions and suggestions were very important to me. Again, thanks to editor, Bill Cecil, for his contributions while editing this novel. To all my readers and followers, thank you for your positive feedback. Without it, this project would never have begun.

A special thanks to my publisher, Salt Water Media in Berlin, Maryland. Stephanie Fowler, Patty Gregorio, and Andrew Heller assisted in bringing this book to its current format and creating a website where you can follow me, order my books, and communicate with me if you wish.

Your reviews of my book are very important to me as they help spread the word and bring readers into the fold.

For those who have not read my first book, *Vengeance*, but enjoyed this read, I strongly suggest you go back and take a look at this dark, cautionary tale of a psychopath who seeks his own style of misguided vengeance on the town of Sandpiper. Brogan will continue to pursue the criminals who dare to enter his jurisdiction and threaten those who just want to have fun at the beach.

www.ingramcontent.com/pod-product-compliance
Lightning Source LLC
Chambersburg PA
CBHW050922030726
47503CB00007BB/2421